REDEMPTION

KILLs

REDEMPTION KILLS

L. W. WEDGWOOD

iUniverse, Inc.
Bloomington

Redemption Kills

iUniverse books may be ordered through booksellers or by contacting:

iUniverse
1663 Liberty Drive
Bloomington, IN 47403
www.iuniverse.com
1-800-Authors (1-800-288-4677)

Because of the dynamic nature of the Internet, any web addresses or links contained in this book may have changed since publication and may no longer be valid. The views expressed in this work are solely those of the author and do not necessarily reflect the views of the publisher, and the publisher hereby disclaims any responsibility for them.

Any people depicted in stock imagery provided by Thinkstock are models, and such images are being used for illustrative purposes only.

Certain stock imagery © Thinkstock.

ISBN: 978-1-4759-1123-7 (sc)
ISBN: 978-1-4759-1125-1 (e)
ISBN: 978-1-4759-1124-4 (dj)

Library of Congress Control Number: 2012906186

Printed in the United States of America

iUniverse rev. date: 5/16/2012

My special thanks goes firstly to Anna for her invaluable and tireless support, and also to my family for always being there.

CHAPTER 1

MEMORIES

They were halfway through the bottle of scotch, and concentration was becoming increasingly difficult. The hotel was small, ancient, and very expensive. It sat atop the sheer cliffs of Monte Carlo, overlooking the Mediterranean, which glimmered mystically in the soft, evening light. A gentle breeze blew onto the stone balcony, sharpening Dane Larusio's senses long enough for him to take careful aim and toss the matchstick into the small, empty glass on the opposite side of the table. The match landed neatly, as if dropped from only a couple of inches.

Koso Dilerenso grinned, a thousand lines erupting over his aged but strong features. "A lucky shot, son," he muttered, the faint hint of an old British accent still detectable.

"I was born lucky," Dane answered.

"I've known a lot of people who were born that way—and died that way too."

"Well, I wouldn't be playing this game if I had any fear of death now, would I?"

"True, old son, true."

"Stop stalling and take your shot," Dane jested.

"Ha, we'll see who's stalling," Koso replied. He pitched the match across the table in an almost casual manner, and it landed perfectly in the tiny glass. "Not bad for an old man, eh?" he said.

"Speaking of luck."

"That there's not luck, not in the least. I was playing this game before you were a twitch in your daddy's pants," Koso said.

Distracted by Koso's words, Dane's throw missed the glass by inches.

"Now let's see how lucky you are," Koso chuckled.

Fighting off feelings of protest, Dane picked up the Colt .45 pistol, spun the chamber, raised the barrel to his temple, and pulled the trigger.

Koso erupted into a bout of laughter.

Dane poured a shot of scotch and looked Koso square in the eye. "To luck!" he bellowed, tossing back the smooth liquid. Immediately, the liquor soothed his frayed nerves. Sometimes Dane wondered why he no longer felt fear like a normal human being. It hadn't always been that way; when he was a child, he'd felt terror like no other. But time and circumstance had dulled this emotion, like it had so many others.

This time Koso's matchstick bounced off the edge of the glass and onto the table. Like a stubborn mule, Koso spun the chamber on the Colt and jerked the trigger. The hammer slammed home on emptiness. "To luck, old son, to luck!" He tossed back the shot of scotch with a well-practiced flick of his wrist.

That was the game. The only real rules were these: One, you had to throw the match in the glass from a distance of at least two feet. Two, if the match missed, you always had to pull the trigger and drink a shot of whatever was in the bottle. Three, you never stopped until the bottle was finished.

Although Koso was Dane's closest friend, there was a lot about him he didn't know—his profession, for instance. Some swore Koso worked for the CIA. Some said he worked for the British Secret Service. Others claimed he worked for everyone except Asians, whom he hated with a passion. Dane knew Koso as a very resourceful, very loyal old bastard who could get any information and fix any problem—all for a healthy price, of course. He'd met him while he was setting up a new resort in Sicily. The local mob had been giving him some heat, trying to cut in on any potential profits. A business acquaintance had suggested Koso as the most effective for taking care of such problems. A hundred thousand US dollars later, the mob was sending Dane gifts and patting him on the back. For better or for worse, however, they had established a friendship that was seemingly impossible to shake.

"So, have you ever seen anyone lose this game?" Dane asked.

Koso looked thoughtful for a moment. "As a matter of fact, there was a time."

Dane leaned back in his chair to make himself more comfortable. He noticed that his old friend had an audible slur.

"We were in a Beirut basement bar," Koso began, scratching the bristles on his chin. "There were two crazy Israelis with us, and for some unknown reason, they thought Lebanon was a good place to make some easy money. That couldn't be further from the truth. Lebanon, at the time, was in the middle of a major conflict with Israel and was being bombed daily. Many areas in Beirut were nothing but rubble, but somehow, you always managed to find a bottle of scotch and a quiet corner in which to drink it."

Lighting a large Partagas-160 cigar, Koso continued, "Anyway, there were these two Syrians in the game, whose reaction to the scotch, I might add, was somewhat more severe than the rest of us. That's where the trouble began. We were all armed to the teeth, but no one could have foreseen there being two Colt .45s within the same room. The guns were identical, except for one crucial difference—my Colt was loaded with only a single bullet, whereas the other gun, which somehow made its way from one of the Syrians and onto the table, was fully loaded."

Dane could guess what happened next, but Koso explained anyway.

"Well into a second bottle of scotch, one of the Israelis was unlucky enough to miss the glass, and with a scotch-enhanced grin on his face, he picked up a fully loaded Colt and blew his brains out."

"Shit," Dane said.

"Indeed," Koso said. "But the remaining Israeli's language was a little more colorful when he figured out what had gone wrong. And then, well, all hell broke loose."

"Let me guess," Dane piped in. "The remaining Israeli brought the guilty Syrian's life to a short and painful end?"

"No, my friend, we are talking of an Israeli here. And as brutal as they can sometimes be—especially at that time in their history—they aren't murderers."

"So he just let the whole thing go?"

"Wrong again, son!"

"Then what?" Dane eagerly asked.

"Then he gave the Syrian a chance." He paused for effect. Relishing the moment, he puffed on his cigar and blew thick blue plumes into the overhead lamp. "Barely maintaining his composure, the Israeli picked up the almost fully loaded Colt, spun the chamber, and handed it to the wide-eyed Syrian, who looked about as afraid as a man could be. 'If you don't pull the trigger, I will,' he demanded. Those words remain crystal clear in my head, even to this day. Well, that room went so quiet you could have heard an ant sneeze. Daring not to refuse, the Syrian took the gun and raised it to his temple. A full minute passed before the Syrian finally summoned the courage to jerk the trigger, and then—*click!*—the hammer slammed home on the spent round."

"That lucky bastard," Dane breathed.

"Well, he was that day, anyway," Koso went on. "Two days later, on a bright and sunny morning, he was walking along a downtown street when the remaining part of a bombed-out, six-story wall decided it was time to collapse. He was crushed to death."

"That unlucky bastard!"

"Anyway, my friend, I believe we have a game of Riviera Roulette to finish, and I believe it's your hand."

Though the game continued, it had lost its previous zest, and Dane frequently eyeballed the Colt .45 with much suspicion. However, the bottle of scotch slowly disappeared without mishap, and when it was finished, they both still had their heads firmly intact.

Later, Dane leaned heavily on the balcony banister, breathing the cool night air and staring blindly out at the sea. He couldn't sleep.

The dark irony of Koso's story had stirred memories of a catastrophe in his own life that had happened many years ago—a catastrophe that had caused him to flee his family and everything he had known. Old emotions he would have rather left dormant surfaced, and an overwhelming remorse clawed deeply into the fibers of his consciousness.

Fifteen years ago …

It all began in Genova, Italy, when Dane was eighteen. He had dropped out of school and spent his time doing errands for his father, a very successful shoe-store proprietor. One midsummer afternoon, during siesta, he was searching for a cool place to pass the hottest hours. He decided on a small, cool bar on the corner of Via Firenze and Via Tevere. He had barely touched his lager when a low but clear voice sounded from behind him.

"Boy … Boy!"

Dane turned from where he sat at the bar. Directly behind him were two men—a short, fat man in a crumpled suit, sweating heavily, and a tall, skinny man. "You talking to me?" Dane grumbled, trying to sound more like a man than the boy that he actually was.

"Yeah, I'm talking to you. Do you see anyone else sitting around here?"

"Then what do you want?" he asked nonchalantly.

"We got a real smart one here," the fat man said.

"How would you like to make a few dollars?" the skinny man asked.

Dane looked closely at him. He was so gaunt that his shoulders stuck through his jacket like a coat hanger, his hands sticking out of his sleeves like witches' claws.

"Why not lira? And what do you want me to do?" Dane asked. He could use some money, but was not about to be swindled by anyone.

"It's US dollars we're paying, take it or leave it. All you have to do is take this bag and drop it into that trashcan across the street, then walk to the phone booth on the corner and look in the phonebook under the escorts section. There you'll find your money."

"What's the catch?"

"No catch; just walk, drop, and collect."

"For a hundred US dollars?"

"That's what I said, didn't I?"

Dane stared hard at the two men. It didn't take more than a few seconds to decide. Smoothly he turned to the bar, raised his glass, and emptied the contents in two deep gulps. He then took the bag from the fat man's hand and walked out of the bar. Just like the fat man said, the money was in the phonebook.

The following morning while he was eating breakfast, Dane couldn't help but notice the front-page headline on the paper his father was reading: "Paul Serge Killed in Bombing." After reading the article and seeing that the bomb had exploded on the corner of Via Firenze and Via Tevere, he did not need to be told that what he'd placed in the trashcan the day before had been a bomb. However, caring about much of anything at all had never been an inherent virtue of his. Knowing he'd been responsible for the death of a powerful diplomat who happened to be parked on the street near the trashcan didn't make him feel the least bit guilty. He'd always maintained a firm belief that guilt was a useless emotion.

The years went by slowly and uneventfully. Dane did more and more work for the skinny and the fat man he soon came to know as Sticks and Stones. Dane learned that they were members in a criminal syndicate of significant magnitude, but this was something that did not rattle him in the least. In fact, he enjoyed the danger. He even reveled in it. The jobs he usually did were fast-and-simple drops, which were always very unfortunate for whoever happened to be on the receiving end. Dane couldn't care less about the result of his work. He was making more money than anyone he knew. There seemed no limit. Each time he was paid, he would search out gifts for his mother or whomever else he decided to please. Everyone loved him. Life was wonderful. And then everything suddenly changed.

It was winter. He was sitting in a bar about three blocks from his father's shoe store. He was halfway through his second lager when Sticks came through the door in his usual easy manner. For the first time since Dane had known him, he didn't have Stones at his side. Something was obviously very wrong.

Sticks' smooth, chiseled features were awash with unknown woe. "Stones has been shot," he whispered.

"What? Who?" Dane asked.

"He died two hours ago in a safe house just outside Milan. He was gunned down by Peter Pordelone."

Dane knew of the Pordelone family. They were the local competition for any of the illicit goings on, and they were extremely powerful. "What would you have me do, and when would you like it done?" he asked, trying to appear calm.

Sticks looked at Dane, momentarily admiring his clarity of thought. "It's not about money this time. This time it's personal. If you're in, I have to know now, because *now* is the time for action," Sticks said.

"I'm in!"

"Good. Let's do it."

The plan was simple. Dane was to walk with Sticks across the street from the Bari Patisserie. He'd stand on the street and keep watch while Sticks went into the Marino Restaurant. Sticks wanted to be up close with this one. He wanted to look into the man's eyes before he pulled the trigger. Nothing else would satisfy him more.

Dane's part was very straightforward. He was the cleanup man. After keeping an eye out for any curious spectators, he would walk into the building, drop his package, and walk out. And judging by the weight of the package—it was *very* heavy—, he knew there'd be nothing left to use as evidence once the job was complete. It held enough explosives to level a good-sized building.

Seeing Sticks exit the building Dane made his move. He slipped into the restaurant and found his target lying face-up on the floor. There was a neat hole between the man's eyes and a fast spreading pool of blood around the body. Carefully, Dane reached inside the bag he carried and flipped the arming switch. He then placed the bag directly beside the body and left as discretely as he'd entered. Five minutes later he was in the bar drinking his lager when he heard a distant thud. He decided to drink two more rounds before heading home. By that time, the initial chaos on the streets should have died down a bit.

Approaching the gates of his family estate later that evening, Dane noticed, for the first time in memory, that they were closed. As he drew closer, he saw Dacio, his father's associate, standing with one hand cautiously reaching inside his jacket. Dacio visibly relaxed as he recognized Dane. The gates opened as he approached.

"What's going on?" Dane asked as he pulled alongside Dacio.

"You must see your mother immediately," Dacio insisted.

Dane hit the gas pedal and sped up the driveway. He found his mother in the garden. Clearly, she'd been crying. Sitting at her side, he put his arms around her in a comforting manner.

"Your uncle Dino is dead," she said, her voice shaky.

The words hit Dane like a brick to the forehead. Out of everyone in his family, second only to his father, Dino had been his closest friend. "What? Who?" He fumbled for words.

"That's not all. Your father is in hospital. He's been very seriously injured." Her words rushed out all at once. "I've been waiting for you. We must go to the hospital at once."

Grief washed over Dane. "What happened?" he begged.

"All I know is there was a massive explosion in which most of the building was destroyed."

"What? What building?" Dane asked.

"The bank. The bank on Via Vico delle Grazie." She burst into tears.

The hospital was an ancient and creepy place filled with evil sounds. Dane hated hospitals. To him a hospital was a place of misery and weakness. He waited with his family in the hall outside the operating room. His father had been in surgery almost five hours. He couldn't get his mother's words out of his head: *Via Vico delle Grazie*, she'd said. *Via Vico delle Grazie.* Why did the street names sound and feel so significant to him?

Finally the doctor came into the hall to face them. A grave look upon his face, he spoke in a low, determined voice, "He'll live."

Dane watched his mother visibly relax.

The doctor went on, "He lost a lot of blood, but we were lucky enough to have stopped the flow in time. However, I'm afraid he will be paralyzed from the waist down. The blast badly mutilated his legs, and there's still a chance we'll have to amputate."

The blast. The words rocked Dane. Everything suddenly slid into place. The bank on Vico delle Grazie ... the blast ... Of course! Via Vico delle Garazie ran parallel to Via Vico Valoria, the same street that the Marino Restaurant was on. Could it be that the bomb he'd planted for Sticks had been responsible for the tragedy? He had to know the truth. He leapt to his feet and rushed from the hospital under the bewildered eyes of his family. Ten minutes later, in a half-dazed state, he parked his car on Via Vico Valoria. There was nothing more than a massive heap of rubble where the restaurant had been. He stood on the sidewalk, staring in disbelief. The bag Sticks had given him had done much more damage than he'd imagined.

It was growing dark, and in a trance-like state Dane ducked under the police barrier and stumbled though the rubble. The last few policemen were leaving, and no one noticed his presence. Sure enough, he could now clearly see that the bank had been attached to the rear of the restaurant—in all effect, they were one and the same building. A heavy cloud of despair fell over him. His mind was a minefield of emotion. He sat heavily in the rubble, unable to move.

It was completely dark when he finally reached a reasonable level of coherence. One thought, and one thought only, rebounded though his head—*escape*. He had to leave Genova and find somewhere to calm down, collect his thoughts, and decide what to do. Standing slowly in the dark, he felt his way back through the rubble, but had taken only a few paces before he fell flat on his face. Painfully getting to his feet, he found his foot was caught on some unseen obstacle. Through the dimness, he made out the faint outline of a chrome handle. His toe was stuck within its grip.

An unusual feeling of curiosity swept through him, and he decided to take a look at what the handle belonged to. He yanked his foot free and scratched at the rubble until he uncovered a large suitcase that must have weighed a good eighty pounds. It was a hard case with a combination lock. Unable to open it, Dane decided to take it with him.

Present day …

Dane awoke to the smell of strong black coffee, which Koso was waving under his nose. He groaned loudly and righted himself in his chair. "A hangover like this makes me think it would be easier if I'd lost the game last night," he said.

"Ah," Koso grunted, "you young ones are all the same—as soft as piss."

Dane sipped the hot black liquid in silence.

"What you need, son, is a little mountain air in those lungs of yours. The skiing in New Zealand is perfect this time of the year. Why don't you come with me and stir up a little trouble on the slopes?"

Dane considered for a moment and came to a solid decision. "I'm afraid I'll have to pass on New Zealand this time. I'll let you do the damage on your own."

"Oh come on, Dane. What's holding you back? It isn't work this time. I know Bryant's running everything for you these days, so there's no excuse."

"No, it's not work."

"Then what?"

"It's family."

Chapter 2

Home

The soft sand ran between Dane's toes as he walked lazily along the beach. The warmth on his feet felt wonderful to the touch. He'd left Monte Carlo the day before and driven down to Genova, the hometown of his youth. The beach was small, not too busy, and situated just south of the old village. There were high, rocky cliffs to the north, and below them was a small car park, surrounded by lush green trees. A million childhood memories flooded back to him as the familiarity of his old surroundings set in. The memory of his flight from home and the events that followed also returned. He could still clearly picture the Milan hotel he fled to—small, cheap, and unclean. The bottle of scotch he'd bought had also been cheap. He'd thought it best, at the time, to conserve what little money he'd had. But when he'd pried open the suitcase, he'd discovered that his money troubles came to an abrupt end. Inside the case was five million US dollars. When he'd recovered from the initial shock of his find, he'd mulled long and hard over what he'd do with his newly acquired wealth. At first all he'd done was run, afraid to pause or so much as look over his shoulder for fear of what he'd find. After almost six months of endless travel he'd met Bryant Wilson while in Jamaica. Bryant was a smooth-as-silk character with a reputation for making money out of thin air. Dane soon realized that meeting Bryant was a stroke of luck equal to that of the mysterious suitcase find. Together, they forged an empire of five-star resorts that started in Jamaica and expanded into seventeen countries. In less than fifteen years, Dane went from a scarred, juvenile runaway on the verge of a nervous breakdown to a world-class businessman. And now, here he was again, home. The circle was almost complete.

Dane's thoughts snapped back to the present as a figure appeared on the water's edge ahead of him. As he drew closer he saw that the figure was seated in a wheelchair. A few moments later he drew up alongside it.

The crippled old man slowly turned his head, his gray hair floating on the breeze, and looked directly up at Dane. At first, there was no recognition, and then a broad smile swept across the wrinkled old face. "Well, aren't you going to greet me with a hug, my boy?" he said.

Dane's heart pounded in shock and emotion as he pulled his father into his arms. "I ... I," he stuttered, finally standing back. He could barely speak.

"You don't think for a moment I'd forget the face of my own son, do you?"

With a mammoth effort, Dane gathered his senses. He'd had hopes of acclimatizing to his hometown before confronting his family, but it was too late for that now. "Papa, it's great to see you," he said, finally finding his tongue.

"For a moment there, you looked as if you'd seen a ghost," the old man replied.

"It's just a bit of a shock. It's been so long," Dane said.

"I suppose it would be a shock after hiding from us for almost fifteen years."

Despite his words, Dane knew his father wasn't angry. His father never got angry; he was gentle by nature. "I haven't exactly been hiding, Papa. I've just been a little busy, that's all."

"Well, my son, whatever business you're involved in must be very serious indeed to keep you away this long. But you always were that way inclined, weren't you? Always finding ways of making something from nothing."

Dane noted his father looked strong and fit, despite the wheelchair.

"Well, don't just stand there, son—help an old man back to his automobile."

"Of course, Papa. How is Mother?" Dane asked.

"Your mother is as mean and as well as ever," he said with a chuckle, "but I'm sure she'll tell you all when you see her."

His father chattered continuously as Dane pushed him through the sand. Dane momentarily wondered how he had gotten to the water's edge in the first place, but then he realized his father had a driver waiting in the car who'd obviously pushed him through the soft sand. Mostly, however, he wondered what he was going to say to his family. Just how much could he tell them?

When they arrived home, Dane noticed the house was the same as ever, magnificent in every detail. It had been built in the mid-nineteenth century for the famous Italian writer, D'Annunzio Gabrieli. The estate covered a total of four acres, with terraced gardens overlooking the Mediterranean. The three-story house had massive windows and balconies overlooking the gardens. The entire affair was grandiose by anyone's standards. As a child, Dane often wondered how his father could have afforded such a home, especially because he was only in the shoe business. But, as Dane grew up, he came to understand that his father had inherited quite a sum of family money.

Later that evening, there was a dinner in the family home, Italian style. Everyone was there—Uncle Gino, Aunt Cecily, and a host of the usual close friends and family. Dane could hardly remember half their faces, let alone their names. They were all full of a million questions, and in a roundabout way, Dane managed to explain what he'd been doing with himself. They seemed all too proud and happy to see him again, and no one delved too deeply into the past. Dane felt increasingly relieved that he'd finally confronted them. The whole affair went warmly and smoothly, but, as the evening wore on, Dane truly began to feel the absence of his uncle Dino.

It was halfway through the evening, and Dane was on his way back from the bathroom when his mother approached him. He had already spoken to her, but this was the first time they were alone together.

"Come, Dane, talk to me a while," she said.

Dane followed her. She was a large woman, but she moved easily, despite the extra weight. Soon they were seated on one of the more private balconies at the west end of the house.

"So, what are your plans?" she said, looking at him expectantly.

Dane regarded the question for a moment. His mother was a commanding woman, with intense eyes and a will to match. Now that he was asked, he had no idea what to tell her—but he had to tell her something. "I have the business, and soon enough, I will have to return to work," he said.

"You're still hiding from us," she said.

"No."

"Then why don't you stay here with us? Your father could use your help, and he's not getting any younger."

Something inside Dane told him that his mother's concern for his father was the last reason she wanted him home. His parents had been at odds with each other for years, and after talking to many of the guests that evening, he had learned that this had never changed. "I wish I could stay," he said "I wish it was that simple."

"Then just stay," she said.

"I can't. Not yet."

His mother looked at him for a long and deafeningly silent moment. "What happened to your father and uncle was difficult on all of us, but we are family. We get through these things together."

Dane was silent. What could he say? Half of him desperately wanted to tell his mother everything, and the other half wanted to run.

He was saved when his father suddenly wheeled through the French doors. "There you are," he said. "Come, Mother, you can't have him all to yourself all evening."

And that was it. Dane stood, excused himself, and returned to the festivities. His mother was going to have to wait until another time—until he had clearer answers.

As Dane lay in his old bed later that night, he couldn't get the image of his uncle's face out of his head. His mother had kept his bedroom just the way he'd left it, and this only intensified his memories. His sleep was haunted by nightmares—scenes from the bombing, his uncle's pleading face, his father's mangled legs, and blood ... blood everywhere. When morning finally came, he'd hardly slept at all, and he dragged himself to the breakfast table with all the zest of a snail. Feeling somewhat better after breakfast, he moved onto the balcony with his father for coffee. On the table were four foreign newspapers, and Dane remembered how his father liked to keep up on world events. He picked up the copy of *The New York Times*. On the front page was a photo of a bombed-out building. His heart skipped a beat as he read the article, and a light sheen of perspiration began to form on his forehead.

Tragedy struck today in Rio de Janeiro when the central police headquarters was leveled to the ground by a massive bomb. Authorities presume the bomb was driven into the headquarters basement, via police van. So far workers have found no survivors. It is believed that more than one hundred and fifty lives were lost in this brutal act of terrorism.

No one has claimed responsibility for the tragedy as yet, but it is alleged that South American drug lord, Benito Santage is liable. Mr. Santage is a known member of the infamous International Underworld Syndicate, or (IUS), an organization of unstoppable magnitude, which is allegedly led by an individual known as Krait.

Today's bombing is the latest in a series of violent events in Rio. Many say that this event is just another indication of how the Brazilian authorities are losing control in the war on drugs.

"Losing control? Hell, they lost control years ago," Dane's father said while glancing at the article.

"I don't understand why they don't do something about it," Dane said.

"I'll tell you why—corruption, my boy, corruption. It's human nature. And some are simply more willing to push their own agenda than others."

Dane knew deep down that his father was right. The article had deeply stirred emotions he would have rather left dormant. But it was the photo accompanying the article that really rattled him. Standing in front of the bombed-out Rio police headquarters, right alongside the police inspectors and bomb-disposal team, was Sticks, the very same man who'd so corrupted Dane's youth. Sticks was obviously still up to his old tricks, and he was now bold enough and powerful enough to not worry about the law at his side. In that moment, Dane realized that he had to do something. He had the power, the freedom, and the ability to take any necessary action. He just wasn't yet sure what that action should be. Above all, Dane was convinced of one thing—he'd made peace with his family, and now it was time to make peace with himself.

Chapter 3

South America

Six months later ...

Benito Santage gave the handle of the bench vice another quarter-turn. The youth screamed in agony as the bones in his right hand cracked. "How dare you steal money from me? How dare you?" Benito screamed. "One last time: where is my money?"

The boy, no more than twelve, was just one of hundreds working for Benito on the cruel Rio streets. He was now barely conscious, and if it weren't for the guard holding him up, he would have collapsed. "My mother, Senor. Please, Senor, my mother," he managed to say, breathlessly.

Taking one last look at the boy's face, knowing he'd finally told the truth, Santage forced the vice handle around again until the jaws were tightly clamped together. Blood spilled to the marble floor, and the boy gave a final, soul-rattling shriek before fainting.

"Throw him into the street," Benito demanded. "And clean this mess up."

The two men simply tore the boy from the vice. They knew he wouldn't survive the night, but they did as they were told.

The money no longer mattered to Benito. He'd tasted blood, and he wanted more. Two hours later, the unconscious boy was thrown into the street, and Benito and his men stood outside the door of the boy's home—a ramshackle second floor apartment that smelled as bad as it looked. Benito's men, Cisco Delmio and Costa Spartal, stood at his side, ready for anything. It was almost eight p.m., but the Rio heat was still sweltering.

Cisco knocked loudly, and moments later, a short, fat man answered. As if it wasn't hot enough outside, a stifling wave of heat billowed from the apartment. The man wore only a tank-top and shorts and was sweating profusely. His eyes widened when he saw the three men standing at his door.

"My name is Benito Santage; these are my friends. We would like to talk to you."

"I know who you are. Please, come in. Please," the fat man said, an audible tremble in his voice.

The apartment was like any other in the area—small, dim, and filthy. The open kitchen looked as if it hadn't been cleaned since it was built, and in many places, the carpet was worn through to the boards.

"This won't take long," Benito said. "I'm here simply to ask you one question. Julio, your son has been working for me for some time now. Whether or not you were aware of this is of no concern. I simply want to know—if he were to hide money here, where would that be?"

Julio's parents and sister stared blankly at Benito. They sat on a torn sofa, which faced a strangely new-looking television. Electric silence hung in the air for a full minute. The family obviously knew something, but, sadly, opted to say nothing.

The silence was the only answer Benito needed. "Thank you," he said. "That is all I wanted to know. Now my men and I will bid you good night." This said, they made their exit.

They walked to the end of the alley and waited. The explosion came only a few seconds later. The blast was so powerful, it shook the alley walls around them and echoed throughout the city. When the dust settled, they walked back to the apartment. Most of the top floor had been wood. The blast had shattered the flimsy construction into matchstick-like pieces. It took Santage only a few minutes to find what he was looking for; a steel ammunition-case was sitting in the corner of what was left of a bedroom, and inside the case was nearly all of the money he was owed. The family had been blown into small chunks of flesh and mangled limbs and these were now scattered throughout the wreckage. The message was clear—the consequences were dire for anyone who stole from him.

"Thank you," Santage said again.

A small crowd was beginning to assemble, and a distant siren could be heard. But Santage and his men would be long gone before the authorities arrived.

There was the Italian, Russian, Japanese and Chinese Mafias, as well as countless other illegal organizations. In a nutshell, they were all about money. All of these organizations made more money than the common man could imagine. But even in the underworld, there always had to be some kind of control. Without it, chaos would ensue, and no organized criminal wanted chaos. Chaos was bad business and had to be prevented at all costs—and chaos-prevention existed under the iron fist of Krait, and Krait alone.

Nobody knew who Krait was, or, for that matter, *where* Krait was. In fact, there even seemed to be some confusion over whether Krait was a man or a woman. One thing was for certain, however— everyone under the umbrella of what was known as the International Underworld Syndicate (IUS) knew that the ultimate control lay in Krait's hands.

When the illicit wealth of an organization exceeded one hundred million US dollars, Krait would show up, one way or another. No one knew how Krait became aware of these details, but, from that point forth, 5 percent of the concerned organization's earnings went to the IUS. If the 5 percent weren't paid in full each month, there would be one less member of the syndicate. It was rare that an organization didn't pay.

The relationship between Krait and syndicate members, however, was not all bad. Krait had black-market supply power that was second to none, and was available to any IUS member. The first players in the syndicate started out running their own shows; they dealt to and from their own sources. It soon became obvious, however, that Krait always had the best deal. And who could argue?

The last member to argue ended up being demolished, along with the thirteen-floor building he happened to be in at the time. The one before that was rumored to still be alive somewhere in Siberia, processing toxic waste.

More important than all of this was the fact that Sticks, Dane's boss from his youth, was working for Krait in Rio, presiding over a man named Benito Santage, a drug lord of staggering wealth and power—a man known for taking a personal hand in the severest of cruelty toward all whom opposed him. If Sticks was working for Krait, that meant that Krait was undoubtedly the individual heading the crime syndicate Dane had worked for as a youth. Sticks had been where Dane's research had begun. Sticks was number four on a list Dane had compiled of the top-five most dangerous people in the IUS. Krait was number one. One thing above all was certain—all of the five on the list were going to die, and Dane was convinced that only then could he put his past to rest.

Most of the information on the IUS, Dane had compiled from a well-paid connection he'd acquired in American intelligence. Money, Dane's greatest asset, could get you anything if you were prepared to pay enough of it. And it was from this information that he had compiled his list. He would have liked to have gone after Sticks first, but, as much as he'd investigated, bribed, and conspired with the Rio underworld, he had not managed to locate him. He decided, therefore, to move onto Benito Santage.

2:47 p.m.
The hotel suite Dane occupied was simply beautiful. It comprised a total of three rooms and a balcony and had the advantage of being located on the top floor of the Chateau Delmain Hotel, giving ample view of the city. He watched Cisco Delmio through a telescopic lens. Cisco sat, sipping his coffee in the Rio street café, laughing and joking with a lady friend. The display appeared strange, considering that Cisco was a completely soulless murderer. But everyone had a day off, and today was Cisco's.

Dane had been watching Benito Santage and his men for three days. Sometimes he'd watched from a crowd, and sometimes from an adjacent building. He was never close enough for anyone to notice his curious eyes. While he'd been observing, Benito had killed a total of sixteen people. This was the time of the year when the notoriously brutal drug lord did his spring cleaning.

Dane had thought long and hard about how to kill Benito. At first he thought of doing it quickly and moving right along to number two, but after studying his target, he'd decided differently; he wanted Benito to suffer—not just with pain, but also with fear. Instead of taking the head from the beast, he would take the beast from the head. Cisco was the first step in that plan.

The weapon Dane had chosen was simple but effective—a .50-caliber, single-shot rifle with a detachable barrel and a scope that could zero down a fly at a thousand yards. The rifle had a handmade silencer screwed onto the end of the long barrel. The silencer was different from others, in the respect that it didn't slow down the exiting bullet or decrease its accuracy; rather, it increased the accuracy and velocity of the bullet by about 25 percent. He'd learned to shoot from Koso, who had a military background that was altogether unclear—but during the tutoring, it became obvious that Koso had been a master sniper in his day. Dane had taken up sharp-shooting as a hobby, and he never imagined he'd actually use the skill on live targets. Presently, however, he was doing just that, and he felt surprisingly calm as he zeroed down on the forehead of Cisco Delmio. The full-metal-jacket cartridge he locked and loaded was slightly modified; a small hole had been drilled carefully into the tip, and the hole had been filled with mercury. The effect the shell would have on a human head would be nothing less than explosive.

Dane took his time. He aimed carefully, taking long, drawn-out breaths, feeling his heartbeat slow. Between a seventh and eighth beat, when he felt the most steady, he squeezed the trigger. The silencer worked beautifully, emitting minimal noise. The accuracy of the rifle was excellent. Through the lens, he watched the sudden expression of aghast horror on the face of Cisco's lady friend. The café erupted into sudden chaotic frenzy, with people running and jumping in every direction.

21

Dane sat back in the luxurious leather chair and took a long pull from a glass of water. He smiled with the knowledge that Benito Santage's circle of trusted friends had been cut in half—he would now only feel half as safe. Dane reflected on the moment, analyzing his feelings about his first kill. He knew he had killed before while working for Sticks and his companion, but this time it was different. This time it was a lot more personal. Still, he was surprised to feel very little emotion about the act at all. Enjoying the cool water in the heat of the day, he relaxed and waited.

At precisely eight minutes past three, Detective Jimmy Wangol placed a call to Benito Santage's mobile phone. He'd just arrived at the crime scene and could barely believe the identity of the victim. He knew there would be hell to pay over Cisco's death. He chose his words carefully when Benito personally answered the phone.

"We have just found Cisco Delmio shot dead," Jimmy said.

Benito listened as Jimmy elaborated on the situation. He was shocked to the core by what he heard, and when Jimmy was finished, he hung up without saying a single word.

Costa Spartal looked at his boss curiously. He knew that there were only three people who knew his mobile number.

"Cisco has been shot. He's dead," Benito echoed. "I want you to see what you can find out. Our friend is in charge of the investigation, so you'll have no problem getting close to the body."

Costa knew better than to ask questions, so he left quickly and without direction. Although his boss didn't show any sign of being shaken by the event, Costa knew otherwise. Cisco Delmio had been Benito's closest confidant. He had been his right-hand man for as long as anyone could remember.

Benito did have emotions, one of which he had difficulty identifying. He then remembered, slowly at first—and then a torrent of forgotten images washed over him.

He was ten years old. He and his father lived in a small town bordering the Amazon. They were on their usual weekend hike, a day's walk into the jungle. The rain battered down relentlessly. Already Benito felt tired, and they had only just begun. Having lost his mother in an accident while he was very young, Benito had only his father, and he loved him with all his heart. He dearly wanted to prove his strength to him, and he was not about to submit easily to fatigue.

An hour or so before darkness, Benito's father insisted they stop for the night. Benito feigned his desire to go on a while longer, but it was decided that they better get their camp set up before it got dark.

As night fell, the rain stopped, and the noises of the jungle began to change. Benito and his father settled down after a small but tasty meal. This was the time Benito enjoyed most. The night became very clear, without a breath of wind—but the very ground they sat on was crawling with life, as though the jungle itself was one complete, moving creature. They chatted long into the evening about what his mother was like, how beautiful she was, about wars, the universe—about anything and everything, until exhaustion set in, and they finally slept.

When Benito awoke, the jungle was alive with a million morning noises, and the tent was hot to the point of his hardly being able to breath. The full heat of the day was evidently upon them, and he wondered why his father had not woken him earlier. They usually set off shortly after dawn. He tried to wake him, but had no luck. Looking a little closer he discovered his face was very pale. He reached out without even thinking and touched his skin. It was warm, but, in the heat of the tent, that didn't mean much. There was no hint of breath coming from his lungs, and Benito finally admitted to himself that his father was dead. He reached to undo the tent zipper in order to escape the tomb, but found it was already halfway open. It was then he realized he must have left it undone when he'd gotten up earlier to relieve himself. Panic crept upon him as the death of his father became a harsh reality. Carefully he pulled his father's sleeping bag back, and with fear in his heart, he inspected his neck. Two septic holes stared at him from below his jawline. The puncture wounds stared at him like the angry eyes of some evil beast. Years of being on his own for days at a time had taught Benito never to panic, but to sit back and quietly think of a way around whatever problem confronted him. Regardless of this, he felt fear like he'd never known.

After burying his father, he took the compass and headed east, knowing that, at some point, he'd stumble upon civilization. It took six days to crawl out of the jungle, and his supplies had run dry on the third. By the time he had made it, something had changed within him. It was as if he were now more beast than man.

The civilization he stumbled upon was a small village named San Androsia. As he hobbled into it, he could think of nothing but his need for food and water. Walking along the dirt road into the village, he couldn't recall ever being so hungry or tired. Each step he took sent up a cloud of dust. It was hot beyond belief. Whatever moisture remained in him was now being sucked from his very flesh by the drought-stricken environment. It appeared that any residents were in their crumbling, tin shacks, taking what shelter they could. No one was in sight.

Benito pushed open a fly-screen door and stepped into the village supply store. The store consisted of a few shelves on each wall and a narrow table running down the middle. Sitting behind a beat-up counter was a large, sweaty Indian, wearing only shorts and a faded tank top. He was unsuccessfully attempting to cool himself under a tiny fan. The tall barstool he sat on sank threateningly into his expansive backside.

What came next had seemingly been an automatic reaction for Benito—a reaction that had come from some dark survival instinct. Before the fat man could bat an eyelash, Benito pulled his father's hunting knife from his belt and drove it into the unwary victim's left eye. That obstacle dealt with, Benito then leapt over the countertop and retrieved the keys dangling from the dead man's belt. Two minutes later he was speeding away in a big Ford. The seat of the vehicle was all the way forward, and Benito still had to sit right on the front edge to see over the wheel. Lucky for him, the machine was an automatic. He'd only had two or three driving lessons in his young life, and he didn't have a hope in hell of handling a stick-shift. He knew speed was critical. He had to get as far from the town as he could, as fast as he could. He had food from the store, a full tank of gas, and a respectable amount of money he'd found under the fat man's stool.

The events that followed that day fell together in a way that seemed unstoppable. The ruthless edge that Benito had discovered came as naturally as breathing. The fat man he'd killed in that store had not played on his conscience even once. That murder was followed by a string of others.

He'd first made his way to Bogotá, Colombia. There he managed to purchase a kilo of high-grade cocaine with the money he'd stolen. The dealer promised he'd make a massive profit, even if he resold the kilo to tourists right there in Bogotá. But Benito hadn't trusted the dealer one bit, and he quickly decided to correct the situation. The following morning, the drug-dealer was found dead in his doorway of his home with his head caved in; a large brick lay suspiciously nearby. By this time, Benito was well on his way to Cartagena, where he stowed away on a small freighter en route to Miami. In his possession was the cocaine and money that he'd retrieved from the dead dealer's body. Once he reached Miami and successfully slipped by customs, he quickly managed to sell the kilo on the street for five times what he'd paid.

From that point forth, things became easier and easier as time passed. With his newfound wealth, he hired a private Brazilian tutor, whom he eventually learned to trust. By the time Benito was sixteen, he was a very well-educated young man—not only in a conventional way, but also in the art of drug trafficking.

After ten years of dealing cocaine and other substances to many midlevel buyers, Benito had enough contacts to take the next step in his career. This step was, at first, tentatively restrained, but it soon became the very fabric of what became an empire. This master step began by approaching Paul Henderson at a political campaign, a campaign that would ultimately make him governor to the state of Florida. Mr. Henderson's passion for power and politics was accompanied by an equal passion for high-quality cocaine. In America, Benito had found that money could buy most anything, and Paul Henderson was no exception to this rule. In exchange for having the authorities turn a blind eye to Benito's business, the esteemed Paul Henderson received all the necessary funding for his campaign and his drug habit. Certainly, it was this funding which had given Henderson his victory. This was a meager investment on Benito's behalf, considering the returns it offered.

Since Henderson, Benito had purchased several key political players in both North and South America. The financial power, together with more than eighty businesses he now had in over fifteen different countries, was staggering.

So it was that the crushing fear Benito felt at the time of his father's death—the fear that had so fueled his success—diminished as the years passed and as his wealth and power grew. But now, with the death of Cisco, things had taken a dramatic turn for the worse. Indeed, the horrors of the past were clawing at the calm shores of the present.

Dane was finishing his third glass of water when Costa Spartal stalked up to the café where Cisco lay. Dane took his time carefully comparing Costa to the photo he had. He had to be certain that he had the right man. Satisfied, he laid down his powerful binoculars and retrieved his rifle. Again, he loaded the weapon and waited patiently for the perfect shot. He watched as Costa conversed with the investigating detective. A police photographer shuffled about, taking the usual shots. An ambulance was parked close by. The futility of this amazed Dane. A hearse would be more appropriate. He adjusted the rifle in its tripod. He watched through the scope in anticipation as Costa turned and looked to the precise spot where Dane was perched. It was as if he knew the exact location of the shooter. For a moment, this startled Dane, but he then realized there was no possible way Costa could see him over such a distance, which was almost two thousand meters.

Costa continued to look in Dane's direction, and Dane decided to brush off his insecurity and use the moment. Again he aimed carefully at the head of his mark. Again he squeezed the trigger and waited to see the result of his work. A split second later, Costa's head exploded into pieces, splattering the detective at his side. Like a scene from some horror film, Costa's body remained standing for a full three seconds before keeling backward. No one waited for a moment to see where the shot had come from. There would be no more investigation on this particular day.

Dane sighed. He'd taken the legs from Benito—and now the body. It was time to turn his attention to the head. He knew that Benito would even now be receiving word that Costa was dead. He relished in the thought that he would now be feeling fear of the like he'd never felt before. What tickled Dane most was the fact that Benito had no clue as to who his enemy was.

Benito Santage was seated at his breakfast table. His maid, Maria, had prepared the usual meal, but he'd not touched a thing. He couldn't remember ever feeling so bone-weary. It had been three days since Costa's death, and he'd not slept a wink during that time. After hearing the news, he'd caged himself into his home like a scared animal, all the while racking his brains, desperately trying to imagine who wanted to destroy him. *Government? It must be government. Yes, but which one?* All his bases had been covered, and everyone had been paid.

He'd hired ten extra bodyguards and placed them in strategic locations all over his estate. All his men were heavily armed and had come highly recommended. The estate had a twenty-foot-high perimeter wall, with cameras every twenty feet. Two Doberman dogs were constantly patrolling the grounds, along with two of the best bodyguards. Nevertheless, he felt no more secure. The only two people on the planet he could really depend on were now dead. Perspiration dripped from his brow, despite the coolness of air-conditioned surroundings. Taking a sip from his coffee, he noticed the cup trembling in his hands. His world was falling apart around him. He felt abandoned and alone.

"Senor," the maid interrupted, "may I take your plate?"

The presence stirred Benito from his thoughts. "Yes, Maria, I think I've had enough. Just leave the coffee."

"Yes, Senor."

Benito stared blindly into his perfectly landscaped garden, deep in thought. His gardener was meticulously pruning one of the many rose bushes, and he looked superbly relaxed and calm in his task. Benito momentarily wished he were the gardener. All of a sudden, there was a massive crash, and he almost jumped clear out of his skin. His heart ached from the shock.

"Sorry, Senor," Maria yelled from the kitchen. "I just tripped. So sorry."

"Do it again," Benito yelled, "and you'll be tripping off the rooftop!"

"Yes, Senor," she replied, an audible tremble in her tone, knowing full well her boss wasn't joking.

The phone in the kitchen rang, and Maria answered it. "Senor, it's one of the guards; he wishes to talk to you urgently," she called out.

Benito instantly picked up the phone from the breakfast table. "Yes," he angrily answered.

"Sir, we have just caught someone scaling the rear wall. We searched him and found a weapon—a gun, sir."

Benito's spirits instantly lightened. Could it be that the assassin had been caught—a single man? He thought for a moment. He would need somewhere quiet to question him. "Bring him into my study," he said.

"Yes, sir!"

Certainly the intruder was the assassin, Benito decided. Finally, he had someone to vent his discomfort onto. He couldn't resist a tremble of anticipation. He sipped his coffee in quiet contemplation. His appetite had returned, and he wished Maria hadn't taken the food away.

Dane stood, finally face to face with the very disturbed-looking Benito Santage. The study was unusually furnished. On the wall behind Benito's heavy oak desk was a painting of the pope, and to the side of it there was a life-sized mannequin of a naked woman. Dane could not decide what threw him off most—the mannequin or the pope. But it was the look on Benito's face that quickly won his attention. On the surface was the cool, bluntly exposed anger Benito was renowned for. But just beneath this shallow façade were the icy tentacles of fear. Benito Santage was truly a man afraid for his life.

Seated behind his desk, fingering Dane's confiscated revolver, Benito eyeballed him for a full minute before speaking. "You know, by the way in which you took care of my two associates, I imagined that you were a man of great intelligence. But now, all I can see is a common fool, no different than any of those other dead people walking out there. It was you who killed my associates, wasn't it?" Benito asked, matter-of-factly.

"Of course," Dane confirmed, his voice calm and serene, as if he were commenting on the weather.

Benito felt dumbstruck by the confession. He'd been anticipating an intense interrogation. Still fingering the revolver, he contemplated using it to beat the intruder to death. Rage boiled within him. The assassin was not reacting in the fashion he'd anticipated. "I'll make you pay for the deaths of Costa and Cisco, and I promise, you will pay slowly," he growled.

Dane remained composed. He snuck a look over his shoulder to find two guards standing directly behind him. One of them was still holding the briefcase that they'd taken from him when he was captured.

"So, my friend, who do you work for?" Benito asked.

"Myself," Dane answered.

Benito chuckled, eyeing the briefcase. "We'll see about that," he said. "My men tell me that there is no way of opening your briefcase without the correct combination. They have also scanned the case for explosives and toxins, so this raises my curiosity all the more. If the case is not dangerous, then it must be for something you were bringing to me, or for something you were going to take away? Either way, I'll need to see inside. So tell me the combination, and I will make your death quick and easy. However, if you give me the wrong answer, I'll cut your fingers off one at a time until the case is open." This said, he placed the gun on the desktop before him.

29

Dane took a long deep breath of relief as the gun was placed on the desk. It had a solid-gold handle and was a beautiful handmade weapon that had inspired Benito's interest—exactly as anticipated. "Okay," he conceded, feigning defeat. "I know you think I'm a fool, but I'm not foolish enough to go losing my fingers in any great hurry. So, to hell with it, I'll give you the damn combination."

Silence settled in the room for moment, and Dane began to call out the numbers one by one, slowly, so he could see them being keyed in out of the corner of his eye. "One ... Three ..."

The guard fumbled with the lock.

"One ..." and again he paused. "Three," and in that moment, Dane's world went into slow motion. As the briefcase opened, he dove face-forward, to the floor in front of the desk. The instant he landed, his gun, still on the desktop in front of Santage, exploded, sending razor-sharp shrapnel that sliced through everything in its path. Inside of the gun had been a shaped charge, specifically designed to explode from the top, bottom, front, and back, and since the gun was lying on the desk when detonated, it sliced through the air directly parallel to the floor, exactly as the engineer had promised.

Dane stayed face-down for a full five seconds after the explosion to make sure the bomb had done its work. He then slowly rose. Aside from some blood and tissue—not his own—he was totally untouched. Standing slowly, he observed blood pouring freely over Santage's still-twitching legs from under the desk. Both the guards and Santage were certainly dead—or only seconds away from being so. Santage's body was virtually cut in two, though his eyes were still open, staring blankly toward Dane, looking frighteningly alive.

Dane moved quickly. Other guards would arrive on the scene within moments. Seized by an amusing idea, he leapt over the desk and tore the pope from the wall. His souvenir safely under his arm, he made for the door, stepping over what was left of the mangled briefcase, which held only a transmitter. In the hall, he could hear the shouts of people approaching. He spotted a flight of stairs he'd seen during his capture, and he hurried down them. Reaching the bottom, he carefully opened the door to check for guards. Almost directly in front of him was a mechanic working under a big Rolls

Royce. Parked about ten feet away was a Porsche 928. Dane smiled. He saw only two problems: how to get to the Porsche without alerting the mechanic, and whether or not the keys would be in the ignition if he did make it.

He spotted a ring of keys attached to the mechanic's belt. He took off his shoes and silently tiptoed over to the jack that was holding the Rolls aloft. The mechanic was mumbling to himself, unaware he had company. Quickly Dane turned the release screw on the jack and lowered the car onto the mechanic's body, just enough so that he couldn't move. The mechanic shrieked loudly, and the sound echoed through the basement. Ignoring the cries, Dane put his shoes back on, pulled the keys from the mechanic's belt, and quickly made for the Porsche. As he did this, the big rolling doors began to rumble open, and shouts came from beyond.

Jumping behind the wheel and carefully seating the pope in the passenger seat, he began franticly trying each key. On his third try, the ignition turned, and the car roared into life. Immediately, he slammed the transmission into drive and roared toward the still-opening door. Lucky for him, the car was built very low to the ground. Still, as he flew under the door, the roof made contact with a loud clang. Guards went flying in every direction as he exited, and before they could recover, Dane was speeding down the driveway toward a pair of iron gates. Bracing for the impact, he glanced at his speed, which was already one hundred kilometers per hour. When he hit the gates, the car was doing a hundred and twenty, effectively bursting them open like a hammer to a walnut. Not believing his luck, he sped off down the road, adrenaline pounding through his veins.

"One down, four to go," he said aloud.

He wished he had the time to celebrate his success, but he had a six fifteen flight to Greece. Number two required his urgent attention, and the clock was ticking.

Chapter 4

Angel Fire

Limnos Skiathos had not had an easy life. His mother had left when he was five, and his father, a four-star Greek general, had had little time for family life. This left Limnos alone much of the time. Until he was old enough to enter the services, he was haphazardly shuffled between boarding schools and nannies, given everything he wanted—and nothing he really needed. By the time he was thirty, through his father's influence, he received his first star and became one of Greece's youngest generals. Still, he wasn't happy. Soon his thirst turned to money, and he began smuggling a few small arms, selling them for a good profit to his numerous contacts. Things then escalated to antiaircraft weapons, grenades, and the like. Each time a sale was made, more and more people became interested. This went on until there was no longer any time to pursue his official military career. To his father's dismay, he resigned his commission. But by then he had enough international contacts to last a lifetime, and his father no longer mattered.

After building enough wealth with trafficking, Limnos invested heavily in a Greek cruise line, with the sole intent of using the ships as a delivery system for his merchandise. The plan was immediately effective, and from that point forth, the world was at his feet, and his wealth doubled yearly.

Limnos now stood on the bridge of one of his cruise ships with the captain. They could see the south of Italy coming over the horizon, under a fireball sunset. Limnos marveled at how the polluted European atmosphere could create something so beautiful. But he had much more on his agenda than admiring storybook sunsets. He had work to do—a lot of work. They would dock at Taranto for two days, and while the passengers enjoyed the sights and sun of southern Italy, he would oversee the stowage of his largest arms shipment yet. He'd been lucky enough to acquire two F-14 jet fighters, which would bring him twice what he had paid once they reached Uganda.

Twenty years ago …

Angelica Skiathos closed her eyes and concentrated on one of the rare moments she and her mother had alone together. They were seated in one of the many luxury cabins aboard *The Best 4U*, an ocean cruiser belonging to her father, Limnos Skiathos. She loved the feeling of the brush being drawn through her long black hair, a ritual her mother performed nightly. Although she was only eight years old, she was already showing the telltale signs of a beautiful young lady. Born to a Greek father, she had olive skin and huge, dark eyes. Her mother, on the other hand, had given her the exquisite bone structure and flawless skin of her Chinese heritage.

Although home was Milos, a quiet island north of Crete, Angelica spent most of her time aboard one of her father's cruise ships. There were three hundred passengers on board this particular ship. Their next stop was Antibes, France.

Later that night Angelica awoke with a start, startled by the familiar sounds of her mother and father fighting. Her father's screaming chilled her to the bone. Whenever they fought, she would put on her headphones and turn the stereo up so loud she could barely think. Tonight was different, however. Tonight really scared her. She could hear rage in her father's voice, unlike anything she'd heard before. Sitting up in bed, she listened intently. Tears of fear stained her cheeks. Her mother shrieked abuse, her father swore, and glass shattered. After one last great crashing sound there was then prolonged silence. Angelica instantly knew something was *very* wrong. She fought off panic, sprang off her bed, and burst into the adjoining cabin. The scene before her would stay imprinted in her memory for the rest of her life. She had grown to hate her violent father, but now her feelings were way beyond hatred.

Limnos was seated with a half-finished glass of scotch in his hand, staring blankly at Angelica's mother, who was sprawled across the smashed glass of a coffee table. A long splinter protruded from her neck, and blood poured freely from the wound. Her white evening dress was soaked red. Limnos's blank look didn't change a bit as he turned toward Angelica.

Her father's eyes told Angelica everything she needed to know. She turned and stumbled from the room, tears streaming down her cheeks. She cried in the knowledge that no one would come to comfort her.

Present day …

Angelica lay with her eyes closed. A soft, warm breeze blew from the Mediterranean and flowed over her tanned curves. To the casual observer, she may have looked relaxed—peacefully asleep even. But peace was the last thing that dominated her being.

She loved Cyprus, and she wished she could spend more time lazing in the sun there. Much of her time, however, was spent plotting and planning how she was going to make her father pay for killing her mother.

Soon after her mother's murder, which her father had had no problem covering up, Angelica was sent to an exclusive private school in the south of France. She eventually studied law at Oxford and was soon hired by a large firm in London. Two years later, she was winning cases most attorneys only dreamed of. But, despite the power and wealth the law profession provided, Angelica remained unhappy.

In the twenty years since her mother's death, plotting to destroy her father was never far from her mind. Now the time had come. In three days' time, he was having his fifty-sixth birthday on Cyprus. Six hundred and fifty of the world's most influential people would be attending. The venue was a large building Limnos had constructed especially for the occasion. She was going to be there, and hell's fury would be her date.

Dane picked up another handful of sand and let the grains slide slowly through his fingers. The soul-warming Cyprus sun did little to lighten his thoughts. He was in one of his darker moods, which he couldn't seem to shake. But he had a task to perform. He couldn't let the enshrouding darkness cloud his judgment. He had to isolate his focus to where it was needed. Nothing less than his full attention was required for Limnos Skiathos, the world's leading arms dealer. Limnos was a man responsible for supplying drug lords, dictators, madmen, and international terrorists with any weapon they required, from the smallest handgun to the deadliest combat aircraft. Technically, Limnos was not a member of the IUS, but it was rumored in intelligence circles that he was about to be initiated into the syndicate. Dane decided he was a high value target that simply couldn't be left off his list.

The termination of Limnos Skiathos wasn't going to be easy. The security that surrounded him was heavily layered, constant, and state of the art. One possibility, however, had presented itself—Skiathos's fifty-sixth birthday, which would take place in just three days. Dane would be there. Limnos, however, was not the sole target. His US intelligence source confirmed that Krait would also be attending, and Dane simply couldn't pass up such an opportunity to at least try to get a look at this kingpin.

Dane had three days for a much-needed rest and a little planning before the event took place, and he intended to make the most of it.

His attention was suddenly caught by a beautiful, young woman who was staring directly at him. The moment he made eye-contact, however, she looked away, as if embarrassed. He dismissed the gesture and tried to return his thoughts to their previous path, but he soon found he could not take his eyes off her. Obliquely, he studied her more closely. She was unusual-looking, in a sense that it was difficult to tell her origins. But she was remarkably attractive, if not beautiful. She had flawless, olive skin, a perfectly symmetrical face, with a defined yet elegant jawline, full lips, a small, straight nose, and almond-shaped eyes. All this was topped by a wash of long, dark hair. He felt a certain rush of fervor he was unaccustomed to. Who was she? Where was she from? Was she married or attached? Why was he thinking such things? He felt surprised by his excitement—intrigued even—but there was no time to dwell on such fantasies.

Dane's indifference toward women was not without warrant. Over the years, he'd taken a number of chances with love. Each time, the experience had crashed and burned due to the greed and apathy of those dispassionate people who were motivated only by money. Impulsively, however, he stood and strolled across the sand to the spot where the beauty was sitting. Some unstoppable force told him he needed to take a closer look. She was reading—or at least pretending to. Not wanting to disturb her, he sat about five feet away and pulled out his notebook.

Angelica lay, staring into that space that was everywhere and nowhere all at once—the space you couldn't quite focus on—the space where you look when you're deep in thought. Unexpectedly, a shape materialized before her—the figure of a man. He seemed to be staring into the same space she was, also deep in thought. She wondered for a moment why he'd caught her attention; and then his vision, like hers, began to focus. He had large, intensely dark eyes and a wash of black hair, and he was obviously in very good shape. She shied away suddenly and broke the contact. She felt self-conscious, as if the man had briefly looked into her very soul. She returned to studying the notes that she had been working on, but her concentration was gone. From the corner of her eye, she watched the dark stranger try to study her inconspicuously.

She'd had only two real lovers during the stretch of her life, and, like all men, they had disappointed her. The first was a young professor at Oxford. She'd fallen head over heels in love from the moment they'd met. Six months later, she contracted a rather nasty STD. This occurrence made her study his sincerity more carefully. Without looking too hard, she found out her lover was sleeping with a total of eight of his students, and took regular sex vacations to China. A short course of antibiotics took care of her physical problem, but it took much longer to recover from the emotional damage.

The second man she'd met while working on an assignment in New York. This man was being prosecuted in a charity-fraud case. He'd allegedly been skimming from fundraising profits; the total figure had been in the ten million dollar vicinity. She'd met him purely by accident. They'd literally bumped into each other in one of New York's many libraries. He was doing research for his own defense. He told her a story about not being able to afford a lawyer, and how he had no choice but to defend himself. After chatting for over two hours, Angelica was completely convinced of his innocence and had been determined to defend him herself. A romance began and intensified after she won his case. A few months after they began living together, Angelica stumbled across a bank statement from a Swiss bank account. The account balance showed 8.5 million dollars, and was accumulating a healthy rate of interest. The heartbreak she'd felt drove deep into her soul. She'd been so sure of his innocence. For months she'd tortured herself, questioning how anyone could have deceived her with such ease. The questions stayed with her long after she packed her bags and walked.

From the corner of her eye, Angelica watched the stranger walk directly toward her. She tried even harder to look as though she was studying her notes, but through her dark sunglasses, her eyes strayed to him. He looked strained, as though he had been working long hours without sleep. But under this rather grim veneer lay a strong and handsome face. Again she attempted to concentrate on her work. She didn't have time for distractions.

He settled a few feet from her and began busying himself with his papers. Her concentration failed miserably. A few minutes passed before he apparently finished his work, picked himself up, and left. Angelica had been sure that he was going to approach her. She watched him disappear, and she felt an unusual pang of disappointment.

Shaking off the intrusion, she went back to her scheming. She'd waited far too long for an opportunity to set things right, and any distraction was totally unacceptable.

Dane decided it was time to leave. Gathering himself, he stood and walked away. There was no time for play. Krait had to be found and terminated. The first critical step in this process was to identify this elusive kingpin. Preparations had to be made for the party where he hoped this would transpire. He also had to finish assembling the explosives package, and this was something he never liked to rush.

On his way back to his hotel, he bumped headlong into a woman bustling along from the opposite direction. It took him a moment to realize exactly who it was. "Mother! What are you doing here?" he said, startled. In the same moment, Dane noticed a massive man carrying several shopping bags behind her, but the moment Dane looked directly at him, he disappeared into a shop doorway.

Celia Larusio's hand flew through the air lightning-quick and connected with Dane's cheek, smacking loudly.

"What was that for?" Dane cried.

"For not looking where you're going." She slapped him again, this time on the other cheek. "And that one is for looking at your mother so rudely. And, for your information, your father and I are here on vacation—the very same place we have been coming to for the past decade. Not that *you* would have noticed." She pulled him into a motherly embrace and kissed each of his burning cheeks.

"It's so good to see you. Such an unlikely coincidence we should bump into each other here," Dane said.

"Your father and I have just finished lunch at the hotel, and I decided on some afternoon shopping."

"So, Father's here too?"

"Yes, of course. He's resting back in the hotel. Come now, let's find somewhere to have coffee, and after catching up, maybe you'll join me with my shopping?" Her words were reinforced with one of her stony glares.

Dane had no option but to obey. He knew better than to argue with his mother. Besides, he had some shopping of his own to do. They linked arms and strolled down the cobbled street.

"So what is it you are doing here?" she asked.

"The thing I'm always doing—working," Dane said.

"You're opening a hotel here on Cyprus?" she asked, stopping and turning to Dane.

"Let's just say, I'm surveying an opportunity," Dane replied.

There was an unusually awkward moment before his mother's look softened. "Well, if you do open a hotel here, then you must let me know. Your father and I will be the first to stay there."

Dane agreed and they walked on.

The afternoon drifted by with the sweetness of a summer breeze, and Dane enjoyed every moment. It felt like old times. They had coffee and talked the hours away. They did some shopping, and then they talked some more. She was surprisingly helpful when it came to finding him a new dinner suit. The tailor turned out to be a genius, and within two hours, Dane was fitted out with a beautiful tuxedo. Handmade, it accommodated every line of his body to perfection.

"Very expensive, but very good," his mother had insisted. "Now all you need is a lady of equal quality by your side."

"Don't start, please," Dane begged.

"Okay, okay. It was just a thought, and you know you deserve it. Besides, you can't be alone all your life, and there must be countless women who would be very willing to fill such a place in your heart."

Dane couldn't disagree more, but he kept his objections to himself.

That night, he lay in his hotel bed, thinking well into the small hours. He thought about his mother and father, about the rest of his family, and about his past. Unanswerable questions taunted him, leaving his conscience raw. Why did his father and uncle have to be in that bank at the exact time of the bomb drop? How could he have been so stupid as to get mixed up with thugs like Sticks and Stones? There was also the money. Where had it come from, and what on God's green earth had possessed him to take it? It wasn't the bank's money—of this he was certain, because the bank had not reported its loss.

Over the years, he'd spent countless hours mulling over the same questions, but there seemed to be no answers. He could contrive only one cure for his gloom, and that was to keep his mind free from such thoughts—to cram his life so full of action and events, leaving little space for anything else. If there was one productive and worthy cause in his life, it was what he was doing now. South America was only the beginning. He had no doubt in his mind that the human race would be infinitely better off without the monsters he was singling out. Ironically, he'd compiled his hit list through the many government agencies that were supposed to be eradicating such scum. Instead of acting, these agencies preferred to sit on the sidelines and watch the game unfold, and this was the fact that miffed Dane the most. Governments seemingly knew everything, but did nothing.

Deep down, however, Dane knew his motives ran much deeper than some private vigilante war against evil. What he hoped to procure most from his actions was a chance at redemption. And then he could possibly enjoy a certain degree of peace.

"The incompetence of people enrages me to the point of insanity," Limnos growled. "Those idiots. How could they have ordered the wrong champagne? I told them—cut and clear, exactly what I wanted, and what did they get? Some cheap Italian shit." He paced up and down furiously.

Paullina, an expensive escort, lay across the king-sized bed, watching and listening. She knew better than to say anything during these moments. This was not the first time she'd seen him in such a rage. She silently decided she'd drop Limnos as her client thereafter. The money was good, but not that good. In his anger, it was common for him to lash out, and she no longer desired to be the target.

"Just days until the celebrations, and suddenly I'm in possession of a thousand bottles of crap I wouldn't let my dog drink." Seething in anger, Limnos's eyes darted around the room, searching for something to vent his frustrations on. "You, you fucking whore. You remind me of my wife—just a lazy fucking whore." The words dripped off his tongue like molten lava.

Terror suddenly welled within Paullina, and it stood out on her face like a witch's wart. This triggered excitement in Limnos. The look reminded him of that last day he'd spent with his wife.

"So you like fucking for money, do you?" he grunted, stepping toward her. "Just another fucking whore who loves money and loves to be fucked. Well, now's your chance. I'll give you your money."

Taking a roll of bills from his pocket, Limnos stormed toward Paullina. She tried to move at the last moment, but was stopped short by a hard backhand across her cheek.

"Stop! Stop! What the hell are you doing?" Paullina yelled.

Grabbing one of her ankles, Limnos dragged her into the bathroom like a sack of potatoes. "I'll give you what you want," he yelled. "I'll give you what you fucking want, you fucking whore!"

In no time Paullina's hands were tied to the towel rail. In one swift movement, Limnos tore the gown from her body. Paullina screamed, but no one would hear her—and, even if they did, they'd do nothing to help.

Limnos was now more excited than he'd been in years. He absorbed the scene with insane delight—the cowering, bent form of the naked whore below him.

Looking over her shoulder, Paullina watched Limnos rolling a stack of hundred dollar notes into a tight bundle that was easily as thick as a broom handle. The horror of not knowing what he was going to do gripped her. The terrible question was answered as Limnos spread her cheeks and rammed the wad of bills into her anus. Ignoring the screams, he pushed the roll further inside her. But Paullina's agony was nothing in comparison to what came next.

"Here comes your fucking money," Limnos yelled. He then stuffed the full length of his penis into Paullina, jamming the bills, painfully toward her belly.

With every thrust, Limnos muttered another obscenity, and with every thrust, Paullina felt a tearing pain. It was as if her insides were being incised. All that kept her from collapsing to the floor was Limnos' hands around her waist. The last thing she remembered before passing out was seeing her blood pooling at her feet.

Sitting in his study later that evening, Limnos felt invigorated from his ordeal with the whore. He hated women with a passion, but he had needs like any other man. For now, his mood was brightened, and the situation with the champagne was a distant memory. And he had every reason to be happy. Krait was rumored to be attending his birthday party, and this meant only one thing—he was about to be initiated as a new member of the International Underworld Syndicate. The union would streamline every part of his business, and revenue would flow doubly into his accounts. A lifetime of hard work was about to pay off. In ten years' time, he'd have enough money to buy an island off the coast of Crete and retire an extremely wealthy man.

Limnos ran his fingers through his thick black hair and reclined further into the comfort of his armchair. He couldn't remember when he'd last relaxed for any length of time, and for the first time in years, his thoughts drifted toward his daughter. The last he'd heard, she had completed her studies and was about to take a job with a firm in London. He'd sent a party invite to her, but he had little expectation that she would show up. He hoped there was some chance that they could patch up their relationship. Soon he would have more time to focus on family, and she was the only family he had left.

Limnos's right-hand man, Samson Zardio slumped back in the restaurant chair making no attempt to hide the erection stretching the fine fabric of his expensive trousers. His greasy black hair clung to the olive skin of his flat forehead, his mud-colored eyes peeking down his hawk-like nose across the table at the exquisite curves of Angelica Skiathos. "So, you say you're now with your father, working as his personal consultant," he muttered in a low, arrogant tone.

"These are delicate times, Mr. Zardio," Angelica replied. "My father is tightening the circles to those he trusts most. If you wish to question my sincerity, you are quite welcome to take this up with him. You know how much he loves unnecessary phone calls." She pushed her mobile phone across the table, daring him to make the call.

Samson had heard how Angelica and her father had parted, and he knew that they hadn't spoken since. He studied her intensely, trying to read into her dark eyes. Limnos must have made her a very attractive offer indeed in order to attain her service. Certainly she was right about one thing—security had dramatically tightened around Limnos. Something was in the wind, though no one knew for certain what that something was.

"Okay!" Samson finally agreed, deciding he'd play along for the moment.

"Okay, what?"

"Okay, I'm sure you didn't arrange this meeting merely to inform me of your new job. There is obviously another matter to attend to. So let's get on with it." He wiped the sweat from his brow with a table napkin and slumped further into his chair.

Angelica imagined Samson was melting under the Mediterranean sun, his very being becoming nothing more than a stinking pool of perspiration. She watched him raise a bottomless glass of wine to his lips and wondered briefly how anyone could drink wine when they were obviously so uncomfortably overheating. "What I have to say is very simple and will only take a minute of your time," she said in a soft, sensual tone, provocatively uncrossing and crossing her long, bare legs. "As you know, in two days time, it's my father's birthday. This so-called birthday party is not only a party; Limnos is going to use the occasion to conduct a meeting with all the key figures in his business. What I am here for is to personally give you the briefing notes regarding the parameters of this meeting." She paused for effect, studying his reaction. "I have no idea what the notes contain, so please, don't ask. Any questions you have can be addressed directly at the meeting. I have also been told to inform you that the briefing contains highly sensitive material and should not be discussed with anyone prior to the meeting."

Samson took the folder without offering any thanks. "You don't have to worry about my loyalty. You can tell your father I'm looking forward to his birthday celebrations and the meeting." He paused for a moment, seduced by her sultry image. "So, now we have business out of the way," he said, "would you care to join me on my yacht this afternoon? It's a beautiful day, and I'm sure we can find many ways to entertain ourselves." A wry smile spread across his greasy features.

"I'm afraid you'll have to spend the afternoon entertaining yourself, Mr. Zardio," Angelica said, slowly standing. "You aren't the only person I have to meet with today," she added, trying to keep her tone as neutral as possible. "Good day to you, Mr. Zardio. I'm sure we will be seeing each other at the meeting."

Sitting at the dockside restaurant table, Dane nodded to the waiter who had handed him the lunch menu. He quickly ordered, and as the waiter left, he caught sight of a face he recognized in the neighboring restaurant—a greasy-looking fellow with a jagged scar on his neck and intense dark eyes. There was something strikingly familiar about the man. Dane searched his memory, struggling to recall the face. It then hit him like slap to the cheek—the man was Samson Zardio. He'd had spent hours studying Samson's CIA file. He felt like kicking himself for not recognizing him sooner. He must be more alert. Knowing all the key players in the game was absolutely imperative, and Samson Zardio, Limnos Skiathos's oldest and most trusted business partner, was indeed a key player. Dane suddenly imagined he was in the hornet's nest of all hornet's nests. All of the most corrupt scum in Europe must be on the island. If only he had a bomb big enough.

Samson Zardio was speaking to a woman whose back was turned to Dane. There was something about her figure he recognized. As he stared, the woman got to her feet and exited the restaurant. For a brief moment, he saw her face and placed her immediately—it was the woman he'd seen on the beach. Dane was intrigued by her sudden appearance and was unable to imagine what reason she'd have for lunching with Samson Zardio. Impulsively, Dane decided to follow her. Half the reason for this was to try to better understand the connection between her and Zardio; the other half of the reason was because he really wanted to get a better look at her.

John Williams was not a bad man. He'd worked for the CIA for almost thirty years, and in that time, he'd not once bent the rules. He'd had one of those careers that never seemed to advance or decline to any significant degree. Despite maintaining a flawless service record, he nonetheless merely maintained a kind of status quo. It wasn't until he'd met Dane Larusio that he had realized there could be more. It was Dane who'd set up a European bank account for him. It was Dane who had opened a window to what would one day be a better life—a life without the monotony of getting up day after day to move meaningless data to meaningless destinations. So, when Dane e-mailed John a photo asking for the identification of a subject, he was nothing short of delighted to serve. A couple more jobs, and he'd have enough money to last him the rest of his days. Goodbye, Virginia, USA; hello, Cote d'Azur.

John began the search at around ten thirty p.m., when there was but a skeleton crew in the office, and the few people who were also working late didn't give him so much as a glance of curiosity. Besides, it was common for him to be working at any given hour of any day.

It took John less than an hour to compile the information on the subject and e-mail it to Dane. His work done, he smiled at the photo of a yacht docked at a Nice mariner, the French Alps majestically towering in the background. The photo had been pinned to the back of his desk since the eighties. Soon his dream would be realized.

Dane sat in a shaded corner of one of the island's many bars, watching the young lady. It was exactly 1:35 p.m. when his iPhone bleeped at him. He opened the e-mail he'd been waiting for and examined the files. He wasn't the type who surprised easily, but this moment was an exception to that rule.

Limnos Skiathos's daughter had grown up a great deal compared to the last photo Dane had of her. Although beautiful as a child, she bore little or no resemblance to the woman in the present picture— the woman he now had sitting but ten feet from him. Indeed, she was as stunning in real life as she was in the picture. But what in hell's name was she doing hanging around her father's right-hand man? Dane's information insisted that Angelica hadn't had anything to do with her father or anyone in his business since she was a child. Something wasn't right, and Dane felt certain he needed to know what that something was. He momentarily wondered if he should head for the hills and regroup, but he quickly dismissed the thought.

L. W. Wedgwood

He sipped his drink and further studied Angelica's photo. "What are you up to?" he asked aloud.

Following the meeting with Samson Zardio, Angelica gave out a total of twelve briefing dossiers to twelve of her father's top people. The day of her father's birthday had finally come by the time the meetings were concluded, and she was so sickened by the effects of her company that she wished the island would sink into the sea.

Feeling filthy from being in the presence of so much scum, Angelica made a vain attempt to cleanse her body with a long, hot bath. As she soaked in the hotel tub, she took solace in the prospect that in a few hours' time, she'd be free. Finally, she'd be able to continue her life without the burden of her murdering father taunting her every thought. Two years of planning, research, and hard work were about to bear fruit.

CHAPTER 5

THINGS GO RIGHT AND WRONG

Limousine after limousine pulled up to the entrance. Figures stepped from the cars and walked the red carpet to the center of the celebrations. Limnos Skiathos had spared no expense. The scene could be described as nothing less than spectacular. Trees surrounding the building were softly lit to compliment their natural beauty, the huge outdoor pool glowed mysteriously, like the waters off Nice on a clear day, and a live band performed soft jazz at the center of the celebrations.

"It's time to play," said Dane to himself as he pulled up in a classic Lotus.

Dane didn't have an invitation, but he did have a very large wad of one-hundred-dollar bills stuffed into the jacket pocket of his tuxedo. As he stepped from the car, a valet was at his side immediately. The valet was more interested in the car than in Dane, which was exactly as he had planned; and the oversized gorilla at the door paid even less attention once he was handed enough money to fund his steroids bill for the coming year. In fact, the only person who did happen to notice him enter the grounds was an exquisitely dressed young lady who had entered only moments before.

Money was not the only tool Dane was packing. Strapped to the small of his back was a charge of explosives and a transmitter. His plan to assassinate Limnos was simple—isolate him as best as possible and blow him sky high. If a couple of the other guests had to go down with him, then so be it.

Angelica was taking note of all the people who had concerned her in the approaching affairs of the evening. Most of all, she was looking out for her father. She wanted to corner and talk to him; she wanted to face him one last time. But then she noticed Dane, and her attention was uncontrollably diverted. He looked different than the man she'd seen casually dressed on the beach three days earlier, but she had an eye for faces and an excellent memory. He didn't just *look* different though, she decided as he slowly walked toward the pool—he looked wonderful. So who was he? And what was he doing at her father's birthday? Hastily, she decided to find out.

Angelica approached Dane, who was now helping himself to a drink at the bar, but he briskly moved away before she reached him. This threw her off, and for the moment, she decided focus her attention elsewhere.

Something had caught Dane's eye in the crowd at the bar, and he decided to have a closer look. He didn't get far. From nowhere, an almost-naked woman appeared before him.

"Sir, is there anything I can get for you? Anything at all?" she inquired seductively. She motioned with her eyes toward a row of curtained enclosures that he'd failed to notice before.

Dane could see some of these were already occupied, and it wasn't hard to imagine how the occupants were celebrating. "A drink would be fine for the moment, thank you," he replied, turning back to the waitress.

"Of course, sir. What would you like?"

"Scotch on the rocks, thanks." Dane watched the waitress walk away, her thin thong covering little to nothing.

She returned with his drink, and he sipped quietly while taking in his surroundings more thoroughly. The architecture was really quite something. Giant pillars placed about ten feet apart formed a massive rectangle and towered fifty feet into the air. Straddling the pillars was what Dane guessed were living, sleeping, and private-entertainment quarters. It was all built in limestone, giving the structure a classic, Mediterranean feel. A pool was in the center of the open-air courtyard, and surrounding the pool were gardens. Dane decided to take a seat among the flowers and observe the growing crowd. It was only eight thirty p.m., and already there were hundreds of people present. Finding a secluded bench he sat, sipping his drink, and idly wondered how many of the guests the host actually knew.

Limnos had planned to use his party venue as his headquarters once the celebrations were over. Aside from an open-air entertainment area in the central courtyard, the estate was outfitted with offices, nine bedrooms, a tennis court, three boardrooms, two swimming pools, a helicopter landing pad, and even an underground shooting range. The boardroom in which Limnos now stood was built at one side of the mezzanine floor of the building. He quietly looked down on the guests, like a lion surveying a herd of wildebeest. His anticipation was at an end. The board meeting would soon commence, and all of his associates were in for a treat; only then would the true celebrations begin. At midnight they'd receive a small token of his appreciation for all that had been accomplished. The thank-you gesture was a small fortune, enough money for a humble man to retire on. There would be twelve people attending the meeting, all of them key components in his business success. But the motivation behind the meeting was also a celebration of acknowledgment—the acknowledgment of the large step Limnos was about to take in his career, one that would affect everyone in his business. And if Limnos Skiathos was going to be initiated as a member of the IUS, then it wouldn't simply be him who benefited from such an outcome; it would also be everyone who did business with him. They all needed to know of this shift that was about to take place. They deserved to know. This was the true reward for their loyalty.

There were a lot of very wanted and very well-known people in the crowd. Dane would have liked to imagine a hint of a clue at which one of the guests was Krait, but he had no such luck. He knew it was a long shot, however, and the thought did not faze him too much. Besides, who would even hazard a guess at what image Krait would portray. He had to reassert his focus to the host and the task at hand, but he spotted the host's daughter, and his attention shifted to her. She was sitting in the garden beside the pool in a quiet little corner, appearing to be daydreaming. He decided it was high time he had a chat with her.

She was a world away with her thoughts, and she didn't notice him at all as he approached. "Is the party really that boring?" he asked, using his Greek, which was not all that good.

She looked up, obviously startled, but she quickly recovered. "Your Greek is terrible," she replied cheerfully, in perfect Italian.

"Excuse me," he said. "Languages were never my forte."

"How did you know I was Greek?" she asked.

Dane's heart skipped a beat. He had not thought of that. "Lucky guess, I suppose. I'm Dane Larusio," he quickly offered, extending his hand.

"Angela Smith. Pleased to meet you, Mr. Larusio," Angelica said.

"A pleasure," Dane said.

"And what, may I ask, is your connection to our host?" she asked.

"Lets just say I'm in the trade," he offered. "So, you're a friend to the host?"

"No," she replied, "I'm here with a close, personal friend." She gestured toward a tight cluster of people gathered around a single man—Samson Zardio.

Dane looked on in amazement. He inwardly laughed at her cover. Every scrap of information he'd ever studied relating to Angelica indicated that someone like Samson Zardio was the last man on earth she'd accompany on an evening out. "Ah, yes. Mr. Zardio's reputation precedes him," he said. "From what I hear, he is a good man to know. I also understand he's a trusted acquaintance of our host." He knew that even this small piece of information was privy to a select few.

"I understand you are right, but I make a point of staying out of other people's business. His affairs are his affairs," Angelica said.

Dane sensed her warning. "If it seemed as though I was prying, then I apologize. I was only trying to make conversation."

"Apology accepted. Though I'm sure you understand that most of these people wouldn't like anyone making conversation about them," she said, gesturing to the crowd with a sweep of her hand.

A waiter drifted by close enough for Dane to snatch up two glasses of champagne. He handed her one and offered a toast. "To the pleasure of making your acquaintance, and may there be peace between us," he offered.

She raised her glass and smiled approvingly. "So, is this your first visit to the island?" she asked lightly.

"I've been here on business a few times, although this is my first pleasure trip. If you haven't already, you must try some of the water sports."

"Actually, I did most of my growing up around here; there isn't much that I haven't experienced in the way of these islands," Angelica said.

"You must have had one hell of a childhood." He sensed she didn't like people asking questions that were at all pushy, so he didn't delve any deeper into the details of her past.

"My childhood? My childhood was shit, to say the least." Angelica replied in blatant honesty.

Dane was startled by her sudden outburst.

"My mother died when I was very young, and my father was strict beyond words. My father loved his business more than his own flesh and blood. By the time I was ten, we had traveled so much, I didn't know where to call home. Any friendships I made were abruptly cut short by yet another move …"

Angelica rambled for a while, apparently oblivious to the mixed emotions in Dane's expression.

"Well, what can I say? That's quite a story. One good thing though—I bet you were never bored," Dane said.

"Never," Angelica said.

Dane was tempted to ask her more about her father, but he suspected he wouldn't get a straight answer, and so he decided to change the subject. "So I presume you've tried the aero-water-skiing in the harbor?" he asked.

"Aero-water-skiing, you say? No, I haven't tried this. Please, do explain."

Dane described the skis and how they were not just made for water, but, when used correctly, could be substituted as wings if one wished to be airborne. And instead of being pulled by a boat, the line was attached to a special biplane designed to stay in the air at very low speeds.

"Surely, you would have to reach quite a substantial speed if you wanted to leave the water?" Angelica asked.

"That's what separates the men from the mice, so to speak. To become adequately airborne for any considerable length of time, you have to reach a speed of over one hundred kilometers an hour. Of course, as you can imagine, it's very dangerous. For example, so much as twitch in the wrong direction …" He left the result up to her imagination.

"What if you panic and slip? Has anyone been badly hurt?"

"I must admit there is not much room for error. However, there is a safety device. This device is a rocket-released parachute, which can only be used when airborne. If it is released while you're on the water, it could spell trouble. There are two release buttons—one for the water ski rope detachment, and one for the chute. Both must be released simultaneously. If the rocket parachute is activated while you are still attached to the plane your neck might be broken."

Angelica considered the sport, intrigued. "So, when can I do it?" she asked.

Dane was about to answer when, out of nowhere, a loud voice bellowed, carrying a still detectable trace of an old English accent. "Well, what do you know? Of all the damn places, it's my old, Italian friend, Dane Larusio. How are you, son?"

Dane couldn't help but shake the wiry little hand so ungraciously thrust toward him. "I'm very well. I see you haven't changed, old man; still chasing the young ladies," he said.

Koso Dilerenso glanced at the waitress standing attentively at his heel. "Oh yes, one of the perks of being a privileged guest of our most generous host." He took a fresh glass of Scotch from her.

Dane scanned his surroundings, but Angelica had slipped away. He cursed Koso's untimely invasion. He had been enjoying the experience of finally meeting her, which surprised him deeply. But something wasn't right; there was something very uncoincidental about Koso's presence.

"I apologize for cutting in on you and your friend's conversation, but I must say that I was doing you a favor. For one, the girl's Asian," Koso said, the word *Asian* rolling off his tongue as if it was the vilest sound known to man. "Also," he continued, "her father is someone you *don't* want to get mixed up with."

"Don't worry, I know you well enough to understand the word *polite* isn't listed in your vocabulary. And for your information, she's *half*-Chinese." Dane found himself on a surprisingly offensive defense.

Koso raised an eyebrow and studied his old friend carefully before replying. "I believe you have a very good perception of what matters and what's just another pile of hogwash, old friend, but never underestimate the motivation's of any Asian you ever meet. They're villains, the lot of them."

Dane cringed at the mention of Asians once again.

Koso ignored his friend's discomfort and continued, "Son, I really don't know what in hell you're up to here tonight, but whatever the reason is, I'm certain it doesn't concern me." He paused a moment to let the words sink in. "However, what does concern me is business, and protecting you may very well serve my clients and my own interests. So I'm guessing you came onto this island with more than a couple of suitcases and a beach umbrella. My guess is, you've got some business of your own happening here. But before you go getting carried away with any commitments, listen carefully—there's something big on the breeze here tonight, and it's more than the scent of some high-class pussy. Watch your back, old friend; all the big boys are in the house and a storm is brewing." On that note Koso clinked his glass to Dane's, turned on his heel, and wandered off into the crowd.

Despite the Koso's less-than-graceful approach, Dane decided he'd better take the warning seriously. Koso was not the type to speak out lightly, and if he offered a warning, one should heed it.

Dane noted the time; it was almost eleven thirty p.m. He looked around for Angelica Skiathos, wondering if he'd have a chance to pick up where they'd left off, but she was nowhere to be seen. The more he examined the crowd, the more he realized that some of the other key guests were missing.

"Mr. Larusio?"

Dane turned toward the voice. He was surprised when he came face to face with the suited gorilla he had encountered at the entrance. "Yes," he asked. "Is there a problem?"

"Not at all, sir. It's just that our host would be very interested in meeting you. If you'll accompany me, I'll escort you to the boardroom, where he's waiting."

Dane was worried by the invite, but he saw no reason why he shouldn't meet the host, and he obediently followed. After all, he had not done anything wrong but crash his party.

Limnos' tension visibly grew as he read the dossier. What it contained was a detailed outlay of how he was going to outflank the IUS and ultimately dominate the global black market for arms. Each of the guests seated at the boardroom table also had a dossier before them, but they seemed all too relaxed; some even appeared excited. Limnos was apparently the only one who recognized the ensuing consequences of the dossier's content.

Angelica's fear cut right to the bone. She was standing at the back of her father's boardroom, where she'd been forcefully summoned by security. She had an invitation to the party, and she had a right to be there. More importantly, she needed to be there. She wanted to face her father one last time—but not like this, not under the heavy hand of his security. She did not want to be made a public spectacle. But none of that mattered now. She could only watch as her father flipped through the dossier. He was not supposed to receive a copy of it until after the party, but, obviously, that plan had fallen through. She was at the edge of a brewing storm that was about to engulf her, and there was nothing she could do about it. The door suddenly opened, and Angelica watched as Dane was led to her side. She was speechless. What was he doing here?

Dane felt the tension in the boardroom the moment he entered. Seeing Angelica again delighted him, but seeing the worry her face gave him no delight at all. He quickly realized that he had arrived on a scene that he had no understanding of—and no control over.

Finally, Limnos completed his skim of the files and carefully placed them at respectful distance, as if he were handling a bomb. He felt chilled to the bone, despite the heat of the room. His skin crawled, and his heart pounded in his chest. He would like to have boasted his money had been well spent toward his daughter's education. The files were very convincing, and it was no wonder that his associates hadn't brought the matter to his attention sooner. But, with each passing moment, he realized more and more just how much trouble he was in. Krait had eyes everywhere, and there wasn't a hint of doubt in his mind that Krait had already seen the files.

"Why?" Limnos asked, coolly eying his daughter.

"You dare to ask why?" Angelica replied, just as coolly, the words dripping off her tongue like venom.

"If you are referring to your mother's death, you know that was nothing more than a freak accident," he pleaded.

"And all the times you lashed out at her. I suppose they too were all freak fucking accidents." She held his eye.

Limnos's fury suddenly came to boil. "How dare you? How dare you insult me in front of my guests?"

"Guests?" she snickered. "What about your family? Your guests are nothing more than a bunch of gutless, deadbeat murderers, and the only reason they bother with you is to make money."

Dane watched and listened—two things he'd always done well. As the conversation unfolded, one of the guests quietly stood and left the room by a side door. Dane hadn't gotten a look at this individual because of his vantage point in the room, and he only saw the guest's back as they left. There was something familiar about the figure that Dane couldn't quite pick out. He wondered for a moment if he himself could also leave so easily, and he considered bolting for the door. If he could just distract the guards long enough, it might be worth a shot. He had a gut feeling that the boardroom was the last place on earth he should be. A family feud was blossoming by the second, and Dane couldn't make up his mind about who looked more fearsome. He noted the guests were getting visibly uncomfortable with the unfolding domestic turmoil.

"Did you really think I'd forget what you did? Has power really made you that fucking arrogant and stupid? You don't deserve to be on this planet. You and your halfwit associates have caused more damage to more lives than anyone would have the guts to admit. This is where it stops—right here, right now." Blatant hatred was now reflected in Angelica's tone, and she visibly trembled with rage.

The events that followed surprised Dane, but gave him the exact opportunity he was after.

The gorilla standing next to Angelica was big, no one could deny this; but the size of the man would certainly make him slower. Angelica must have also recognized this fact, and she seized the opportunity. Obviously possessed with rage, she snatched the guard's holstered pistol with lightning speed and swung it around until it was roughly leveled at her father. But this was where her luck ended; the moment she pulled the trigger, the guard's arm came crashing down over hers, and the guard watching Dane tackled her.

Angelica's bullet did not hit its intended mark, but instead tore through Samson Zardio's throat. Dane didn't see any of this—he instead seized the moment and turned his attention to escape. In five short, fast strides he made it to the exit, grasped the door handle, turned, and pulled. Nothing happened. He tried turning the handle the other way. Nothing. There was no lock on the door that Dane could see. Suddenly his nostrils filled with a foul odor, and seconds later, everything went black.

Chapter 6

The Rock

Angelica woke up afraid. She couldn't decide which part of her body hurt more. But what really scared her was the total darkness and complete ignorance of where she was.

She began feeling around her, searching for something to connect with—something to prove that her other senses still existed. The floor felt filthy, and the only object her hands came in contact with was something soft under her head. Exploring more carefully, she soon realized the object was a body. She felt arms, legs, and something sticky. She pulled back with a jerk and resisted a surge of nausea. She had no way of cleaning the blood from her hands. Feeling around further, trying to find something to wipe her hands on, she soon came across a second body. Although not soaked in blood, this one was equally lifeless.

Panic began to well within Angelica. She breathed deeply, forcing herself to calm. Eventually her head cleared, and her nerves steadied. The steel will she'd inherited from her father prevailed, and she set her mind to work on where she was and how she'd got there. The last thing she remembered before waking was seeing Dane Larusio trying to get the boardroom door open. She desperately tried to remember more—she'd snatched the gun from the guard and had managed to get a shot off at her father before being pinned to the ground. An overpowering scent had then filled her nostrils, possibly gas. And then there was nothing. Finally, she was awake in the darkness.

She had an unnerving feeling that she'd become a victim of her own vengeful plan. Surely Krait had received a copy of the dossier she'd distributed to her father's associates and immediately acted. She'd presumed Krait had her father under surveillance, but she never dreamed justice would be served so quickly.

The darkness suddenly felt overwhelming. And she could do nothing but listen and wait. Her only company was what sounded like the whine of a jet engine.

When Dane woke, a pain at the back of his head throbbed sickeningly. He felt motion beneath him, and a whistling sound filled the darkness. He quickly realized he was on an airplane. Feeling carefully with his fingers, he found a lump the size of a golf ball. He wasn't sure if he'd been hit or had hit something.

Sitting up, he quickly realized he couldn't see. He ordered his thoughts. There were two simple possibilities for why he couldn't see: one, his sight had been damaged by the bump to his head; two, he was in absolutely darkness. He gently touched the lump on the back of his head again—it hurt badly. He then felt under his jacket, where the explosives had been earlier. They were gone.

Sounds of shuffling and stifled groans escalated around Dane, and he realized he wasn't alone. "Hello? Is someone there?" he whispered. He noticed his voice had an echo, which convinced him he was in an enclosure that was fairly large.

"Yes, who's there?" came a tentative whisper.

Dane recognized the voice. "Angelica, is that you?" he asked.

"Yes, who are you?" Angelica asked.

"Just another unfortunate like yourself. And I'm not just referring to the lump on the back of my head or the fact that I can't see anything."

"You're not the only one who can't see," Angelica replied.

New voices began to pierce the darkness. Some voices were angry and some were clearly frightened, but each held an edge of desperation that came with the inability to act on the unknown of the surroundings. Dane soon had to raise his voice in order to be heard. He decided to shuffle closer to Angelica, but, after a couple of feet, his head hit the solid steel of the enclosure's outer wall. He couldn't hold back the tears forming in his blinded eyes. He groped along the wall in the direction he felt sure her voice had come from. "Where are you?" he called.

"I'm right here."

The voice was so close it startled Dane. "Just thought you could use a little company," he said. "Do you have any idea what's going on here?"

"No ... maybe," Angelica said. "There are some things you should know," she nervously whispered. "And if we are going to get out of this alive, then we should keep our voices down." And then she quietly explained her history with her father, taking on a tone of desperation toward the end of the story and finishing with the plan she'd concocted to turn Krait against him and ultimately deal out the justice he deserved. "He deserves nothing but death," she finished.

Dane was awestruck by Angelica's scheming. He'd been picking off the scum like Limnos Skiathos one at a time while she'd managed to get a whole bunch of them in a single clever swoop. But none of this served to relieve any tension from the crisis at hand. He silently mulled over the facts for hours, desperately trying to digest the situation's gravity.

The hours passed slowly. Angelica slept and woke and slept, as did Dane. The darkness would have driven Dane crazy if it hadn't been for the sound of Angelica's presence. Yet, through the darkness, something niggled at the back of Dane's mind. He felt sure he'd missed something during the course of their capture, but, for the life of him, he couldn't pin it down. It was like an event that passes in a moment when you are too distracted to recognize its significance.

As the hours went by, the inevitable happened, and people gave in to nature, emptying their bowls. The odor of human excrement became unbearable. What bothered Dane most, however, was the fact that his sense of smell began to all but disappear. Soon enough, he couldn't smell anything.

A cold, hard wind blew across the desolate landscape. Ankle-high tussock grass stood firm against the icy breeze, just as it had done for millions of years. The rolling landscape boasted sporadic rocks as well as an occasional low-weather beaten bush. But this was all there was.

Dawn was approaching, but it wasn't the advancing daylight that had roused Elvis from the comfort of his bed—it was a sound. Elvis had lived in isolation for a long time, and his senses had become highly sensitive to foreign noises. Standing atop a steep hill outside the camp, he listened intently and was soon rewarded. The sound was closer now, and was accompanied by dull throb reverberating through the air. A strong gust of wind blew back his tattered black hair, revealing a face as weathered as the surrounding landscape. The Gobi desert was not a place for soft people, and Elvis was a man who'd never known softness. In fact, he didn't know much about anything other than running the camp. He didn't even know who had given him his name.

History had taken Elvis from his family when he was only five. His parents had been unable to care for him, due to their heads being in the way of two Kremlin bullets. Around the same time, a high-ranking KGB officer had earned a punishment surpassing death and was sent to the Gobi camp as commander of operations. He was given building material, supplies enough for six months, and fifteen prisoners. He was also given a young boy for a servant. He named the boy Elvis. The commander had three reasons for naming the boy Elvis: one, he was nameless; two, the thick black mass of hair sprouting from the boy's head; and three, he didn't really care enough to give the matter more thought. One day he'd been eating Russian caviar and drinking French champagne, and the next, he was posted to one of the most godforsaken places on earth. His one consolation was a never-ending supply of vodka.

Within two months, the commander's prisoners had built a sound officer's quarters and were working on living quarters of their own. They worked under the strict supervision of automatic rifles that quickly reduced their numbers. It quickly became known among the prisoners that anyone who came into the camp would die there.

Many nights, the commander sat alone, vodka in one hand, service revolver in the other, desperately trying to summon the courage to pull the trigger. Years passed. More prisoners died, and every six months, a fresh load of supplies and prisoners was delivered.

When Elvis was about twenty years old, the commander finally pulled the trigger. His death did not bother Elvis in the least. Death was a part of his everyday life; he'd seen it in *many* forms. It was simple for Elvis—his master was dead; therefore he was now in charge. It was no mystery as to what he had to do—his master had spent years studying the plans and had often asked Elvis's opinion on matters. The transition was seamless.

There was one thing unique and enigmatic to Gobi that only a handful of people were aware of; these people referred to this enigma as the Rock. There is one of these in Georgia, USA, called Stone Mountain, and another in central Australia called Ayers Rock, and various others around the world. However, the Rock in the Gobi desert differed from many of the others—it was almost completely underground. At sixteen kilometers wide and eight deep, it was almost perfectly oval.

It didn't take long before a Russian scientist pointed out that the Rock offered the perfect attributes of a dumping site for toxic waste. Presenting simple calculations, he proved the Gobi desert Rock, formed from solid granite, was more stable than concrete. Disposing of toxic waste was an expensive process, and money was in short supply, especially in Cold-War Russia, and key party members quickly leapt at the solution the scientist offered. A three-step plan was all that was needed—drill some very large holes in the Rock, pour the waste in, and seal them. Proper machinery required for this was altogether unaffordable, so instead Russia's less-desirable prisoners were put to work digging the holes with the use of basic hand tools. The system had worked perfectly for over twenty-five years.

Life was simple for Elvis—keep the prisoners digging, keep emptying the shipments of waste into the pits, and quickly seal the pits. The less time the waste was exposed, the longer the camp's occupants would live. Every six months—not a day early or a day late—a new shipment of waste, prisoners, and supplies were dropped.

The noise assaulted Elvis's ears again—louder this time. He strained to hear over the whistle of the wind. As if in answer, a small dot then appeared on the horizon, and it was gone, and it was back again. This happened over and over again, until the dark little dot began to take shape. The shape continued plowing through the air, winding its way over the rolling landscape in a powerful, purposeful manner. All of a sudden, the sound of huge rotors could be clearly heard beating against the chilly air, and just as suddenly, a massive Chinook HC Mark One helicopter rose into view no more than a kilometer away.

Elvis noticed a large shipping container dangling from the chopper's undercarriage. He watched silently as two of his guards scrambled to his side. Elvis didn't say a word. The three of them stood in stunned silence as the Chinook carefully dropped the container before them and settled to the ground beside it.

A single man leapt from the cockpit. He was dressed in the full Russian military uniform of a high-ranking officer and was most direct with his manner. "Where is the commander?" he asked Elvis.

"The commander is dead. Now I am master. If you have any business here, you may deal with me, and me alone," Elvis replied in short, halting Russian.

They faced each other, both with their own stony gaze.

The officer studied Elvis for a few moments before answering. "First," he finally said, "I have prisoners. I don't know how many. Second, I need fuel. I understand there is a fuel dump here."

Elvis knew better than to question a Russian officer. He decided quickly it was in the camp's best interest to meet the demands and get rid of the man as quickly as possible.

Elvis watched as the last of the nine semiconscious prisoners were dragged from the container and into the central courtyard of Camp Five. Two corpses followed, and were thrown into a heap next to the living. He became grimmer by the moment as he considered the condition of the living. He didn't like their chances, but he needed the workers. He would give them two days' rest and food. If they couldn't work by then, they'd be thrown into one of the pits with the rest of the waste.

The trembling, pitiful prisoners were covered in everything from vomit to feces. Elvis turned the knob of a powerful fire hose and pointed it into their midst. Within minutes, all were fully conscious and fairly clean. Some scrambled to try and catch the water in their mouths. Others attempted to protect themselves from the powerful blast that had enough force to knock the strongest man off his feet. As quickly as it had begun, the jet of water retracted. A guard stepped forward with a massive heap of worn clothing. No one waited to be told; they quickly stripped and dressed in the ragged garments, which were at least warm and dry.

"Well, at least they smell a little better," grumbled Elvis. "My name is Elvis," he yelled, "and these are two of my assistants." He pointed to the guards standing behind him, carrying a couple of beat-up automatic rifles that looked as if they were of World War II vintage. The guards didn't look much better.

"There are three things you must understand," Elvis continued. "The first is that you are now a prisoner of Camp Five, from which there is no escape. We don't need walls here, you see. In that direction is desert." He pointed. "And it is the same in every direction. I don't know how far it stretches, but, believe me when I say, it's a great distance. The second thing you must understand is that you are here for only one reason—and that is to work. If you do not work, you'll die. Finally, you must do what you're told. If you don't, you'll die. The choice is simple people—live or die. Really, it doesn't matter to me."

The group stared at Elvis in silence, their expressions as bleak as their future. Elvis realized most of them couldn't understand a word of what he was saying, but he also realized he didn't give a damn about the matter either way.

Dane did understand what Elvis said. He'd learned a little Russian from his business activities over the years.

Limnos Skiathos also understood Russian, but he was too busy eyeballing his daughter with raw hatred to express any real fear or concern at the severity of his predicament. He knew she was responsible for the hell he was in, and she was going to pay. He had thought he had heard her voice in the container while they were in transit, but he had not been sure, and he had not been willing to go groping around in a pitch black and unknown environment in search of revenge. But now, here she was.

Dane looked up the seventy or so feet to the lip of the hole. "Water," he yelled. A rusty can was lowered, and he drank deeply.

It had been over a month since their arrival. He had been sent to the pits, and Angelica had been sent to work in the kitchen. They toiled twelve hours a day, seven days a week. Dane's soft hands had begun to bleed from the constant friction of the jackhammer handle on the first day as he dug. There was a point where the pain was almost unbearable, and he had to put down the bloodied tool. But his strength was renewed when a rifle was fired in his direction. Not wanting to test the sincerity of Elvis's warning, he'd again picked up the jackhammer and forced himself to work. When each hole was finished, they would move on to the next site and start all over again.

There were four men to each pit—two with jackhammers, two with shovels. They alternated tasks in a vain effort to relieve the strain. The first week had been the most difficult, their muscles not accustomed to the intense labor. But, after a time, the pain eased, and those that survived slowly recovered and regained their strength.

The men accompanying Dane in the pits were different every day, but they all had the same hopeless look in their eye. Sometimes some would try speaking to him, but mostly they stayed quiet, fearing shots from above if they displeased the guards with idle banter. Today, however, one of the men with him was Limnos Skiathos, and during one of the rare periods when the guard was away getting more water, Limnos decided to risk a conversation.

"We never got to speak earlier," he said, putting a hand on Dane's shoulder before he started the jackhammer again.

Dane couldn't resist jumping when he felt the touch. Quickly he forced himself to calm down. "No," he said. "I was wondering why you called me to see you. In fact, the thought has been at the forefront of my mind since we arrived here. If you hadn't called me to your little meeting room, then I wouldn't be here right now."

"You didn't have an invite to the party. That's reason enough for me to be curious of you, isn't it?" Limnos said.

"If it were my lack of an invitation that caught your attention, then you would have simply had me thrown out."

"Quiet, or we'll be shot," said the other man in the pit.

Limnos picked up a rock and swung it into the man's head. He went down like a sack of potatoes. His skull crushed in at the temple, he was obviously dead. Limnos resumed the conversation like nothing had happened. "You were seen talking with my daughter, and I wanted to know what your connection to her was."

"I spoke to a lot of women at your party; which one was your daughter?" Dane asked, trying to stall for time.

"The woman who took a shot at me in the boardroom, you idiot. The woman responsible for both you and I being here."

"She was just a pretty face to me, nothing more," Dane lied. In reality, Angelica had become much more than a pretty face to him, but he did not want to involve himself with the family feud. Survival as it was, was difficult enough.

Limnos eyed him with a penetrating glare, but the guard then came back. The body was removed from the pit, and no questions were asked. It was a common occurrence for workers to die from falling rocks. The remainder of the day unfolded in silence.

Dane's empty drinking can was raised back to the surface on a thin piece of rope for refilling, and he returned to work with his three companions. Thankfully, he'd spent a full three days without being stuck in the pit with Limnos. He wondered how long his luck would hold. The hours passed, and another day drew to an end. His wounded hands had long since healed and formed rock-hard calluses. His body was now leaner and harder than ever; he judged he had lost about five kilos, and he was already lean before he'd arrived at the camp. All things considered, he was in surprisingly good physical health.

For the first time in memory, Dane felt a desperate appreciation for life. He saw people dying horribly around him often, and it made him wonder when his time would be up. The real possibility of death from a multitude of angles had intensified his passion for living in a way he'd never dreamt of. His purpose in life had suddenly been isolated to survival alone. This raw instinct was invigorating to his every sense, and he spent his darkest hours pondering it, like a scientist contemplating a new species.

The top of the pit was now growing dark, indicating it was almost time to finish for the day. They had nearly reached the end of the measuring rope. They wouldn't be told to start on the next pit until morning.

"Finish now," one of the guards called from above.

Dane didn't need to translate to the rest of the men. Among a few others, "Finish now," were two words they had come to understand well. In silence, they began to scramble up the measuring rope, which was knotted every two feet to serve as a crude ladder. Whoever didn't make the climb at the end of the day didn't leave the pit. Today, they all reached the top.

Lying in front of the guard were two corpses. Dane recognized one of them as number four on his hit list. The man had been a corrupt American politician, well known for manipulating powerful people with blackmail. Under any other circumstances Dane would have been happy to see the man dead. He'd been allegedly involved in everything from share-market crashes to oil-tanker spills. Now the man was just another reminder of how fragile Dane's own existence was—and how inevitable death seemed.

"How deep have you dug?" the guard asked Dane.

"Two feet from the end of the rope," he replied.

"Good. That will be deep enough. Throw the bodies in the pit and then you can go and eat."

Dane observed that one of victims had had their skull smashed in, most likely from a falling rock or the butt of a rifle. The bodies were stiff as boards, and it felt like carrying furniture rather than flesh and blood. Both corpses made an echoing thud as they hit the bottom. The sound would have sickened most, but food was waiting, and the workers were already walking briskly back to the camp.

Dane watched the other three prisoners in front of him in silence. Talking was a waste of energy. Two of the men were stumbling rather than walking. He'd seen this before, and he knew they wouldn't last much longer. Most of the men associated with Limnos were way out of their league with the physical exertion of hard labor. The most exercise they'd had was lying on their back getting blowjobs from high-class hookers.

The light was fading as they trod along, and despite the bone aching fatigue, Dane found himself marveling at the beauty of the surrounding desert. An icy breeze swept across the plains and brought the sweat on his body to near freezing. The sensation was invigorating after being in the bottom of the pit for much of the day.

Week five ...
Shivers ran up Angelica's spine. Once again, she felt the cook's greasy hand brush against her. Again and again, as she went about her work in the kitchen, she could feel him trying to make eye contact. Again and again, she managed to avoid it.

Chief was the only name she knew him by; it was all anyone called him. In the past few weeks, she'd observed him doing two things only: eating and eyeballing her. She calculated he was consuming a good third of the camp's daily ration. And he didn't seem to care what he ate. Once she'd caught him eating spoonfuls of butter directly from a two-gallon tub.

She knew her patience was not going to hold up much longer. She knew, sooner or later, that there was going to be a confrontation, and that was the last thing she needed. Despite her difficulties, she counted her blessings that she wasn't outside digging with the others. She knew she wouldn't have lasted more than a week.

But Angelica had one tiny shred of relief in the hellhole of Camp Five. Each evening, when everyone else was too numb with fatigue, she would meet Dane on the camp perimeter. There, looking over the harsh desert landscape, they would talk. They would languish in the sheer pleasure of conversation—something they were denied throughout their daily toil.

One night, they had wandered off into the desert for over two hours. But despite their apparent freedom, they felt more isolated and trapped than ever before. The landscape had not altered in the least during their two-hour walk, and they'd had the feeling they could've walked for a week, and it still wouldn't have changed. With no other choice, they'd returned hopelessly to the camp.

Angelica finished up her work and grunted to Chief that she was leaving.

"Always in such a hurry, huh?" Chief stood at the door, blocking her way. "You know, if you could just show me a little more gratitude, I could make your life here a lot easier. Elvis *thinks* he runs this place, but where do you think that bastard would be without food? So why don't you and I make a deal?" Spittle began to gather at the corners of his mouth, raw lust in his eyes.

Her thoughts scrambled to find a way out of the situation. The perfect solution came from nowhere. She began explaining coolly, "I really do not know what it is you have in mind, but you should know that Elvis and I are lovers. And as for control, well, I think you underestimate him. I believe he is, and always will be, very much in control of this place." She didn't hang about for a response but used Chief's shock to push past through the door.

Walking away through the camp's central courtyard, she grinned. Yes, she'd won that round, but she wondered how long the fragile security would last. The thought of being molested by Chief intensified the hopeless reality of her captivity and the need to escape. But escape from where? Escape to where? She looked around the concrete courtyard and the buildings she had come to call home. She imagined life before the camp being nothing but fantasy. Cold, dismal concrete surrounded by never-ending desert was her world now. There was nothing more. She finally arrived at the place where she and Dane met each night.

"Angelica, over here," came a voice.

She turned to find Dane sitting against a large rock. Deep in thought, she'd walked right past him. It had been a long, hard day, and the confrontation with Chief had drained her. She sat heavily at Dane's side.

"Are you okay?" Dane asked. Looking through the darkness he could clearly see how tired she was. She barely resembled the beauty he'd seen back in the bayside restaurant only weeks before.

"Just a long day," Angelica lied.

Dane didn't believe her. He could imagine the hell she was bearing while working in the kitchen with Chief. With a little prodding, he got her to open up and explain the events of her day. As she spoke, he had a growing feeling that something terrible would soon happen to her. It was high time a serious attempt at escape was made.

Dane looked up at Chief after receiving yet another unusually small portion of daily slop. It was the third day in a row he'd been underserved, and he'd had enough. Even if the stuff did look like something a cow had chewed on and spat back out again, he had to eat.

"How do you expect us to work without enough food?" Dane asked.

Chief snatched the bowl back and handed it to the next man in line. Dane didn't know what to do. He turned to see everyone looking right at him, intense pity in their eyes. They knew as well as he did that missing even one meal could mean sickness and death. There was no room for weakness.

Dane watched, stone-faced as the remaining food was served. He was in for a hungry night. His anger almost got the better of him as he recognized the raw contempt in Chief's eyes.

Little did Dane know that a week earlier, Chief followed Angelica to their meeting place. He had watched and listened as they spoke. The more he heard, the more he realized what a fool Angelica had taken him for. He'd planned his vengeance. It was simple—first he'd starve Dane to death, and then he'd have his long-awaited way with Angelica.

Dane hadn't felt such anger since he'd been at Camp Five. But now, facing Chief, his true nature materialized, and he snapped back into the vengeful reality that had previously consumed him. In seconds, the anger boiled into a hysterical rage. And then it exploded. He had two options—kill or be killed.

Before Chief could blink, Dane leapt across the counter and pinned him to the kitchen floor. He had the momentary advantage of surprise, but he was weakened by malnourishment, and Chief's strength was superior. Chief quickly struggled from his grasp and got to his knees. Dane followed suit, and Chief rewarded him with a sharp left. Dane managed to dodge the blow and lash out at Chief's kneecap. The blow didn't have enough momentum to do any real damage, but it was enough to send Chief crumpling to the floor again. Seizing the moment of reprieve, Dane stood. Chief also scrambled to his feet, but he visibly supported his weight on one leg. Unexpectedly, Chief then drew a large carving knife from the bench. Dane responded by picking up the closest implement at hand, a large cooking pot; he held the pot protectively in front of his body as Chief advanced.

Dane dodged the first knife thrust by a hair. He then made his own advance, viciously swinging his pot through the air toward Chief's head. The sweating cook easily dodged the move. Dane began to feel the last of his strength slipping away. Sweat ran down his brow and into his eyes, and he wiped at it feverishly. The distraction was all Chief needed. He pounced at Dane, and again he pinned him to the floor. As the knife was raised for the final thrust, Dane could barely muster the strength to raise his arm in a flimsy blocking maneuver. The knife blade brushed by the block and sank into his shoulder, slicing straight through, its tip scraping noisily on the concrete floor. Wide-eyed in agony, Dane screamed, and in the same moment, saw something flash from the left and connect with Chief's head. Blood sprayed over Dane's face, and Chief's enormous body collapsed onto him. The pain was more than Dane could handle, and he fell into the tended arms of unconsciousness.

Elvis was seated in his office, fingertips gently placed on his forehead, as they always were when he was faced with a problem. It had been years since the camp had had trouble, and now this. Killing Chief hadn't been what he'd wanted, but he'd had no choice. Chief had been a hair away from killing one of the best workers. As if in slow motion, he could still see the whole event unfolding—the heavy pot crashing down on Chief's head and cracking it open like a coconut. The wounded worker had lost consciousness under the twitching bulk of Chief's corpse.

Elvis had never killed someone like that before, and he was surprised how traumatized he felt. To make matters worse, a new shipment of waste would soon arrive in only a couple more months. If twelve more pits weren't dug by then, everyone in the camp risked being exposed to it. Last time that had happened, half the camp was dead or dying within a week.

Elvis needed every man he could muster. There was simply no choice, he decided. He was going to have to work everyone sixteen hours a day until the shipment arrived. There would be deaths from overwork, he knew, but nowhere near the amount of deaths that would result from waste exposure. He would give the workers extra food—have it delivered right to the pits if he had to—in order to increase their chances of survival. He would give the injured man a week to recover before putting him back to work. As punishment, he'd be worked harder and longer than anyone else. Disorder would not be tolerated.

Dane lay in the hospital bed, looking at the ceiling and feeling the fire in his shoulder as if the knife was still there. It was late evening, and he'd had an exhaustingly painful day. He'd been in the hospital three days, and he *was* recovering; but the medical attention he'd received was minimal, and the painkillers nonexistent.

The room was sparsely furnished. There were two beds and a stainless steel surgical table. A small set of cupboards hung from one of the bare concrete walls, and under the cupboards was a small sink and bench. There was a doctor, and Dane had become quite friendly with him. He was a tall Ukrainian in his seventies with a polished bald head and a slight limp in his left leg and was the longest surviving prisoner in the camp, having been there over twenty years. He was in astonishing health, both mind and body, considering the length of his stay. Having been moved to Camp Five after a fifteen-year term in a Siberian labor camp, he'd been a prisoner for much of his adult life.

The door suddenly opened, and the doctor walked in. "How are you feeling?" he asked in English, walking to the bed.

"Like I've been stabbed," Dane jested with mammoth effort. He also used English. He was glad the doctor could speak this language, as his Russian was nowhere near as good.

"Your sense of humor is returning. This is a good sign," said the doctor, smiling as he sat Dane up and removed the rough bandages. "You will live."

Dane winced as the last reel of bandage was removed. "Not if you keep that up," he said.

"The nearest dose of penicillin is about six hundred kilometers north of here. Fresh bandages are the only things stopping you from getting an infection, so don't complain too much."

"You know where we are?" Dane asked, his heart skipping a beat.

The doctor looked at him, a twinkle of fear in his eye. But then his eyes twinkled anew with the professional intensity necessary to examine a serious wound. "Don't worry about where you are. Just focus your energy on getting better. The sooner you get your strength back, the more chance you'll have of living once you get back to the pits. And believe me, that won't be long.

"How long?" Dane asked.

The door opened again, and this time it was Angelica. Dane found he was immensely glad to see her again, despite the risk she was taking. He had been worried about her since entering the hospital. "Good to see you're alive, Angelica," he said.

"And you," she said. She looked at the doctor. "How is he?" she asked.

"He'll live," repeated the doctor as he began wrapping the fresh bandage. This time he was smiling, and if he was at all surprised to see Angelica show up, he didn't show it.

"I can't stay long," Angelica said, "but I did manage to get this for you from the kitchen.

Dane watched as she unwrapped a large piece of stewed beef and handed it over. His eyes lit up. He'd not seen so much meat since before the camp. "Thank you," he said, truly grateful for the offering. "How is the kitchen?"

"A lot better," she said. "I'm in charge of the cooking now, and I am on my own there most of the time, except for one old guard who spends most of his day looking out the window."

The doctor finished putting the fresh bandage on. "I'll leave you two alone," he said.

"Thank you, Doctor," Dane said.

Angelica stayed for a while longer, and they talked like they had every night before he'd been stabbed. Dane found great relief in her presence. It was as if her just being there was the best medicine he could have had; even the pain didn't feel so bad. But all too soon she had to leave, and when she did, the pain returned.

Dane was startled to consciousness by a hand on his good shoulder. He saw the doctor's face, and he calmed down. Dim light filtered through the windows. It was still night.

"What is it?" Dane asked.

"We need to talk," the doctor said. "There is something I need to tell you."

Dane painfully sat up and turned on a small lamp at the head of the bed.

"You asked me earlier if I know the location of the camp," the doctor said.

"Yes, and you looked scared out of your wits," Dane said.

"I am scared, but I do know where we are."

"How?" Dane asked.

"I was here when the camp was being built. One day, a supply plane crash-landed just south of here, and when all of the fuss had died down, I wandered out to the wreckage late one night. I was curious to see if I could salvage any medical gear, as I knew they always had a full medical kit on the planes, and I could have used the supplies. The medical kit was gone by the time I got to the wreck, but I did manage to salvage two things—a map with the camp's location and an old army compass."

Dane's eyes widened. "Why are you telling me this?" he asked.

"Because I see the way you are with Angelica. You two don't belong here. You have to leave, and you have to leave soon. I play chess with Elvis most evenings, and earlier this evening, he hinted that you would be worked to death once you got out of the hospital. You have another few days here at most."

Dane was stunned by the revelation. He knew he was going to be punished, but being worked to death was the furthest thing from his thoughts.

"I made some calculations," the doctor continued. "If you travel south, the distance to the edge of the desert is about five hundred kilometers. There you will find smatterings of civilization and a few authorities. And with the right planning there is a chance you can make it on foot. I would have done it myself ten years ago, but a healthy leg and the advantage of youth were not on my side. And I'm not getting any younger. You have a much better chance. So take that woman and go live life," the doctor said, handing the map and compass over.

Dane could hardly speak. The whole thing was so overwhelming. But he managed to thank the doctor. And then he was gone, obviously afraid of what might happen if he were caught giving the means of escape to a prisoner. Dane was left to his thoughts, which wouldn't allow sleep.

The following evening ...
The doctor had hardly spoken to Dane all day, sticking to his duties and avoiding the usual friendly conversation they engaged in. So Dane had been largely left to the torments of his thoughts, and it

was close to midnight before Angelica arrived to see him. He was massively relieved by her presence.

Angelica didn't waste time on small talk. "We must leave here soon," she said, touching his hand. "Everyone is saying you're going to be severely punished. Some say you'll be worked to death. Others believe you'll be chained up in the courtyard and starved. Either way, your chances of survival are probably higher in the desert."

"I know," he said. "The doctor told me as much last night." He then told her everything else the doctor had said.

"Can we trust the doctor?" she asked.

"Yes, I'm sure of it. Even so, what choice do we have? He's our only chance."

"We must leave as soon as we can get organized then," Angelica insisted.

"Tomorrow. We'll leave tomorrow," Dane said.

"We'll need food," she said. "I can get it from the kitchen. And blankets, of course, we'll certainly freeze to death without some kind of warmth. Water, as much as we can carry."

Dane choked back his relief that she had resigned herself so quickly to the task. And he was slightly shocked by the passion she projected about embarking on such a demanding journey. He saw a fresh determination blooming within her, seeded by new hope.

"I can steal bedrolls from the store room," Angelica continued. "And there are some old plastic containers in the kitchen, we can use them to hold the water. They carry about fifteen liters each. That should get us far away."

"You must go now or there will be trouble," the doctor said, appearing at the door. "At midnight, Elvis always comes to drink and chat and play chess. But if he finds someone here who's not supposed to be, it could mean trouble for me. And, at my age, I don't need trouble. All I need is peace. So please, you must go. He will be here soon."

Angelica stood to leave. "I'll send word to you tomorrow," she whispered before quietly slipping from the building.

Dane didn't sleep until the early hours. He felt useless not being able to help Angelica with the preparations.

Angelica was worried. It was almost two o'clock, and she had not yet had a chance to ready all the things for their journey. A guard had been assigned to her to take extra food to the overworked prisoners, and in between runs, he helped her with the meal preparations. Out of the corner of her eye, she watched him as she hung a heavy pot back on its hook. She just needed a little more time with him not around.

Another hour passed, and her nerves began to fray. They had served the last of the extra food for the day, but the guard insisted on hanging around, obviously avoiding his other duties. She kept telling herself not to panic, but fear was beginning to overwhelm her. She began to imagine he could sense her discomfort. Over and over, she tried to think up ways to get him out of the kitchen. All she needed was fifteen minutes. Ten would do.

She finished the last of the post-meal cleaning and began removing food from the huge storeroom for the evening meal. It was then that she noticed the guard looking through the kitchen window and into the courtyard. He had his back to her, his attention captivated by something out there. She suddenly realized what she had to do—she was going to have to knock the guard out. She wondered if she had the nerve. She'd never physically harmed anyone before, and now, when her life depended on it, she felt terrified.

She had to act. She had no other choice. Not wanting to make the same mistake Elvis had, she quietly selected a pot that wasn't overly heavy, and she then began edging across the kitchen toward the guard. He thankfully continued to stare intently out of the window, daydreaming. Perspiration accumulated in tiny droplets on her forehead. Reluctant to make unnecessary movement, she refrained from wiping it away, and it ran freely into her eyes, stinging them. She desperately forced herself to calm down. Only a few feet now separated them. She detected a slight tremble in her hand, and she gripped the pot handle tighter, her knuckles whitening. She knew she would only get one chance—if she failed, all bets were off.

Without warning a loud gunshot rang out, startling her. She dropped the pot to the floor in shock. The guard turned almost instantaneously, and if he was surprised to find Angelica at his heel, he didn't show it. In a very relaxed manner, he wandered to the door and left.

It took Angelica only seconds to regain her composure and remember to breathe. Finally, she stumbled to the window to see if the guard had left her in peace. The guard who had been in the kitchen was nowhere in sight. But she saw another man, a prisoner, obviously trying to sneak up on two other guards, who were in intense conversation in the middle of the courtyard. The prisoner was about a hundred feet away, but through the gloomy evening light, Angelica saw he had a rifle. The man was her father, and neither the distance nor the gloom dulled the malice in his eyes. There wasn't a doubt in her mind that he'd finally chosen his moment, thinking she was alone in the kitchen; he was coming to kill her.

The guards had obviously heard the shot, but it was normal for there to be shots throughout the day. Oblivious to Limnos's approach, they stood, idly chattering. Angelica watched helplessly as her father took advantage of their ignorance. He raised the rifle and skillfully let two bullets fly. Immediately both guards dropped to the ground. Not taking any chances, he ran with startling speed to where the two lay. One wounded guard, still alive, looked up as Limnos Skiathos raised his rifle a second time. Angelica watched in horror as he shot the guard in the head. Blood and tissue exploded onto the filthy ground.

Picking up a second rifle and slinging another across his shoulder, Limnos turned toward the kitchen. Two of his comrades were at the perimeter of the compound protecting his rear. He had time, but his patience was obviously all used up. He came at Angelica like a lion to a fallen zebra, his stride now strong and confident. His weeks of waiting were over—he was going to murder her.

Angelica was riveted to the spot with fear, but she forced herself to back toward the rear exit, unable to take her eyes from her father's. He would be in the kitchen in seconds.

Suddenly, another shot then rang out from the courtyard wall. The guard who had been in the kitchen had flanked Limnos and shot him from behind. Limnos stopped dead in his tracks. Still holding the two rifles, he looked slowly down at his chest, where he found that a bullet had made its ragged exit. As blood began to pool at his feet, his expression changed to a bland visage, and he lifted his eyes one last time to meet his daughter's. Just before he toppled over, Angelica imagined she saw a flash of sorrow in his doomed eyes.

More shots resounded in the distance, accompanied by screams.

Angelica waited only long enough to see Elvis slipping from the shadows, rifle in hand. She then bolted. Although her apathy toward her father's death shocked her a little, she knew it was basically his own arrogance, stupidity, and greed that had sealed his demise. She had no time to dwell on the event. She had to seize the moment to do what she needed to. Ironically, her father's death had given her the chance to escape and live.

Delivered to Dane by a guard with his evening meal, the message was short, sweet, and scrawled on a piece of ten-year-old newspaper: "The usual place at the usual time," it read.

Dane was massively relieved; Angelica had apparently completed the preparations for the journey. He had heard the shots earlier and was very worried. He checked the wall clock for the thousandth time.

The old doctor appeared in the doorway.

"I will go tonight," Dane said.

The doctor nodded, smiled, turned, and left. Moments later, he returned with an ancient army backpack. "Here, this may help," he said, handing it to Dane. "It's old, but it will still hold much of what you need to carry."

"I don't know how to thank you," Dane said.

"Just never forget how precious your freedom is. That will be thanks enough," the doctor said.

"Thank you, from the bottom of my heart; thank you. If, or should I say, *when* I do make it out of here, is there anything at all that I might do for you? If you still want your freedom, be assured I can arrange it with ease," Dane said.

"I appreciate your offer, and thank you, but I wish for nothing more than to live out the rest of my days in peace. And in a funny way, peace is something I have found in the isolation of this place," said the doctor.

"As you wish," Dane begrudgingly agreed.

Angelica waited quietly at the meeting place. She looked over the provisions she had carefully accumulated. She calculated she'd gathered just enough food and water to stay alive for ten days. By that time, they should be well out of the desert. She'd bundled the food together into two sacks and tied them to the ends of a broom handle. She'd done the same with the water containers. Two heavy blankets were tied around the center of each broom to cushion their shoulders and make the carrying more comfortable.

She judged the time to be close to ten p.m. Dane would arrive within minutes—or not at all. Her nerves were on edge. A cool, light breeze blew across the plains, chilling her skin.

Dane tapped her from behind, startling her. They embraced without speaking. She saw he had a backpack, a much more efficient and comfortable piece of luggage. Quickly they transferred the food and one of the blankets. The water they would still carry on a broom handle. Finally, they decided to keep the remaining broom handle as a walking-stick-come-weapon. They did not know if there was any predatory wildlife in the desert, but they felt more comfortable having at least some kind of defense if there was. This done, they set their direction with the compass, and, with somber delight, they began their walk over the ancient desert plateau.

CHAPTER 7

FLIGHT

The quarterly meeting was held in a cool, dark cellar. Anxious guests nervously fingered the cracks in the long, ancient table. Seated at the end, Krait overlooked the sordid assemblage, gazing through the gloom like a primitive predator. The gloom was a vital component in Krait's anonymity, and had been for many years.

Koso Dilerenso peered across the table at Krait's shadow. He knew exactly what was coming. His chair creaked beneath him as he shifted uncomfortably.

"First, I would like to thank everyone for being here today," Krait began. "As you all know, it has been three months since we last assembled. You also know of the latest threat to our organization and how swiftly it was dealt with. For this, I have to thank certain people present here today. You know who you are; I don't feel the need to single you out. Despite the success of the operation in question, however, one mistake has recently been bought to my attention. An individual was mistakenly caught up in the events. This was most disappointing, as this individual has a direct effect on our business." Krait's voice became gruff, determined, and suddenly directed at Koso. "You, Mr. Dilerenso, are the most qualified to make the necessary correction, wouldn't you agree?"

"I do," Koso said.

"Good. Here is the information you will need."

A small file was passed to Koso, who picked it up and placed it in his jacket.

"Do you have any questions?"

"No. And I thank you for your confidence." He stood up and excused himself; he had preparations to make and a long journey ahead.

Leaving the meeting, Koso vigorously scratched his ruffled gray hair and lamented about how he'd gotten involved in such a mess. If Krait wanted to simply ask him for help, he wished it had been by phone call. He did not want to have to fly four hours and travel another two by car just to hear a few words. He would have at least liked to stay for the entirety of the meeting. But he knew Krait hated using phones or any other modern communication technology, and the trip was necessary. The quarterly meetings were the only contact Krait had with anyone, unless it was a dire emergency.

He had no idea how he was going to do what Krait asked, but he had to find a way—and he needed to move quickly. Dane's time was limited at best.

They found the remains of the Russian plane during the first evening of travel, the very one that the doctor had taken the map and compass from many years before. Seeing no harm in it, Dane decided to rummage through the wreckage. Possibly the doctor had missed something that might be useful. The remains of the pilot and co-pilot were still inside the shattered cockpit. This came as no surprise. He searched the wreckage for a few minutes but found nothing.

"Dane, I found something," Angelica suddenly called.

Dane scrambled forward to the cockpit to see what she'd found. He was just in time to see her removing a wristwatch from the dead pilot's skeletal wrist.

Angelica handed it to Dane. "Merry Christmas," she said, smiling—strangely not in the least perturbed by the ghastly human remains.

Dane took the watch from her, sure that the years of exposure to the elements would have rendered it useless. He looked at its face and saw that it was an Omega Speedmaster. It had a green nylon, military band, which had not decayed with its owner's wrist. The stainless steel case, although scratched, was still in relatively good shape. He gave it a few winds, not really expecting it to work—but he was proven wrong. Sure enough the old Omega kicked into life and began steadily ticking away. He shook his head in wonder and looked up at Angelica. "Thanks," he said, "but I don't have anything for you."

"Well, we'll just have to see what we find in the next crashed aircraft, won't we?" she replied.

Dane grinned at her. "Indeed we will," he said, strapping his Christmas gift to his wrist and setting the time by making his best guess.

They started off again at a steady pace, and the plane crash was soon far from their thoughts. The Gobi was desolate, and aside from the odd scrawny goat, signs of life were zero.

They soon decided it would be best to do the majority of their travel at night, which were cold enough to blow steam. The days were much warmer, averaging about twenty degrees Celsius. Night traveling kept them warm in the cold hours and conserved their water in the warm hours by minimizing dehydration. And the bewildering beauty of the nights helped lift their spirits, as they felt as if they were walking through the stars themselves, so clear were the skies.

It was early in the second evening of their journey when Angelica suddenly asked, "What are your passions in life?"

Dane was startled from his thoughts. It had been hours since either of them had spoken. It was a dark, moonless night, but the stars had provided enough light for them to pick their way over the barren landscape.

"For the past year or so, killing bad people," Dane said, startled by the truth in his tongue. And once he'd begun, he couldn't stop. He told her everything, from his childhood to the moment of unparalleled coincidence in which he had blown his father's legs away and killed his uncle. He told her of the guilt that followed, his consequential hatred for crime, and eventual loss of his passion for life. He told her of his pursuit of wealth, only to find loneliness and suffering. When he came to the part where he had decided to find redemption by taking the lives of those who caused his suffering, he felt relieved to find that Angelica's expression hardly changed. She only listened. He explained how he'd intended to kill her father before she'd had a chance to do so. Finally, he ran short of words, and a tense silence settled between them as they trod along.

"If you'd only been a day earlier, we wouldn't be here right now," Angelica piped in.

"I know. But I am not one to dwell on what could have been. I prefer to put my energies into what will be," he said. He felt suddenly drained. "I don't know what was in those files of yours back in that Godforsaken meeting, but by the look of things, I presume they had the effect you desired."

"Yes, my father is dead. This is something I have more than desired since the day he murdered my mother. I finally feel as though I can start living my life, and my mother can rest in peace," she said.

"Well, if we are going to be doing any kind of living, we'll have to get out of here first," Dane said.

Without breaking their stride, they locked eyes, both holding identical expressions of determination bordering on obsession. At that moment, they knew that they would somehow make it back to the world.

At dawn, they lay down to rest. For shade, they propped up one end of a blanket with the broom handles. Dane lay looking at the morning sky, thinking of the night that had just passed. He wondered if he would really ever be able to get on with his life if they managed to get back to civilization. Did he really have a chance of ever finding Krait? And if so, how? How could you find someone who had no real name and no face? How could you find someone that no one had ever seen?

When Dane awoke, the afternoon was wearing into evening. He could hear Angelica's slow, deep breathing over the warm breeze. They lay on top of another blanket, the backpack and supplies between them. He looked at his watch and saw it was a little before eight in the evening. He wished he'd managed to sleep a little longer, but he took that wish back as his eyes became transfixed on Angelica's sleeping face. She looked so peaceful. He had the feeling that, since the death of her father, she'd been resting better than she had in years. After some time, he tore his eyes away from her and studied their surroundings. His gaze eventually came to rest on the backpack, and he instantly noticed that the canvas at the bottom was soaking wet. His heart leapt, and he dug frantically into the pack to find that the second water container had somehow split and leaked almost all of its contents onto the dry ground. He cursed loudly. There were only about three liters remaining.

Angelica stirred at the sudden movement. "What's wrong?" she asked, coming up on one elbow and looking at him groggily.

"Only that while we were sleeping, almost half our water leaked away," Dane said.

Angelica grabbed at the container and examined it, feeling its emptiness. The plastic was old and brittle where it had cracked. The seam had probably opened up after the pack had been dropped a little too heavily that morning. She hesitated, and then shrugged uselessly. "What's done is done, Dane. And if you think for one moment that I'll turn around now because of this, you're sadly mistaken."

"Good, because I'm not planning on turning around either. But from here on out, we're going to have to strictly ration the remaining water," Dane said.

They nodded solemnly at each other, committing themselves to what was obviously a massive risk.

They ate a small meal of dried beef and the last of their bread and packed up their gear. Very carefully, they poured the remainder of the water from the damaged bottle into the good bottle, which they methodically checked for any defects. They had seven liters of water left and an uncertain distance to walk. Time and many other circumstances lay heavily against them.

In the dull, dawn light, whenever they reached the top of one of the rolling hills, they could now see what the map indicated to be the Yinchuan Mountains in the distance. However, with each passing hour, they appeared no closer. The effect heightened their anxiety as the morning wore on. The map indicated that civilization in the northern direction was much closer. But Dane had insisted that going to the towns to the north would invite trouble, especially if some of the citizens were Russian. The last thing they wanted was to end up back where they had started because of some local do-gooder. But it was too late to change direction now. South was now the only direction. They were committed.

Dane was mesmerized by the intermittent view of the mountains that lay ahead. They were breathtakingly beautiful. But, at the same time, he was worried. They still had hundreds of kilometers of desert to cross before reaching water. They had ample food, but the threat of dehydration was becoming more real as each hour passed. They had to find water, and soon.

"Fuck!" Koso cursed loudly, another gust of wind rocking the undercarriage of his plane. It felt like someone had fired a cannon under him, sending a wrenching shudder through the Cessna 185's framework. He would have preferred a larger, more powerful plane, but pickings had been slim in northern China. The larger planes he'd considered at the Lanzhou airfield looked as through they wouldn't make it through takeoff, let alone a lengthy trip. The Cessna 185 wasn't perfect for the job, but it was reliable, and that was what mattered most.

As the sturdy, three-hundred-horsepower engine chugged through the mountain air, he put the controls between his knees and lit another cigar—a skill he'd practiced many times in the roughest of flying weather. He'd flown bombing runs over more than one country in more than one war, and the horror of flak fire still hadn't dulled. Not even the worst weather could compare to such an experience.

He looked at the aircraft thermometer; it showed minus-thirty degrees Fahrenheit outside. It wasn't much warmer in the cockpit. He had been in the air for about two hours and was now plugging his way through a thick fog toward the Yinchuan Mountains. Through the dim dusk light, he occasionally caught a glimpse of the wild landscape below. Soon it would be dark, and already he was using the plane's instruments to do most of the flying. He hated having to trust instruments.

There was a refueling station of sorts near the small alpine village called Bayan Obe, where he hoped to refuel and rest. When he'd asked for navigational directions, he'd been rewarded with some coordinates scribbled on a map that looked as old as the mountains themselves. The more he flew, the less confidence he had in the coordinates. The fog was thickening, the darkness was growing, he was on reserve fuel, and, to make things worse, he was down to his last readily available cigar. From the corner of his eye he then saw something flash brightly. He stared directly at the blackness, but nothing else appeared. He was about to put the strobe of light down to fatigue when it came again, almost directly in front of him—and surprisingly close. This time it didn't disappear. Circling, he decided to take a closer look. There were eight lights in total. Someone's idea of a landing strip, he supposed.

With the heavy fog, it didn't prove to be an easy landing. If he'd been less experienced, he would have certainly been killed. As it was, he put down hard, the undercarriage jolting and flexing many times. He finally came to a rough halt outside what he supposed to be a control tower, which was nothing more than a rusty tin shack that someone had clearly thrown together in a matter of hours.

Koso had few near-death experiences under his belt, but the post-adrenaline rush never failed to put a few trembles through his old bones. First came the realization you were alive. And then came the one-by-one movement of different body parts—no bones broken, no mortal wounds.

Finding he was still intact, he let his jaw relax. He needed a drink. He discarded the now-severed cigar, which hit the frozen ground about the same time his boots did. He briskly made his way toward the tin shack, and, as his eyes adjusted to the darkness, he spotted an old man sitting by the door under a kerosene lamp that swung from the rusty porch ceiling.

Stepping onto the porch, Koso pulled out a roll of cash. "Scotch?" he asked.

The old man seemed to understand. He took the hundred-dollar bill from Koso's trembling hand and motioned him inside. Moments later, they both sat at a makeshift wooden table. A large fire was blazing to their side.

The burning liquid of an unusually good scotch hit the bottom of a dirty shot glass. Koso tossed the liquid down and stole a weary glance around the shack. There was a set of bunks to one side of the room near an open fireplace. The shack was no larger than a double garage, with a floor that was a mixture of dirt and wood. And there was only one small window near the door. On his way in, the old man had carefully placed an antique elephant gun against the wall. It looked like something from a museum, but Koso had the feeling it would be most effective if circumstances called for its use.

Day three ...

For some hours they'd been walking across a vast, barren plain that appeared absolutely level. Previously, there had been wide dips and basins in the terrain that served to make things a bit less monotonous, but the plain made it seem as if they weren't moving at all, and with the passing hours the mountains looked no closer. To try to counteract this misconception, they stared at the ground before them. This at least made it feel as though they were moving.

With the mountains now in sight, they decided it was best to travel in the early hours of the light so they could keep their destination in plain view. It was their hope that this approach would keep them on the most direct course and increase their chances of success.

"You know, I never thought I could miss the comforts of civilization as much as I do right now. What I wouldn't give for a cool drink and a warm meal," Angelica mumbled.

Dane looked sideways at her and wondered if this was all she had thought about for the past two hours. In that time she'd not said a single word. "A glass of good red wine and some of my mother's ravioli is what's been making my mouth water." He smiled lightly at her, deciding any conversation was better than none, even if it was about something so unobtainable.

They walked again in silence for a while. Angelica busied her thoughts with trying to decide if it was worth taking a break to remove a pebble that had worked its way into her shoe. "Do you still plan on going after Krait if we manage to get out of this mess?" she asked, trying to ignore her aching heel.

"That's something I haven't put a lot of thought into lately. What do you think?" Dane said.

"What do I think? I think you're the sort of person who'll never quit," Angelica said.

"Well then, I guess you know me better than I thought," Dane agreed.

"Aside from Krait, how many others are left?" Angelica asked.

"Only one, thanks to you and your ingenious plan. Two from my list were back at Camp Five, and both are now dead. So at least something good came of this rotten situation."

Angelica opened her mouth to speak, but held back at the last moment.

"I have been having a recurring thought for some time now—a memory, or, much rather, a lack of memory of the meeting at your father's party. It's as if I missed some small detail that should have been obvious. Now, out of nowhere, I know what it is that's been bothering me all this time," Dane said.

Angelica peered across at him curiously.

"Think back to the meeting," Dane said.

"Not really something I want to think of at this stage. But now that you've brought it up, go on."

"In the meeting room, for the few moments we were there, just before everything went out of control, do you remember seeing someone leave?" Dane asked.

Angelica thought aloud, "There were the guards beside and behind me. My father was sitting at the opposite end of the table," she said. She then remembered. "There was someone sitting directly in front of me. I remember them quietly leaving before everything turned to hell. It was a woman. I didn't see the face, but the hair was definitely styled in a feminine way."

"I think you're right. And now I think about it, there's something else bothering me," Dane said.

"You think she had something to do with what went on in that room, and the events that followed?"

"Truthfully, I'm not too sure what to believe at this stage, but I'd have to say that that woman was a damn sight more lucky than anyone else in that room," Dane said.

Koso tried the starter again, and again he swore loudly. It was very cold, and the plane engine was in no hurry to come to life. To make matters worse, he had a skull-cracking headache.

Backing the choke off a little, he tried the starter once more. The heavy motor turned over and over until he was sure the battery was almost dead. The engine then fired once, twice, and, with a loud, rushing roar, burst into life. Ice flew from the single propeller as the motor settled into a healthy idle. Looking down from the cockpit, Koso found the old man grinning up at him, a large cup of coffee between his gloved hands. He didn't hesitate in accepting the offer, as a coffee break would give the engine time to warm up. He jumped down and took the steaming cup of liquid in hand. The old man's grin broadened, and he gave a happy nod. Koso drew another hundred-dollar bill from his pocket and gave it to the funny little fellow, whose head bobbed in approval once again.

Sipping, Koso noticed how filthy the cup was. It probably hadn't had more than the odd rinse since it was made. But the coffee was strong, hot, and comforting, and he was grateful. As the plane's engine warmed and the oil circulated, the pistons relaxed into a healthy, rhythmic beat. A strange but comfortable calm settled as Koso sipped his coffee and absorbed the panoramic surroundings. Thankfully, the fog from the previous evening had cleared. It was going to be a perfect day for flying. Slurping down the last dregs of coffee, he thanked the old man once more with a nod of his own and leapt back into the fully fueled plane.

The takeoff was only a little smoother than the landing, despite the luxury of renewed visibility. Heavy with fuel, the plane barely made it into the air. But eventually Koso gained a respectable altitude, and he crossed himself and sincerely thanked God for helping him cheat death yet again.

Soon he was flying out of the Yinchuan Mountains, their majestic peaks bordering the southern edge of the great Gobi desert. Thirty minutes later, he was over the plateau. For the first time in days, he had a few moments of calm to sit and wonder why it was that Krait had asked him to find, and, if at all possible, rescue Dane. He also wondered how his old friend had got himself into such a mess to begin with. What connection could there possibly be between Dane and the IUS? The more he racked his brain for answers, the more they seemed to elude him. Eventually he decided to focus on the job at hand and think of nothing more.

Day five …

The energy for lengthy conversation had long since dissipated. The last of their water was long gone, and they knew that, if they didn't find more very soon, they would begin dying. To make matters worse, their mouths had become too dry to eat the dried, salty beef, the mainstay of their food supply. They cut the brass buckles from the now very light backpack and sucked desperately on the cool metal. This gave them some relief from thirst by producing saliva, and at least made their mouths felt somewhat moistened. The mountains now looked heartbreakingly close, and if they only had a good, two-day ration of water, Dane knew they could make it. Still, while they could walk there was hope. That and sheer willpower was now all that drove them on.

Angelica was a shadow of her former self, her sunken cheeks giving her a harrowing appearance. Her focus was now narrowed to the length and strength of her fragile steps, which felt like a steady crawl into the arms of death.

The day before, they'd walked up and down through shallow dips in the desert for hours. The change in terrain was short-lived though, and now they were crossing another vast plain. The weather felt warmer, and this intensified their desperation all the more.

That evening, they stopped sooner than they would have liked. They tried again to chew on some dried beef, but only managed to swallow a little. Finally, in a bid for comfort, they lay down closer together. They were too exhausted to speak. Angelica pulled her arms from under the blanket and put them around Dane, who gratefully moved into her comforting embrace.

Angelica was slow to wake. They'd only been sleeping for about six hours, and dawn hadn't yet broken. She realized suddenly why she'd woken so early. Dew, as heavy as a wet blanket, covered everything in sight. It wasn't something she'd seen until now, due to the dryness of the desert atmosphere. She wondered briefly if it was because they were closer to the mountains. She didn't analyze it too much. Quenching her life-draining thirst was the only thing now demanding her attention. She had to get as much of the dew into her as possible before the sun came up. She roused Dane, and hardly a minute had passed before they were both crawling around their camp like overgrown lizards, licking dew off anything from their backpack to the surrounding rocks. Almost thirty minutes had passed before they stopped. Their knees were sore, and their tongues were raw, but their thirst was somewhat quenched, and they even managed to eat a little.

They judged that they must have drunk at least one good cup of water each. Their energy levels were lifted, as were their spirits. They wished they'd somehow managed to fill the empty water bottle, but they were grateful all the same.

Their renewed energy was short-lived. Four hours after they set off, Dane was showing signs of extreme dehydration. He was beginning to get partial blackouts, and on two occasions, he almost keeled face-first into the ground. Angelica began to complain of severe cramps, and by late afternoon, they had no choice but to stop.

"I can't move anymore," Angelica croaked. "I've never had cramps like these before. It feels like someone is stretching my every muscle and tendon with a pair of pliers."

Dane wanted to express his sympathy to Angelica, but he was finding it difficult to maintain consciousness. They flopped to the ground like a couple of stunned fish. They were too tired even to spread out a blanket. Eventually, they passed out in a helpless heap, lying still, silent, and not so far from the edge of the great Gobi desert.

Chapter 8

Dune

Koso saw Camp Five from about twenty miles to the south, and he landed his plane about three miles out. He hated walking any great distance, but he would rather walk than be shot at. Stealth was his ally, and the longer the camp occupants were unaware of his presence, the better. He covered the ground on foot very quickly, a small pack across his back, an HK UMP 45, universal machine pistol, grasped in his right hand, and four extra twenty-round magazines in his belt. It was a little after dusk as he approached the buildings. He used a few minutes to closely study the camp before moving in. To his relief, there was no one to be seen. His information showed, however, that there were more than a dozen guards within the camp, and he wondered where everyone was.

Reaching the wall of the first building, Koso carefully edged his way around. From the corner he saw that the central courtyard looked clear. He waited a full two minutes before gingerly stepping around the corner and making his way toward one of the larger buildings. Keeping as close as possible to the wall, he edged along to a window. A smell pervaded his nostrils, and he glanced around, trying to locate the source of the foul odor. After looking up toward the central courtyard, his suspicions were answered. The severely decaying corpses of three men were strung up on a makeshift framework. Apparently, some of the prisoners had been made an example of. Koso wondered why he hadn't seen the corpses before.

He made a mental note to be more observant. He didn't want to wind up slogging his guts out with the rest of the soul-weary inmates. Warily, he turned his attention back to the window and peered inside, finding a hall filled with ragged and beaten-looking men. All of them were eating from bowls in a mechanical fashion. The scene was mesmerizing. Memories of a long-forgotten past flashed through Koso's mind, but he quickly shook them off and refocused.

There were four guards in the hall, looking all too relaxed. Some of the prisoners looked ill, gaunt, pale, and were obviously close to death. After a couple of minutes of close observation, Koso could clearly see Dane wasn't there. A door slammed somewhere in the distance, and Koso quickly slipped back behind the corner of the building. Peering even more cautiously around the corner, he observed a stocky, dark-haired man striding toward the mess hall. The man had a grim look that Koso guessed constituted his full range of expressions. The man purposefully strode into the hall and closed the door. Koso used this as a cue to go back to the window and investigate the scene inside.

The dark-haired man was talking to one of the guards, who stood attentively and listened closely to what he was being told. Obviously, the dark-haired man was someone of authority. Once he'd finished speaking, he stalked off into the kitchen. Losing sight of him, Koso slipped back to the safety of the shadows. Sitting in the gloom, he watched dusk turn into night. He decided his best chance of finding Dane would be by having a chat with the dark-haired man. But it would be best if he waited until everyone was settled and sleeping before making his move. Again, Koso lamented on just how in hell Dane had gotten himself into such a jam to begin with. Dane Larusio was not the kind of man to make mistakes, and it was certainly a huge mistake for him to have been at the Skiathos birthday celebration. However, he must have had a very good reason for being there.

The time passed slowly, and the stinking corpses hanging in the courtyard made the wait all the worse. He pulled out a cigar and placed it between his yellowing front teeth. It gave some comfort, even if it wasn't lit.

It was eleven o'clock before Koso decided to make his move. Once again he looked carefully around the corner. The courtyard was clear, except for a single guard slouched and snoring against the outer wall of the mess hall. A rifle lay on the ground next to him. Creeping around the corner, he quickly snuck up on the man and put a bullet into his head. The machine pistol made only a dull thud. This relieved Koso greatly, as the gun was one he'd not used before, and he was always a bit edgy about unfamiliar weapons. He removed his cap and placed it on the guard's head to conceal the wound. He then headed for the door from which he'd seen the dark-haired man exit earlier. Thankfully, it opened easily and silently. Confronted with narrow set of wooden stairs, he began climbing.

At the top of the stairs, a thin shimmer of light shone from under a rough, wooden door. Koso put his ear to it and listened for a full five minutes. Not a single sound came from the room. Whoever was inside was either sleeping or very relaxed. Gently, Koso tried turning the handle. It didn't move. He carefully relaxed his grip and tried turning it in the opposite direction. It still didn't move. Staring through the dim light, he studied the handle as best he could. There didn't seem to be any lock. Pulling out a small flashlight, he took a closer look. He almost laughed aloud; he'd not seen such a trick in years. The handle was on the same side as the hinges, giving the impression the door was locked. In reality, it had no catch at all and would just push open from the opposite side. It was a simple security precaution, but could be very effective if it had not been encountered before. At very least, it would slow a man down. He shoved lightly once again, this time on the correct side. It gave way easily, swinging inward altogether too hastily. He just managed to catch the door before it banged against the wall.

The room was more dimly lit than Koso had imagined. He held his breath for a few moments before doing anything more. No sound pierced the silence, and he took this as his cue to enter. Lightly stepping inside, his gun barrel quickly followed the fast movements of his alert eyes. The room was sparsely furnished with a single bed to one side and a battered old dresser beside it. Set in one wall was a glowing fireplace, in front of which sat a worn, but comfortable-looking chair. Apart from this, there was very little else. The room appeared empty, but, as he was about to turn around and leave, he glimpsed a wisp of hair protruding from just over the top of the chair's back. Relieved, Koso pulled a photograph of Dane from his pocket. The seated man barely even flinched when he felt the cold gun barrel pressing into his temple, and the photograph was thrust before his eyes.

"This man, where is he?" Koso demanded in halting Russian.

Elvis hesitated for a few moments before answering. "This man has gone," he said.

"Gone?" Koso inquired. "Where has he gone? Is he dead? Where is he?" He pressed the barrel of the gun harder into the unusually calm individual's head. He had a nagging feeling the man didn't really care much about anything, least of all life, and without due care, such a man could cause serious trouble.

"The man in the photograph has been gone for almost a week. Before that he was in the hospital recovering from a wound. The last person to see him was the doctor. Aside from this, I know nothing," Elvis said.

"Where do I find this doctor of yours?" Koso asked.

"In the hospital, two buildings right of this one as you exit," Elvis growled. The gun popped twice, and he was asleep again.

Koso was out of the door and down the stairs before Elvis's heart stopped beating. He entered the door of the so-called hospital, which consisted of two rooms. The first one he entered was obviously where the patients were housed. There was no one in sight, so he quickly made his way to the other one, where he found an old man reading a book that looked older than he did. A wrinkled face looked up at him with no hint of surprise. Koso didn't even bother to lift his gun. The old man wasn't going to give him any trouble.

"I'm not here to hurt you," Koso said. "I understand you are the doctor around here."

"That is correct, yes. How is it I may be of help?" said the doctor. "Help is what you want, isn't it? I'm sure you would have used that gun slung under your arm by now if you wanted anything else."

"Yes. I need to know anything you can tell me about this man." Koso asked, again holding up Dane's photo.

"Dane Larusio was his name. Is that correct?" The doctor spoke, his eyes wandering from Koso for only a moment to look at the photo.

"Dane, yes, that's right. I just spoke to the man in charge, and he told me you were the last one to have seen him," Koso said.

"He was going to be punished, it was certain," said the doctor. "Apparently he'd got a little hot-headed with the late cook. Dane, the man you are looking for, was sent to me with a minor stab wound as a result of the incident. Upon his recovery he would surely have been worked to death."

Koso listened carefully to the doctor as he explained how he'd given Dane the map and a chance of escape. When it was explained that Dane was not alone in his flight, Koso was surprised. But there was no real time to theorize about Dane's traveling companion. There was a desert to search, and Koso had a limited amount of fuel.

The doctor was kind enough to show Koso to the fuel dump and scribble a rough copy of the map he'd given Dane. Finally they loaded the jerry cans into an old wheelbarrow for the trip back to the plane.

"Thank you for your help," Koso said, shaking the doctor's hand. "I would give you a lift out of this place if I had enough room in my plane."

"As I explained to your friend, I have no need for the outside world at my age. It was crazy enough out there during my day. God only knows what it's like now. However, I did notice the scent of a good cigar on you," the doctor said.

With that Koso pulled out a silver box, which contained his last five cigars. "Your sense of smell is pretty good. You can have these." He handed the box to the grateful doctor. "Compliments of Havana."

"One more thing," the doctor said. "The man you saw before me, is he still alive?"

The question surprised Koso a little, but he answered without hesitation. "I had no choice but to kill him," he said, prompting a flash of sadness in the doctor's eyes.

Their goodbyes said, Koso jammed a half-smoked cigar in his jaw and began pushing his wheelbarrow of fuel back to the plane. When he'd reached it he was exhausted, and decided to sleep for the remainder of the night. He knew that he was going to have a long day to follow, and the rest was much needed.

It had been two days since they'd licked away at the dewdrops, which had turned out to be entirely inadequate to offer any prolonged relief. Their throats were now too dry for them to understand each other's speech.

Angelica lay on her back beside Dane, trying to think of a time in her life when she'd felt so close to death. They had been resting for almost two hours. They were dehydrated, starved, and too exhausted to move for more than a half-hour at a time. They were dying, and Angelica knew it. She couldn't even summon the energy to cry, and she knew Dane was no better off. But, however hopeless their situation seemed, they still clawed their way toward the mountains whenever they had the strength to move. If they could just find water, they might still have a chance.

With a mammoth effort, they weakly rose into a crawl-stagger and moved off with snail-like speed. It seemed as if everything was slowing down. Angelica watched Dane's weak movements as he feebly checked the compass. She drew a dry, raspy breath into her lungs before following his lead.

"Is this where I'm meant to end my life? Is this what everything has been for, what everything's been leading to? How is it that I came to be here at all? Why? What use has any of my life been?" Dane realized he was croaking the words aloud, and he quickly checked himself. Thankfully he knew that his speech was completely inaudible.

Angelica gave Dane a feeble version of one of her curious, sideways glances.

Dane tried to order his thoughts by concentrating on the dip in the landscape they were coming out of. The dip had been big enough to put the mountains out of sight for several minutes. They slowly inched their way to the top until they again had a clear view of the horizon. As they did so, their mouths dropped open in perfect unison. About a mile ahead, swelling menacingly out of the surrounding desert, was the biggest sand dune either of them had ever seen. As if a massive hammer had dealt them a final crushing blow, they crumpled to the ground. A feeling of utter defeat engulfed them. They knew that there was no way they could climb the dune, which was at least a thousand feet high.

They lay close together, their energy spent. They hadn't moved an inch from where they had stopped upon seeing the sand dune.

Dane looked down at his hand, which was cramping like the rest of his body, the skin taut and stretched from the final stages of dehydration. He reached out for Angelica's hand, and their fingers entwined. Unblinking they lay, staring into each other's eyes, unable to move, afraid to let the moment go. Her lips moved, but Dane only heard the harsh rasp of a dried throat. She seemed to be making a massive effort to summon enough moisture to speak.

And then it came. At first, the noise was almost undetectable, as if it were coming from a very great distance. Slowly it grew louder and louder. A glimmer of recognition shot through Dane. From somewhere within, he mustered a reserve of strength and stood, swaying on his feet like a homeless drunk. The powerful noise of the airplane engine filled the air as it roared over their heads only meters above them. Dane would have waved his arms, but it was all he could do to stand. His heart leapt as the aircraft made a long, sweeping turn and flew back in their direction. Dane vaguely felt the presence of Angelica at his side, but he couldn't take his eyes from the plane, afraid it might disappear.

But the plane didn't disappear, and they both watched in stunned silence as it landed and came to a halt only a few feet from where they stood. The motor was cut, and a familiar silence settled. Dane tried to see through the dusty windshield. Who was the pilot?

The plane's side door opened, and a familiar, lanky figure leapt to the ground. "Well, fancy that. Of all the goddamn places, if it isn't my old friend, Dane. And looking the little worse for wear I might add," Koso gruffly said.

Dane tried to speak but the effort proved too much. He fell into a crumpled heap, unconscious, but nonetheless alive. Koso Dilerenso had somehow found them, and somehow they were saved.

Angelica was conscious long enough to see Dane hit the ground before she followed suit.

Koso looked down at them, shocked. "Was it something I said?" he grumbled. But he turned more serious as he realized their condition.

When Angelica awoke, her head was swimming, awash with images, old memories, and daydreams. Her eyes didn't open easily, and when they did, she gathered her thoughts for a few minutes, yet she felt all the more confused. She was still in the desert, that much was certain. But above her, a thin piece of linen was flapping in a gentle breeze and sheltering her from the sun. She felt completely disorientated, and her mouth tasted like chalk. She wondered where the linen had come from. She then remembered the airplane and the man who seemed to know Dane. She must have passed out. But where was Dane? She turned her head, looking to her right. Pain jabbed her sharply, firing though her body and head like a bolt of lightning. She was still dehydrated and cramping, her muscles far from recovered. Dane lay only a couple of feet away from her, breathing deeply. She let out a raspy sigh of relief when she saw he was okay. She was about to try to move when a knurled, old hand gently restrained her.

"Try not to move. Just rest and try drinking a little," came the voice.

Looking around Angelica discovered the man from the plane. His face was somewhat familiar, but she couldn't place it. A small cup of water was pressed to her lips, and she gulped at it. But the cup was quickly withdrawn.

"No. That'll be enough for a little while. It won't do you any good to drink too much too soon," came the voice again.

Angelica tried to object, but she knew the man was right. At least her mouth felt a little better, and she could speak again with some degree of clarity. "Who are you?" she croaked, looking up at a face lined with immeasurable character.

"For the moment, let's just say I'm an old friend of your partner's."

She looked at him quizzically.

"If you really need a name for the face, then you can call me Koso," came the voice again.

Angelica would have cried, but there wasn't enough water in her body to do so. "Thank you," she said. "Thank you. We thought we were done for." With that she laid back, exhausted from the effort of her meager speech. She then fell asleep again.

Koso looked closely at Angelica. Despite the desert grime, he could tell she was very beautiful. Admittedly he stared in awe, for to have lasted the distance with Dane, her beauty must have been combined with incredible strength.

For three days Dane and Angelica did nothing but sleep, drink, and finally eat. They now sat around a small camp cooker. Hot coffee was brewing. Koso had known when he'd found them that it would have been dangerous to move them right away; they needed to get stronger before he could risk the flight. But they were now doing surprisingly well, and there was enough water for them to have a brief, but satisfying wash.

The coffee fully brewed, Dane poured the contents into two alloy mugs, one of which he and Angelica shared. The evening was turning into night, and the sky slowly started to fill with stars. Now that they were safe, they looked at their surroundings with a whole new appreciation.

They talked long into the night before falling into the most peaceful sleep they'd had in months. The next morning when they awoke, Dane knew they were well on the way to full recovery, and it was time to make a move back to the world. Koso readily agreed with Dane's suggestion, and they spent the morning packing the plane. Dane was glad to be finally making the escape.

Angelica was listening to one of Koso's many stories. Lost in his thoughts, Dane watched them. Koso still hadn't told Dane the truth of how he'd found them. When he had questioned Koso on the matter, he'd been rewarded with nothing but the thinnest of stories. This troubled Dane a lot, and he was beginning to wonder if Koso had dealings with Krait. Such a scenario would explain a lot. Krait was the only person Dane could think of who knew of Camp Five. The Russian government knew, yes, but Dane doubted Koso was connected to them.

"Dane? Dane? Are you asleep with your eyes open, or have you gone stone deaf?" Koso asked.

"Sorry, I was just a bit distracted by my thoughts," Dane said, suddenly snapping back into the moment.

"I was just telling Angelica that you made quite a friend back there at the camp. If it wasn't for him, you two would undoubtedly have been baked into this desert floor by now," Koso said.

"True. Actually, if it hadn't been for him, I would more likely be lying dead at the bottom of a pit under tons of toxic waste." Dane thought for a moment. "It's not very often you get your life saved twice by the same man." He rubbed his still-healing shoulder in remembrance.

"I wish there was something we could do for him in return, but he insisted on spending the rest of his life at the camp, right Dane?" Angelica said.

"It may well be that he's right in doing so. He will probably find more peace doing what he's doing there than he ever would in the outside world."

"I still wish we could give him something in return for everything he did for us," she pleaded.

"Well, if it makes you feel any better, I gave the old fellow my last five cigars," Koso offered.

Dane's cracked lips spread into a painfully broad grin. He'd been wondering why Koso hadn't been smoking. "When we get back to the world, I'll be happy to buy you a dozen boxes of your choice—that is, of course, if you don't want to use your current predicament to give up smoking altogether," he said.

"Why in hell do you think I'd want to give up smoking at my age? Hell, the shock of withdrawal would probably kill me faster than lung cancer. You know, my old man smoked a pipe from the age of ten, right up until ..."

It was a story Dane had heard many times. He and Angelica looked at each other, and it was everything they could do to not burst out laughing.

"So you think that's funny, do you? Well, of all the goddamn nerve. I'll tell you something—the first city we get to I'm going to buy a dozen boxes and chain-smoke them until they're all gone."

Dane and Angelica finally lost control and broke into fits of laughter. Dane had never seen the old man so uptight about anything.

They finished their breakfast, continuing to chuckle the whole way though, and then they followed a frustrated Koso into the aircraft. They were airborne before they were able to contain their amusement.

Despite his grumbling, Koso was glad at Dane and Angelica's returning energy. But his thoughts were not entirely untroubled. He knew Dane must be very confused as to how they'd been found. Koso explained that he'd got a tip from his more corruptible Russian associates. Dane had seemingly accepted this explanation, but Koso knew that he had his doubts.

The Great Wall of China could now be seen passing beneath them. They would be back in Lanzhou by nightfall at the latest, and Koso secretly wondered if there would be a decent cigar in the old city.

CHAPTER 9

SERENITY

Three days later ...

The evening sun shimmered across the cool Mediterranean waters, a gentle breeze was blowing, and the massive cruise ship had departed from the port of Antibes only a few hours earlier. Angelica lay upon her king-sized bed and looked out over the balcony, deep in thought. She'd spent most of her childhood on ships, but this time, things were different.

Lying in the luxurious comfort of the cruise ship's cabin, Angelica's experience at Camp Five seemed so far away, almost dream-like. But it hadn't been a dream. Only one week ago she'd been hours away from death.

Dane had left her in China, insisting he had urgent business to attend to in New York, and they would reconvene later. Angelica had been upset, but she couldn't bring herself to express her disappointment openly. She recalled his words as she saw him off at the Lanzhou airport: "My business in New York will only take two days, and when I've finished, I think we should get together for some celebrating, don't you?"

She'd chosen the cruise chip for their celebration. The feeling of being surrounded by water seemed very appealing after the ordeal in the desert.

Somehow, the three days they'd been apart felt more like a year to Angelica. They had so much to talk about. So much had happened—so much that no one else would ever know about, believe, or even understand. For the first time in memory, Angelica desperately longed to be with a man. She desperately longed to be with Dane. This both scared and excited her.

Sliding off the bed and standing, Angelica studied her lingerie-clad body in the full-length mirror. Although she felt physically well, she could clearly see signs of the stress her body had been through. Her body-fat was very low, and one or two extra wrinkles had popped into existence. Matted and tangled from the desert, her long black hair had been beyond recovery, and with a little encouragement from the beautician in Nice, she'd decided to take it off. Surprisingly enough, she quite liked the new look. It set her stature off with a sharp, crisp tone of elegance. Instinctively, her hand ran to the back of her neck where her hair had been for longer than she could remember. Its absence felt foreign, and the skin on her neck was sensitive to touch. Closing her eyes, still standing in front of the mirror, she tried to imagine Dane's arms sliding around her, pulling her close to his body, his hands moving over her skin.

Her eyes flew open. She was startled by her thoughts. She wondered briefly when she had started to think of Dane in such an intimate way, but she quickly realized this was the first time she'd had the freedom of mind to do so. Even though they'd been very close for weeks, they had been in no position to think of anything other than survival. But now there was no denying how she felt; the chemistry between them was certain. She wanted him more than any man she had ever known. For the first time in years, she began to feel like a woman.

Dane didn't go to New York. He felt in his bones that Koso was involved with Krait somehow, and he'd decided to follow him. As much as it pained him, Angelica would have to wait.

Dane flew into Rome precisely twelve hours and forty-five minutes after Koso. He knew which hotel Koso would be staying in, because Dane owned it, and he knew Koso wouldn't stay anywhere else while visiting the old city.

Dane sat in a quiet corner of the hotel foyer, drinking from a coffee cup that was frequently replenished by vigilant waiters, and his attention was fully focused on the elevator door.

At exactly seven thirty a.m., a long, white limousine pulled up at the hotel entrance. Roughly thirty seconds later, Koso exited one of the elevators. He made his way smoothly through the foyer, out of the exit, and into the waiting vehicle. He was unusually well dressed. His regular attire was khakis, collared shirts, and good walking shoes. Today he obviously prepared for a very formal meeting of some kind.

Dane also had a driver waiting outside, and he quickly exited the hotel and ordered his driver to follow the limousine. First, Koso made a brief stop at a bank, and then, before getting back into the car, he had a long and frustrated conversation on a satellite phone. Dane was surprised at this. He'd never known Koso to use any kind of portable phone.

Rome's early morning traffic made it increasingly difficult to keep a comfortable distance from the limo without losing it, but Dane's driver proved to be quite talented at his job. Predicting the limo's direction correctly on two occasions, Dane realized his driver had significant pursuit experience.

Two hours of tailing Koso finally ended at an ancient, small, three-story building, where the long limousine pulled into a small basement car park. Dane and his driver waited patiently, parked at a safe distance across the street.

"Are we close enough, sir?" asked the driver.

It was the first time the driver had spoken during the entire trip.

"Yes, this is perfect. You've done well. Leave the engine running so we can have a little air-conditioning, we may be here for some time," Dane said. He was bone weary, having not slept a wink since leaving China. He wondered if he could trust the driver to keep a lookout. His weariness brought him to a snap decision. "I'm dead tired," he said. "If anyone goes in or comes out of that building, then wake me, okay?"

"Yes, sir. There's a blanket in the trunk if you'd like me to get it for you," the driver offered.

"Thank you, that won't be necessary. I don't want to get too comfortable."

"Of course, sir."

When Dane awoke, it was dark. This startled him, and for a moment he wondered if the driver had also fallen asleep. Looking up he found quite the opposite—the driver was sitting bolt upright, staring unblinking at the building. The air outside was now cooler, and the driver had turned the engine off to conserve fuel.

"How long have I been asleep?" Dane muttered.

"Almost twelve hours, sir. No one has gone in or come out of the building," the driver confirmed.

The latter surprised Dane less than the amount of time he'd been asleep.

"Did you sleep well, Mr. Larusio?" the driver asked.

Dane stiffly moved back into a more comfortable position. "Yes, thank you," he said, wincing with pain, his shoulder still healing from the stab wound.

They waited in silence once more.

An hour or so passed, until suddenly the building's basement door opened and a flow of cars began exiting. Dane crouched in the backseat and told the driver to follow suit. As the cars dispersed in every direction, an idea suddenly entered Dane's mind—he opened the door and quietly stepped onto the sidewalk. "Wait here until I return," he said to his driver.

Casually, Dane walked toward the open roller-door. He added a slight stagger to his walk, to make it look like he'd just come from a local bar. Just as he was nearing the entrance another car came speeding up the ramp and onto the street. When it was out of earshot, he briefly listened for other cars coming, but heard nothing. Anticipating no immediate danger, he slipped into the underground basement. The roller-door closed noisily behind him. Moving cautiously, he checked for any threat, but there was no one to be seen. However, three cars remained parked in the basement—the white limo, a Silver Shadow Rolls Royce, and a battered BMW that looked very out of place. Muffled voices suddenly sounded from the door at the top of the stairs, and Dane quickly went into hiding behind a trash container.

"That's nothing compared to what's happening in Nevada at the moment, you know ..."

The voices were clearer now and Dane braved a peek. There were three figures, but they were cast in shadow, and Dane couldn't identify them. He silently cursed the darkness.

"Do you know if Koso found him?" one of the men said.

"All I know is that Koso's here, and he wouldn't be here to see Krait if ..." The roller-door began to open again, drowning out the words.

Dane strained his ears desperately, but the noisy door obscured all clarity of the conversation as the three figures climbed into two of the remaining cars. But Krait's name *had* been used in the conversation. Koso *was* here to see Krait. Dane had what he'd come for—Koso *was* the key to finding Krait. But Dane had seen enough for the moment, and he didn't want to push his luck too far in one evening. He waited for the two cars to leave, and then he ducked out of the lowering roller-door. Rain was now falling heavily on the street.

Dashing through the thick drops, Dane reached the car and jumped quickly into the backseat. It was wet to the touch, and Dane wondered if he had accidentally left the widow open in his absence. In the dull evening light he quickly realized the backseat was covered in blood, not water.

"Bastards!" Dane screamed, leaping from the car. "You bastards!" He boiled with rage.

The driver had been shot through the head, and his eyes had been removed, leaving a ghostly pair of sockets.

"Bastards! Bastards! Bastards!" he exploded beyond control. But his cries were lost in the pounding rain. With a massive effort, he forced himself to calm down.

As the rain soaked Dane to the skin, an idea popped into his head. He opened the driver's door and shifted his body aside so he could get to the controls. Almost sitting on the driver's knee, Dane started the car, stuck the transmission into gear, and pulled swiftly away. The car accelerated toward the closed roller-door.

"If you bastards are going to make a mess, then you can keep it in your own fucking backyard!" Dane screamed as the car crashed through the door and came to a halt deep inside the basement.

Dane moved quickly. Carefully he moved the body back into the driver's seat, wiped his fingerprints from any surface he may have touched, and slammed the door closed. The scene set, he ran off into the night. After running steadily for a few blocks, the heavy rain had washed most of the blood from his clothing, and he slowed his pace to a walk.

As Dane walked and collected his thoughts, he realized just how close he'd been to Krait. The driver's gouged eyes were a multifaceted warning to the unwelcomed observer—a message that Dane didn't fully understand. Why was he being warned? If Krait was aware of what Dane was doing, then why not simply kill him? There were no obvious answers to these questions, and Dane quickly decided to focus on the facts. He had been warned; this was the only apparent fact. He quickly figured he shouldn't risk getting another warning. But his spirits were not shaken, and the murder of the driver only hardened his resolve. He *would* put an end to Krait, and nothing but death would stand in his path.

A dozen great crystal chandeliers hung from the high, tastefully decorated ceiling, casting a warm glow through the ship's five-star restaurant. Delicious, rich aromas filled the air while waiters drifted elegantly about, serving the guests. An elaborately constructed fountain bordered by a beautiful walnut bar centered the room. At this bar, perched atop an art-deco-style stool, Angelica lounged while sipping quietly on a cocktail and waiting for Dane. She'd only had time to sample her drink when she caught sight of him making his way down the staircase.

Angelica was dressed in a very clingy shoulder-to-ankle, black silk dress. It had an extensive split up the left side and was styled so it showed off her back and shoulders—not to mention a brief-but-classic measure of bust. She knew from the looks she'd received that her appearance met the approval of every man within view. She'd forgotten, however, how good Dane looked in a well-tailored Spanish tuxedo, and she felt somewhat humbled by his presence. It was as if time slowed down as he descended the stairs from the mezzanine floor. She stood at his approach, and without a word, they embraced for what seemed like an eternity. She couldn't believe how good it felt to have him in her arms at last. When they finally pulled apart, tears of joy pushed at the corners of her eyes.

"I don't think you know how much I've been looking forward to this," Dane said.

"I could take a guess," Angelica offered, a slight quiver in her tone. "How was your urgent business?" she asked, trying to take the edge off the energy between them.

"It went well," Dane said, unable to hide the strain in his voice when the subject was raised.

The waiter brought champagne.

"I can see you have things well organized," Dane said.

"Well, we have an overdue toast to make," Angelica said, picking up her glass. "First, I'd like to make a toast to our miraculous survival. And second, I'd like to toast the adventure of a lifetime— an adventure I'd rather not repeat, I might add."

"I'll second that," Dane returned. As the crystal clinked, he tried to remember the last time he'd had sparkling wine.

"Can you ever remember a glass of champagne tasting so good?" Angelica asked.

Dane chuckled aloud. "I don't think so. It's amazing what a couple of months in the desert does for your taste buds. I would have walked ten miles for a clean glass of water when we were out there. Now it almost seems too much to be able to drink what I please, when I please."

"So when do you plan to leave?" Angelica asked.

"Leave?"

"Oh, come on, Dane, I know you well enough by now. Your not going to give up on your list, so don't try white-washing anything with me—not here, not now. So please, when do you plan to leave?" Angelica demanded, determined to have the truth.

"I have a lead to the identity of the infamous Krait," Dane said, startled at his honesty. "The lead I have is in the form of a man. In two weeks and two days, this man shall be contacting me at my New York office, just as he always does at that time each year."

"Why would someone who can lead you to Krait be contacting you?" Angelica asked.

"Let's just say he has no knowledge that I know of his association with Krait. He is also someone I have known and trusted for many years," Dane finished.

Angelica noted a flash of pain in Dane's expression. She tactfully decided to change the subject; she didn't want to destroy the evening completely. She had the information that she wanted. Thankfully, the waiter arrived to seat them at their table, thus breaking the moment of tension. The conversation took a lighter turn once the waiter had gone, and it remained so throughout the meal.

"The new hairstyle suits you—it's stunning," Dane said.

"Thank you," Angelica said, blushing slightly.

Coffee arrived, and she peered at him over her cup. "So, I have you for a whole two weeks," she stated rather than asked.

Dane just smiled in reply.

Angelica stretched her hand across the table and slid her fingers between Dane's. "What would you say to a stroll around the deck?" he asked, smiling.

The evening breeze was warm, but refreshing, as they strolled. Seduced by the surroundings and warmed by Angelica's company, Dane couldn't remember ever feeling so good. The last time he'd spent such time with a woman, the experience had felt so alien compared to what he felt now. Now there was a halo of warmth surrounding him, and he knew it wasn't simply the result of the warm sea breeze.

The stroll passed in blissful silence until they reached the stern of the ship. Turning to Angelica, Dane was about to speak when she put her fingers to his lips, silencing him. Looking into her eyes, questioningly, he saw that familiar "I know" look, and suddenly the distance between them closed, and their lips came together.

Angelica lost any remaining control as they kissed a long and lingering kiss. She could barely believe how good it felt to hold Dane's strong body against her own. She completely surrendered to the moment, and minutes had passed before she broke the kiss and opened her mouth to speak, but this time, Dane raised a silencing finger. They were soon kissing again.

As Angelica's hands began to explore, she could feel Dane hardening against her. "Don't you think we should head for the cabin?" she asked, momentarily breaking the kiss. But the words were drowned by the fully unfolding passion.

Eventually, half-kissing, half-embracing, they edged back to the cabin where Angelica wasted no time. She tumbled onto the king-sized bed and pulled Dane onto her. Words were no longer necessary; their hands, eyes, and bodies did all the talking. They made love all night, their bodies blending together as one. It was noon the next day before they became too exhausted to continue and fell into a deep, restful sleep, lying in the comfort of each other's arms.

Soft light shining though the cabin blinds woke Dane. Angelica was still sleeping, and the light appeared magical as it cut across her half-exposed body. His mind wandered over the events of the previous evening. If Angelica wasn't now lying at his side, he could have sworn the whole event had been a dream. But even in his wildest dreams, there had never been such pleasure before. He wished with every fiber of his being that the ecstasy would never end.

Angelica stirred in her sleep, and then relaxed, still breathing deeply. Dane was mesmerized by her sleeping form—the contours of her face and her long, dark eyelashes closed over the olive smoothness of her face, perfectly framed by her lush black hair. Dane couldn't help but reach out and touch her seductive form. He ran his fingers softly along the curve of her naked frame, as if he were a sculptor examining a masterpiece. He'd lost count of the number of times they'd made love, and he was surprised to find he still wanted more. He was happily lost in the moment of pure perfection. Whatever doubt there had been was swallowed whole by a power previously unknown to him. He willingly opened his arms, embracing whatever fate chose to deal.

Ostrov Putin loved his job. Now in his early fifties, he'd been a high-ranking officer of the Federal Security Bureau since the FSB was the FSB. His office was poked away in a quiet little corner just outside the city of Rostov. It was not exactly FSB central, but it was an impressive step up, nonetheless.

He was having a bad day. One of his men had raped a suspect during a special operation. The unfortunate culprit now stood, shaking in his boots, against Ostrov's office door. The rapist was receiving a rather brutal punishment for his actions. A piece of fine, nylon fishing line protruded from the open zipper on his trousers, one end tautly tied to the door handle, and the other end noosed around the culprit's testicles. With hands cuffed behind his back, the rapist was desperately trying to maintain balance on the tips of his toes, but he was quickly tiring, and the moment he let his ankles relax, the nylon would rip his testicles clear from his groin. This was a treatment Ostrov had administered many times. The longest anyone had previously lasted before having their testicles torn from their bodies was three hours. Ostrov delighted in the fact that the man would *never* rape again. He hated rapists.

"I see you're still getting off on your old tricks," Koso said as he entered the room and sat in one of the comfortable chairs opposite Ostrov's desk.

"You know me, my friend. The oldest tricks are always the best!" Ostrov said.

"How long do you think the bastard'll last?" Koso asked.

"Most of the office say another hour, but after the kick in the thigh I gave him a few minutes ago, I'd give him forty minutes, max. The hat's still going around for last bets if you want in."

"Why the hell not? I'm always up for a few extra rubles." He slapped fifty Euro-dollars down on the old, steel desktop. "That do?"

Ostrov grinned, flung the note into the officer's cap along with the rest of the money and smiled a yes. "So, what's your bet?"

Koso flashed a glance at his watch and the sweat-soaked rapist. "I give the miserable bastard fifteen minutes at most. In the meantime, let's get down to a little business, shall we?"

"Ah yes, old friend—business," Ostrov agreed. "Krait, has been putting a lot of pressure on Russian Mafia heads of late. Knowledge of their dealings with Krait has wormed its way to our ears, and corruption has reached epidemic proportions. Even the FSB is riddled with dirty officers. Once responsible, respectable men are now only too happy to do business with the likes of Krait. Already the IUS has its hooks in some of our heavier military hardware, and we can't afford to let this continue. Thank God—if there really is a God—we now have full control over our nuclear capabilities. But Krait's infiltration into our ranks is a serious step in the direction of our darkened past. I'm feeling anxious, and we are running short of money and time, both of which you've taken plenty of. So I hope you bring good news, Koso?"

"Ostrov, my old friend, regretfully, I don't have much to offer in the way of information since the conclusion of our last meeting," Koso grumbled. "I have been in direct contact with Krait twice since then, but both times were at different locations, and both times I knew nothing of the location until five minutes prior. The security measures surrounding Krait are beyond extravagant. Krait is certainly making fools of us all. I've been so close I was tempted to make a lunge right then and there. Only deep down I knew I could have never fully closed the distance. Even if I'd had a gun, I would have been dead before pulling the trigger. But I promise you this—I *will* get Krait. It's only a matter of time. I'm just looking for the right opportunity, and as yet I haven't seen it."

"I don't doubt this, old friend. And again, forgive me if it seems that I'm pushing you, but you must also understand the pressure that is being put on me from my superiors. The days of Krait's kind being tolerated are long gone, and we don't want to be taking any steps backward. Krait's progression must be stopped now, before it expands beyond control. If you need more money, just say so. If you need anything at all, just say so." This said, Ostrov pushed a thick envelope across the desktop. "Here's your cash. Though I have to say, I'd still prefer you to be on our official payroll."

Koso cringed. "Bankers are worse than common criminals. Giving those bastards money would be worse than handing it directly to Krait. There is only one place I trust to keep my money, and no one but myself will ever know of it. And if that isn't security, then I don't know what is," Koso said. Slipping the envelope into his coat pocket, he stood. "You'll be the first to know of any progress I make. And don't go offering me any of those gun-happy rookies of yours. If I needed your goddamn help, I'd ask." He walked to the door and turned to face Ostrov. "Oh ... when I win the bet, you can just add the cash to my next payment," he said. He then left without another word.

Ostrov grinned as Koso walked away. If any other man had spoken to him in that way, he would have taken him out into the courtyard and put a bullet through his skull right in front of anyone who cared to watch—preferably the entire office. However, he and Koso went back further than his vodka-weathered mind could recall, and communication in its raw form was normal between them. It might take time, but, like all things, Krait would come to an end, and Ostrov was sure that Koso Dilerenso was the key to that end.

Soon, Koso's insults were pushed aside and Ostrov's attention returned to the rapist. He leaned back, put his feet up on the desk, and pulled the revolver from his desk draw. He took careful aim at the man's chest and momentarily enjoyed the look of outright terror. He then made his decision. The following morning, when the rapist awoke, he would have a gun to his face. If he didn't die of a heart attack from the sound of the firing pin dropping upon an empty chamber, then, and only then would his punishment truly begin. A fresh command post in a labor camp, deep within Mongolia had become available, and balls were not necessary for the posting.

Koso had freelanced for the FSB for three years. It wasn't the first time he'd worked for the Russians, and it probably wouldn't be the last. Over the years, he'd done work for pretty much anyone, from the English, to the Spanish, to the Americans, and back again. He'd gone freelance twenty years before, after working for a nameless, black-budget US agency, and getting paid far too little for far too much.

Officially labeled as retired, and despite the fact he was no longer in top physical shape, Koso was able to continue working by use of improvisation, a sturdy measure of patience, and a lifetime on contacts and experience. But, despite his endless experience, his patience was now stretched to its threshold. His only luck with the IUS so far was working his way into its ranks. He did this by acting as a rogue agent and selling valuable information to the existing members of the IUS. This quickly brought him into Krait's inner circle, but never close enough. If only he could ID Krait.

His next meeting with Krait was in Athens, Greece. As always, he was to have lunch at one p.m., sharp. The process would be standard—at a downtown restaurant, he would be handed the house phone by one of the waiters. A computerized voice would give him a set of instructions, which would eventually lead him to the meeting.

Before the last scheduled meeting, he'd been instructed to leave the restaurant and cross the street to a waiting car. He'd then been casually driven to a nearby parking building, where he'd found six identical Mercedes waiting. He was then transferred to one of the cars and driven from the building. Twenty minutes later, they had entered the basement of a modest building and led to a meeting room. As with every meeting he'd had with Krait, the entire process had been carried out in an entirely different fashion, making the connection procedure impossible to predict.

Sitting in the back of the car while being driven to the airport, Koso's focus was lost on the bleak Russian scenery, and his mind was a thousand miles away. He'd pay a king's ransom to learn why Krait wanted to have Dane removed from Camp Five; the situation puzzled him to no end. Dane must have been important to Krait in some way, or the rescue would have never been ordered. Yet Koso couldn't put his finger on what the importance could be. The more he thought about the situation, the further he felt he was getting from the truth. Stretching, he realized just how weary he was.

He could barely recall when he'd last rested at length. A tingle ran the length of his spine. He wasn't just feeling weary—he was feeling old. He frowned. He didn't have time for getting old. But he had a plane to catch, and if he were lucky, he'd have a chance to sleep on the flight.

The two weeks Dane and Angelica spent together were magical. During the first week, they had hardly left their cabin, unable to tear themselves from each other's arms. Finally, one afternoon, they had docked at a small Greek Island. There they stayed in an ancient resort, which was nestled in a private bay. They had just spent the afternoon on the water, water-para-skiing—something that Angelica had wanted to do since the day she'd met Dane. The sport was indeed exhilarating, but it was also very physically draining. The boat now sped over the water, the powerful engines propelling them quickly back toward the island.

"Let me come with you?" Angelica said.

Dane had been dreading this moment. He knew she was going to ask, and as much as he mulled the anticipated question, he'd still not come up with an answer he felt would satisfy her. "You know you can't," were the only words he could muster.

She just stared back at him, a grimace in the place of her usual smile. They only had two more days together. An unstoppable feeling of despair was welling inside of her. She only now understood how much she cared for him. "I could help you," she insisted. "You saw what I managed to do with my father. Taking Krait on your own is a massive risk, and you know it."

Dane slowed the boat's engines as they neared the small dock and pulled up to the jetty, where men waited with ropes. Taking a deep breath, he summoned his strength and softly took Angelica's hand. "I'm sorry, but this is something I have to do on my own. You know what happened the last time we came even close to Krait, and I feel much too strongly for you to let you endanger yourself for my purposes. Please understand."

"So, you'll just leave then?" Angelica said, her emotions unraveling. "You're going to let a freak childhood accident destroy your life. Why, Dane? Why can't you just leave your past behind where it belongs and get on with your life?"

"I just can't," Dane said.

Angelica popped. Her tone turned from pleading and teary to bitterly harsh. "Answer me this," she growled. "If what happened to your father all those years ago really means so much to you, then why aren't you with him now?" She didn't wait for his answer. "I'll tell you why—it's because you don't have the guts to just come out and tell him what you did. The real reason you are doing all this is to prove you're not a coward."

Dane instantly walled up. He again became his usual detached, unreadable, and stolid self. From that moment, the showdown was over.

That evening passed slowly. They dined together in silence. With each passing moment, they felt the distance between them grow.

Angelica regretted her outburst, but she didn't know how to make things better. The following morning, when she awoke, she wasn't in the least surprised to see Dane gone. However, the note he left was a surprise. It lay on his empty pillow; scrawled in bright red ink were the words "I love you."

Chapter 10

The Cambodian Twist

The morning Dane left Angelica, he was consumed with emotion. But his old habits had not abandoned him, and instinct threw him back into work. Having no viable lead on Krait, he turned his attention to the only other remaining target, Qui Trang.

During the Vietnam War, Qui Trang had worked for a SVA medical-supply unit close to the action. One day, a soldier was brought in—the son of a general. He'd needed a kidney, and he'd needed it fast. Being constantly in contact with the dead or dying soldiers, Qui had instantly seen a very lucrative opportunity. He managed to acquire a healthy, compatible organ in less than twenty-four hours. He presented it to the general's overjoyed medical staff, and no questions were asked. The payment for the organ had been more than Qui made in a year, and he decided to turn his one-time stroke of luck into a career.

When the war ended, Qui's money dwindled fast, due to his indulgent lifestyle. Soon he was no better off than any other common Vietnamese of the time. But then the tide drastically turned when an American doctor who'd served in the war contacted him. The doctor had heard about Qui's knack for fast organ supply, and offered him thirty thousand US dollars for a healthy kidney. Qui quickly agreed to the deal, and from that point forth, he never looked back. His organ-trafficking turned into a global empire of harrowing proportion. He even had his own fleet of ships, and, to most, he was known to be a respectable businessman. Nonetheless, Qui Trang was a world leader in the organ-supply business—famous in the shadier circles for shipping living people to numerous parts of the world, where they were butchered and sold to the highest bidder.

Thus was the nature of Dane's fourth mark, and now, he examined Qui's Cambodian jungle headquarters through a powerful telescope. The jungle was thick and lush, providing him with excellent cover. Qui's headquarters were elaborate by anyone's measures, and Dane cursed the difficulty of his task. Outside the thirty-foot wall surrounding the complex lay a hundred feet of heavily mined open ground. The mines could be deactivated remotely, but only from inside the compound. The oval-shaped circumference of the wall measured about one mile and was topped by a walkway for patrolling guards. Razor wire as thick as the surrounding jungle lay at the base of the wall, coiled some way up its outer side. Even if Dane did make it through the minefield, climbing the wall would be a suicide mission. There was no apparent entrance into the complex, but he knew there must be one—he just hadn't seen it yet.

Dane adjusted the position in which he lay and gasped as a cramped right leg complained. He'd been lying on the trunk of a fallen tree for two hours, and there was no escaping the consequences. He'd parachuted in at dawn and had landed right on target, about three miles south of Qui's stronghold. It'd taken him an hour to find the package that had been dropped along with him. The alloy canister held an American-made, Asian-modified, rocket-propelled grenade launcher with a half dozen rounds. Also enclosed was a very lightweight HK-UMP45 universal machine pistol with a half-dozen, twenty-round magazines. A more experienced jumper would have had the gear strapped to their body, but Dane was not an experienced jumper. He'd made his first solo jump only a week earlier, and he knew that he was taking enough of risk as it was merely by making a dawn jump into a complex landscape.

The loaded grenade launcher lay in front of Dane on a moss-covered tree trunk. Dane knew from the Chinese intelligence files he'd acquired that Qui always returned to his headquarters upon completion of each shipment of his live merchandise. This was a big relief to Dane, since it meant there would be no innocent people in the buildings.

Dane's plan was simple—he would open fire the moment Qui made his scheduled morning landing inside the compound, make sure he was dead, and then head for a location a safe distance from the compound. Then he'd call in a pick-up. All he had to do was wait. But wait he did, and soon enough, the morning turned into afternoon, and his patience began to wear thin. As evening settled, Qui still didn't show. The delay compounded his frustration and discomfort more and more with each passing minute. He revised the information John had sold to him again until he was convinced his timing was correct. Qui simply *had* to show up.

But as the day came to an end and the nighttime noises of the jungle took hold, Dane realized he would have to accept that Qui wouldn't be arriving as scheduled. He'd wait one more day, and if Qui didn't show up by then, he'd pack his things and go back to the drawing board. Setting the grenade-launcher aside, he maneuvered into a position where he could sleep—or at least rest more comfortably. As he did so, the jungle suddenly became very quiet. Moments later, large raindrops began pouring from the darkening sky. Dane groaned and pulled a camouflaged, waterproof sheet over his head. The meager protection proved to be of little comfort as the night wore achingly on with the rain persisting.

Two things sharply registered in Dane's weary mind as he awoke from his damp and uncomfortable slumber—one was the fleeting bewilderment at how he had managed to sleep to begin with, and the second was the distant sound of a dog barking. Quickly, he snatched his telescope in order to investigate. His heart leapt as about thirty armed guards came into focus, methodically moving through the minefield toward the jungle's edge. Each guard was being towed along by a vicious German shepherd, leashes strained to the limit.

Dane momentarily wondered how they'd come from behind the wall, and then he saw the crane-like structure with an attached cage. The device had raised and lowered a makeshift lift over the wall. He furiously searched his empty head for an explanation for the search. He then heard the *chop-chop-chop* of a helicopter in the distance. Dane quickly realized the guards were doing a routine security sweep before their boss arrived. In the dull dawn light, the helicopter emerged from the fog.

Dane anxiously watched the scene unfold—the proximity of the dogs, the impending target; if he stayed where he was he'd soon be discovered. The choices were clear—he could quit the mission or proceed with his original plan. It was a lousy situation, but, either way, his departure would be a long and strenuous jostle between life and death. Quickly, he made his decision.

The helicopter descended lazily over the center of the compound, as if tempting Dane. He had to wait, though; he had to identify Qui as he exited the chopper. Two guards with dogs straining in front of them reached the foot of the hill Dane perched on. The dogs looked eager, as if they'd already picked up on his scent. Dane tried to concentrate on the landing helicopter, but it was difficult with the dogs so close at hand. His only consolation was that the dense foliage on the side of the hill would slow the dogs enough to give him an edge. Finally the chopper landed, the door opened, and three smartly dressed men climbed out. Frantically, Dane searched their faces, but none of the men remotely resembled Qui. He was about to turn from the telescope when a belated fourth man followed the first three out. It was Qui. Dane recognized him instantly. Acting fast, he swung the RPG unit into position. As calmly and carefully as his panic would allow, he lined up the modified scope directly toward the center of the group and squeezed the trigger. Nothing. His heart leapt in his chest; he had forgotten to release the safety catch. Fumbling, he corrected his error. He aimed again, allowing the extravagance of a deep breath. He exhaled slowly and squeezed the trigger again. This time, the weapon fired, and a moment later, the grenade exploded, right on target. Immediately, gunfire rang out from directly below him. Dane didn't hesitate. He reloaded his weapon and fired two more grenades at the guards closest to him. A clean getaway was no longer an option.

The two leading guards were all but gone, but twenty more were on their way, their frenzied dogs barking as if Satan possessed them. There were three RPG rounds left. Dane knew he couldn't afford to waste anymore rounds on the guards. He had to be sure that Qui was dead, or all his efforts would be in vain. He fired at the helicopter, and it exploded far more dramatically than anticipated, taking three surrounding buildings with it and setting fire to two others. His last two shots finished anything that might have survived. Qui Trang was undoubtedly dead. All of the main buildings within the complex were burning. Moreover, his efforts had somehow caused an electrical malfunction and rearmed the surrounding minefield. Fresh explosions boomed from the perimeter, and guards everywhere were in a panic, too afraid to move. But five guards had already made it to the edge of the minefield and were fast closing the distance to Dane's position. He grabbed his pack, slung the machine pistols over his shoulders, and leaped down from the fallen tree; he had to go. Taking a quick bearing from his compass, he set off. With luck, he would reach the river before his pursuers got close. Once there, he would travel downstream, hoping the dogs would lose his scent.

Night was close at hand. He had been on the run for hours and had headed south out of the river over an hour before. He was now hidden in dense foliage. He had not heard the dogs' bark or a single shout from a guard in over two hours. He was certain he had time to rest a little. The blackness of the night was enough to hide him, but the brush he lay upon also proved to be excellent camouflage. Time ticked sluggishly by as he tried to sleep, but sleep would not come. The luminous hands on his Omega watch indicated it was one a.m., and his restless thoughts returned to Angelica. Squeezing his puffy and tired eyes shut, he rolled uncomfortably in an attempt to relieve the ache of his shoulder. In a happy twist of fate, this tired movement saved his life, for, just as he turned, a bullet bored its way into the still, warm soil of his former position. His thoughts sobered immediately. He sprang to his feet and grabbed his pack and a pistol. Judging from the accuracy of the shot, the shooter had night-vision equipment. This was something he'd not anticipated. He couldn't accurately shoot back, and this left him with only one option—run.

With bullets whistling past him, Dane dashed blindly through the jungle like a possessed animal. Branches and leaves tore at his flesh, but he had to run or die. A bullet passed by so close to his head he could hear its tiny vibrations as it cut through the air. His fear amplified, and he increased his pace. He hadn't been running long when suddenly the ground disappeared, and he was sliding down a steep, muddy bank, out of control. Someway down, a low tree branch barred the way, offering to stop him—but his head connected with the branch before his hands did, and he was knocked out cold.

An agonizing throb pulsed through Dane's brain when he woke. Looking up, he saw he'd slid at least a hundred feet into an overgrown swamp. A massive lump was forming on his skull, which had effectively absorbed the impact of the tree. Distant voices echoed through the jungle as he sat upright, fighting back the terrible pain. Mud squelched under him, and his head spun. Dawn had broken, and shadows loomed everywhere in a ghostly fog. He quickly realized he must have been unconscious for at least a few hours. Astonishingly, he'd remained safely hidden. The bushy swamp he'd landed in provided unbelievably effective coverage, and, somehow, even the pursuers' night vision had failed to locate him.

Trying to ignore the slithering creatures brushing against him, he surveyed his remaining resources. His pack lay in a nearby shrub, so he had food and water. And his machine pistol was still slung over his shoulder. But his compass and the satellite phone that had been belted to his hip were nowhere to be seen, and he cursed the implications of the loss. Below such a thick jungle canopy he couldn't easily determine his direction from the sun's movement. And the loss of the phone meant there was no way of calling in a pick-up. He had no choice but to head for the village of Lumphat, which was over two hundred kilometers to the south. But his pursuers were dangerously close, and he had no time to dwell on the negative. He had to move. He had to find high ground, climb a tree, and get some idea of direction.

Collecting his things, he began his trudge through the wetlands, which lay in a long, low valley surrounded by steep hills. He knew his best chance of escape was in traveling across the swamp and away from the pursuers for as long as possible. But he hadn't gone more than a few yards when he heard a triumphant yell behind him. He'd been seen. He cursed loudly and almost panicked, but he couldn't run in the knee-deep sludge. The best he could do was a hurried wade. The guards then began shooting. They were out of range, but were getting closer by the second, and Dane realized he had no choice but to change tactics. He didn't want to die from a bullet in his back in some stinking Cambodian quagmire. With all possible haste, he waded to an area where the mud was deeper, and there were some bushes between him and the pursuers. He then submerged himself. The vile mixture of water and slime instantly soaked him, but he ignored the discomfort and quickly pulled masses of thick moss over his head, leaving peepholes to see.

The gunfire stopped, and Dane patiently awaited the approach of the enemy. The more time that passed, the greater his awareness became of the surrounding filth and what was living in it. He desperately tried to remember if his trouser legs were tucked into his socks. He then heard a nearby splash, and moments later, three guards materialized from the gloom. They spoke softly together before spreading out and moving in separate directions. Two of them disappeared from view, and one headed directly in Dane's direction.

He focused intensely on the fast-approaching gunman. He prayed silently for mercy, but mercy was not at hand. A sticky swamp creature began edging its way up the inside of his left leg. He hadn't tucked his trouser legs into his socks as he'd hoped. Grinding his teeth, he resisted the urge to seize the beast before it got too far. The guard steadily closed in until Dane could see the alert expression on his weather-beaten face. Suddenly, the guard stopped and looked directly down at Dane, as if sensing his presence; but then, much to Dane's relief, his attention wandered elsewhere. Dane seized the moment of opportunity. As smoothly as he could, he silently curved his wrist until his automatic pistol was pointed upward. He took the best possible aim toward the unsuspecting Cambodian and squeezed the trigger. A stunned expression passed across the guard's face, and he fell, face down, into the mud.

The noise of the gun wasn't as loud as Dane had hoped. He wanted the other two guards' attention. But the approaching curses indicated the shot was loud enough. Splashing through the swamp, the second and third guards came rushing to their comrade's aid. Moments passed in which Dane didn't move an inch. The infernal creature was still making steady progress up his left leg as the other two guards came to an abrupt halt and stood silently over their fallen friend. Both men cursed harshly in Khmer, feverishly looking in all directions. Dane opened fire again. The second guard went down, but the bolt on the pistol then jammed. Dane discarded the weapon and sprang. Reaching the remaining Cambodian in one desperate leap, he wrapped his hands around his neck and squeezed.

The guard brought his knee up into Dane's body, momentarily winding him, and pushed him backward to the ground. The guard's hands clutched Dane's throat. In blind desperation, Dane grappled for anything that might serve as a weapon. His left hand found a hard, oval object attached to the man's belt. Recognition struck him—a grenade. He tugged the grenade free and swung it in a wide arc into the guard's head. He reeled back in pain, and Dane used the moment to stuff the grenade into the front of his pants. The guard frantically fumbled for it, and Dane dove back into the cover of the sludge. A split second later, a thud convulsed through the swamp.

Dane waited until he thought his lungs would burst, and then he slowly surfaced, feeling something akin to a hippopotamus. All seemed silent. He wiped the mud carefully from his sore eyes, and his stomach turned as the gory scene before him came into focus. The man whose heart had been beating strongly only a few moments before was now reduced to a few large chunks of steaming flesh. But Dane's remorse was quickly overcome by a pressing need. He feverishly undid his trousers, dug at the inside of his leg, and pulled out the largest bloodsucking leech he'd ever seen. He was stunned that he'd managed to peel the thing away without having to burn it, but he guessed the creature had had its fill and decided there was no real reason to stick around. He flicked it away in disgust, collected his filthy belongings, tore a compass from the second guard's corpse, and moved out. As he walked, it began to rain.

Despite the present surer course, there was still every chance of running into the arms of the enemy. Lumphat, the nearest town to the south, was about two hundred kilometers away, and a committed enemy was still hot on his heels.

But the rest of the day passed smoothly. He headed south, and had covered a good distance before he decided he could risk a few hours rest. The rain stopped just before dusk, but he didn't stop walking until two hours after dark. He found a relatively comfortable spot and quickly dropped into a deep, dreamless sleep. When he awoke, it was dawn, and he felt fairly well rested, despite the discomfort of the damp ground. He then heard voices. They came from the bottom of the ridge he'd camped on. He splashed water on his face, crawled silently to the edge, and peered about two hundred feet down into a small clearing. Half a dozen guards sat in a small circle, talking to an authority figure standing at their center. When the man turned, Dane, with an involuntary gasp of horror, recognized Qui Trang. Instantly he understood why he'd been hunted so relentlessly—Qui was still alive and intent on capturing his would-be assassin.

Precious moments passed as Dane calmed his nerves and reassessed his situation. They would undoubtedly have a good tracker, so there was little chance of shaking them loose. Deciding his best course of action, Dane gathered his gear and set off again. Qui being still alive left him with no choice; it was time to turn the tables and pursue the pursuers.

It took Dane just minutes to widely circle the enemy and reach the opposite side of the clearing. He was just in time. The seven-strong crew was already moving out in hot pursuit. They were spread about fifteen feet apart, giving them a broad field of coverage while still enabling them to call to each other. The tracker was dressed in civilian clothing, and he walked in the center of the bunch, right next to Qui Trang. Dane observed with delight that he was not making use of a compass.

As they trudged through the jungle, Dane widely circled the clearing once more and began closing in on the party. Using the cover of the dense brush, he methodically began closing in on the left-flank guard. Hardly a minute passed before the man came into sight. Dane moved quickly ahead of him, ducked deep into the thick plant growth, and switched his pistol to semiautomatic. He took aim at his first victim's moving head and squeezed the trigger. A dull thud resounded from the silenced barrel, and the guard fell silently to ground. Dane snatched up his military cap and put it on. Thankfully, it had escaped being splattered by too much blood.

Dane's plan was simple. Without using a compass, the tracker wouldn't immediately realize that he and his companions were being led in ever-widening circles. As the party pursued what was ultimately at their tail, Dane would pick them off one by one. The length of time it took before the ruse was exposed was a gamble Dane had little choice but to take. He knew for sure that the guide would eventually realize he'd been had. With this in mind, Dane moved quickly into step with the next guard, smoothly taking the place of his unfortunate companion.

Within twenty minutes, Dane had successfully removed both guards off the left flank and one on the right. His task was almost complete, but he felt sure that Qui and his tracker were becoming suspicious that something was amiss. The group had made three complete circles, and Dane decided it was time he to drove home the final resolve. Quietly, he worked his way toward the two remaining guards. He would have to deal with them very swiftly. He slid through the foliage until he was keeping pace only yards behind them. He switched his gun onto fully automatic, unscrewed the silencer, and patiently followed until they reached a clearing. Choosing the moment, Dane squeezed the trigger and swept his gun in an arc from one man to the other. Shrieking, they fell before they could move a muscle in defense.

Dane didn't waste a second. He dashed through the jungle like a ghost. Minutes passed as he ran, and for a moment he wondered if he'd misjudged his position. But then he finally reached the clearing where he had spotted the hunting party only an hour earlier. Locating the exact spot he had started from, he settled down to wait. If his luck held, the tracker and Qui would be confidently on his tail, believing they had strength in numbers.

Dane's luck held.

With a wild rush, Qui and the tracker burst through the trees and into the clearing, where they abruptly halted. Confusion spread over their faces as they recognized the area. They turned and peered back into the trees, expecting their men to be hot on their heels. Dane opened fire, and the tracker collapsed, useless.

The vulnerable Qui Trang didn't hesitate; he leapt back into the undergrowth. Dane sprang after him, knowing full well that the cat-and-mouse game was now a cat-and-cat game. Qui was an armed man—and no less dangerous than the weapon he held. The disadvantage was equal, and the prize was survival.

Qui scrambled through the dense jungle, his heart thumping hard against his chest. It had been years since he'd undertaken any strenuous physical activity, and the previous two days had taken a serious toll. He was weak. His body was strained to the limit, and his mind was reeling. Who was the madman on his tail? He thought it would take a small army to penetrate his headquarters, but the tracker had repeatedly insisted that they were in pursuit of a single man—a man who'd murdered Qui's only brother.

Qui had invited his brother to his headquarters in the hope of making him a business partner. He desperately needed some release from the pressure of his work; he needed someone that could be trusted. But any chance of that was now gone—everything was gone, and all in one massive inferno. He could still picture the explosive flames as he'd fled the scene. But his rage had now curdled into mortal fear. In a matter of hours, his bodyguard had been reduced to nothing, and now an invisible enemy was running him to the ground. His assassin was a professional, more than likely a government agency recruit. But which agency?

Sweat poured from Qui's burning skin. He tripped on something hard, rolled once, got to his feet, and continued his desperate flight. He was as the beast is to the hunter, and nothing more.

If Qui hadn't been armed, Dane would surely have had him within minutes, but he was now forced to use extreme caution in his pursuit. He couldn't actually see Qui clearly, but he could see movement ahead and hear the noisy rustling of the jungle undergrowth as it was aggressively pushed aside.

Dane momentarily wondered if he should merely walk away and let the jungle claim Qui; he had no visible compass, and his talented guide was long dead. Surely he would eventually die, lost and starving. It was an attractive thought, but Dane knew he couldn't take the risk. Qui had to be finished, and he had to be finished with certainty.

Qui couldn't go on. Very shortly, he would have no choice but to stop and collapse. It was time for him to turn and face his opponent, for better or worse. He franticly ducked behind a massive tree trunk and tried to muffle his gasps for oxygen. But his heart pounded like a hammer, and he was convinced the entire jungle could hear it. With enormous effort, he forced himself to take deep, slow breaths. He listened attentively for the approach; he didn't have long to wait. Taking the barrel of his rifle firmly in both hands, he raised the weapon to his shoulder. Listening hard over the sound of his heartbeat, he desperately tried to determine from what direction the enemy would approach. A cracking twig alerted him, and he leapt from behind the tree, swinging the rifle hard and in a wide arc as his panic took hold.

Dane caught the flash of movement from the corner of his hyperaware eye and jumped blindly to the side. The blow missed his body, but knocked his gun to the ground. He leapt at Qui before he had time to recover, and they were suddenly rolling on the ground, both struggling for control of Qui's rifle.

Dane soon found his strength overcoming Qui's. He pinned him to the ground and forced the rifle lengthways down to his neck. It was obvious to Dane that Qui was resisting with all of his strength, but his resistance was easily overcome.

Qui then spoke. The words were strained but unmistakable: "The IUS protects me ... protects me ... You cannot do this ... Krait will come for you ..."

The shock of hearing Krait's name momentarily threw Dane's concentration. He slackened for a fraction of a moment, and Qui's right knee jabbed at his groin with painfully accuracy. The blow was not hard, but it was enough to send Dane tumbling in agony.

Too weak to make another attack, Qui instead made run for it. Impulsively, but still in much pain, Dane grabbed his automatic from a nearby shrub and emptied an entire clip into Qui's back. Blood spurted generously over the jungle foliage, and Qui crashed, face down, in a mangled heap. Desperately, Dane ran to his side, knelt down, and rolled him over. He cursed his irrational stupidity. Qui was dead. He had mentioned Krait, and if he were willing to talk, he would have liked to have asked a few questions before Qui began his slow rot in hell.

With immense frustration, Dane sat back and mulled over things. After some time he began earnestly searching Qui's blood-soaked pockets in search of clues: a wallet containing a thick wad of foreign cash, various credit and business cards, a photograph of him with a young Asian woman, possibly his daughter—nothing of any great relevance. In another pocket, he found a crumpled packet of cigarettes and nothing else.

Despite having won his survival, Dane somehow felt defeated. He sat heavily next to Qui's body. Absently, he picked up the photograph and stared at the pair of smiling faces it boasted. He then noticed something peculiar about the picture. At the top left corner, the printed paper was peeling away from the back layer. Gingerly he tugged at the top layer and easily managed to peel the photo in half. He examined the finely cut false-picture backing with surprised anticipation. In tiny, but clear print was a list of dates and numbers. The dates went back three years, each one exactly four months apart. The numbers listed beside the dates held no meaning for Dane, but his curiosity was certainly sparked. He pressed the photo back together and buttoned it safely inside his shirt pocket. Again he looked at the now pitiful sight of Qui Trang. For a moment he considered burying him, but he abandoned the idea. He needed all his energy, and there was no point in denying the local wildlife an easy meal.

It took Dane three days to find his way out of the jungle. Fortunately, he stumbled into a small village north of Kip Trabek that wasn't marked on the map. From there, he managed to make a phone call to Bryant Wilson, his company's CEO. Bryant answered his cellular in the middle of the second ring.

"Bryant Wilson here."

"Bryant, good morning to you," Dane said.

"Dane, good to hear from you," Bryant said, making no mention of the fact that it was three thirty in the morning, New York time. He was a man thoroughly dedicated to what he did best—running a big business. He'd been an IRS bigwig before Dane had gotten his hooks into him and seduced him with stupid amounts of money. But the paycheck was well-earned. Bryant doubled Dane's assets in a matter of years. Above all Bryant had earned Dane's trust as an associate whose reliability was absolute. When Bryant was asked to do something, he did it, no questions asked. So it came as no surprise when Dane asked him to organize air transportation out of an unknown village in northern Cambodia.

Dane's mind reeled for a few moments in response to Bryant's final words:

"Oh, before you go, Koso Dilerenso called asking of your whereabouts. I asked him for a contact phone number, but he insisted he'd find you himself."

Chapter 11

Fallen

Dane called Koso while flying back from Cambodia, and the old man insisted in meeting him in the flesh. "We need to talk about something face to face," were Koso's exact words. They decided on Rome and breakfast. Dane couldn't hide a look of apprehension as he approached the Antico Café della Pace at a little after nine in the morning.

"Another hard night on the scotch, was it?" Dane asked upon seeing Koso slumped over one of the patio tables, looking dead tired.

Koso stood bolt upright and extended his hand to Dane. "Good to see you, my boy," he said, offering a firm handshake that contradicted his deflated appearance.

"And you, Koso," Dane returned, noting the uncertainty in Koso's eyes.

"Recovered fully from the Gobi ordeal, I see."

"Yes, I suppose you could say that," Dane said, sitting.

"Dane my boy, we've known each other for a long time now, so I'm not going to fool around with small-talk," Koso began. "I wanted to meet you today to get a couple of things out in the open."

"What's on your mind?" Dane asked.

"Before I begin, you should know that I'm aware of your current hobby," Koso said.

Dane tried to keep his expression neutral.

"I know about Benito Santage. I also know you had a hand in—or at least tried to have a hand in—the demise of Limnos

Skiathos, who was without a doubt the world's most powerful arms dealer. Last, but not least, I know what you did to Qui Trang."

Dane's fragile composure suddenly slipped and was replaced with wide-eyed concern and astonishment. He'd just returned from Cambodia, and he couldn't imagine how Koso already knew of Qui's demise.

"I know that your next move is to find Krait, and to kill Krait," Koso pressed on, glancing at his watch.

"Who?" Dane asked.

"Don't bullshit me, please. It is my business to know, so let's not make this anymore embarrassing than it is," Koso insisted.

"Fine. Why are you telling me this?" Dane asked.

"Because, son, I know where your life is going. When I plucked you out of the desert with that stunning young woman, I thought you might've had a change of heart, but this recent fiasco with Qui tells me I was wrong."

"How can you know? You don't know the half of who I am." Dane was indignant. He felt utterly humiliated.

"I do know, Dane; I know how it feels to lose family, and I know what guilt is. I know what happened to your father, and I know you feel responsible, but the fact is, you are not."

At the mention of his father, Dane stood sharply and made a move to leave.

"*Sit down!*" Koso demanded.

Seeing a frightening emptiness in Koso's eyes, Dane bit his lip and stiffly sat.

Koso's words turned unexpectedly soft. "I've spent my entire life doing what you're doing now. I was popping bad men with a .22-caliber before you were even born. I lost count years ago of the people who have fallen under my hand. I've forgotten their faces and their names. You're thirty-five, Dane. Things can change for you," Koso pleaded.

"Your words make more sense than any I've heard in a long time," Dane said, "but I cannot stop. Too much has happened. I have to see this thing through. Rational thought can do nothing to defeat this, and what happened to my father and uncle was my fault. After all, I was the one that set the explosives."

Koso shook his head. "I understand you're at the mercy of your drive, Dane, but I also know that going after Krait is the one thing that you shouldn't do," he pleaded.

"I have to!" Dane insisted.

"I've always respected you, Dane. You are the closest I've come to caring about anyone in over forty years, and I simply cannot watch you destroy yourself. I must ask you to trust me. Please, please do not go after Krait," Koso said, desperation now in his voice.

Dane said nothing, and a fierce tension pulsed through the air between them.

Finally Koso spoke. "I know who Krait is," he said.

The sentence had the impact of a punch. Dane visibly rocked backward in his chair. Still, nothing could have prepared him for what happened next. Koso opened his mouth to continue his disclosure. The thought visibly formed, but never made it from his lips. His eyes suddenly glazed over, and, with a gargle, his body went limp.

The shot had come from behind Koso. It had been silent; its only evidence was a spray of blood over the pure whiteness of the tablecloth. A second shot was then fired, and Koso's chest exploded in a crimson kaleidoscope. Dane was frozen to his seat in shock, and before he could react in any way, two police officers yelled at him from the sidewalk, pointing pistols:

"Get down on the ground, now!"

"Get down and stay down, now!"

Dane still couldn't move. A police officer knocked him clear out of his seat and pinned him down.

It took three hours of questioning and investigation for the authorities to figure out Dane was not the shooter. But when his innocence was proclaimed, he felt no better off. Koso Dilerenso, his dearest friend, was dead.

Angelica lay on the hotel room bed, unwinding after another busy day. When Dane had left her, she'd done what she always did when trying to take her mind off something—she went back to work. She'd called Thomas Beckerman, her partner at the London law firm, and he had her working twenty-hour days from then on. Now, as she lay fully clothed on the bed, she felt as if the weight of two worlds lay on her shoulders.

The flickering television suddenly caught her attention:

"A shooting today in Rome … Police are investigating a murder that took place today in a popular Rome café. The investigation has identified the victim as Mr. Koso Dilerenso. The only witness in this tragedy is the international resort tycoon, Dane Larusio."

Dane's photograph popped up in the corner of the screen, and Angelica's heart leapt. Suddenly, she was wide awake.

"Mr. Larusio was breakfasting with the victim when the shooting occurred. He is currently being questioned by authorities in an effort to shed some light on the situation." A broad smile swept across the reporter's face. "We'll have more information on this tragedy later. Now, we'll go to the weather."

Without a thought, Angelica was on the phone, booking the next flight to Rome. Two hours later, she sat in the airport's first-class lounge, waiting for her flight to be called. Her mind was awhirl, her body heavy. Koso was dead. What had happened? Her thoughts screamed. Her desire to be with Dane was suddenly unstoppable. It was as if she'd been holding her breath since she left him and had just now realized it.

The plane touched down at Fiumincino, International airport a little after three thirty in the morning. An hour later, Angelica entered Rome's central police headquarters.

A burly Italian with a somber expression sat behind the front desk. "Good morning, madam," he said in a surprisingly tiny voice. "How is it we may be of help to you?"

"Good morning, Gino," Angelica said, reading the officer's ID tag. "I understand you've been questioning a Mr. Larusio in regard to yesterday's shooting."

"Well, I wouldn't say we've been questioning the man. It's more like we've been working with him trying to shed some light on the situation."

"I would very much like to see Mr. Larusio," she braved.

"I'm afraid you've missed him by almost an hour, madam. A Russian friend of his came to see him just as we were finishing up. They both left shortly after."

"They left together?" Angelica asked.

"That's right," said Gino.

Angelica's heart sank with disappointment. "Have you any idea where he's staying?" she pleaded.

"We don't normally give out that kind of information, but you seem harmless enough. He'll be at the Ritz, on Via Eboli," offered Gino.

Angelica was already moving to the door, her hopes renewed. But when she reached the Ritz, they told her that Dane had checked out. Only with the help of a healthy tip and one of her most pleasing smiles did the concierge confess that Dane hadn't left alone.

"I heard them exchange a few words before the elevator door closed," the concierge said. "I think Mr. Larusio's friend may have been Russian."

"And you have no knowledge of where they were going?" Angelica asked.

"No, madam; I wish I could help you, but no." He glanced at the jacket pocket from which Angelica had pulled the previous tip.

Disheartened, Angelica stumbled back onto the cobbled street. The morning air was surprisingly chilly, and the street was as empty as her heart was heavy. Cold, alone, and very disorientated she wandered, her footsteps echoing off the ancient walls of the surrounding buildings.

Ostrov Putin being in Rome when the news of Koso's death was publicized was no coincidence. He'd been flown down from Moscow the previous night at Koso's request for an urgent meeting. Koso's murder said one thing only—he'd gotten too close; he'd found something. Koso had discovered something vital about the infamous Krait.

Ostrov had enjoyed a friendship with Koso that spanned decades, and he wasn't taking his death lightly. But he had a job to finish, and dwelling on Koso's murder was not an option.

Koso had spoken of Dane Larusio many times. Ostrov knew a little about his involvement with Limnos Skiathos and Benito Santiago, and he knew of Koso's suspicion that Dane was on the move for Krait. Most importantly, Dane was the last person to speak to Koso. This in mind, Ostrov was convinced he needed to speak to him.

Strangers to each other, Dane and Ostrov now sat in a basement café, which was very private and very empty. Ostrov introduced himself as Alex Munstrov, a close friend of Koso's. Dane didn't buy the stranger's story for a moment, but he was too tired to care, and, not wanting to sleep, he welcomed the chance to talk to someone. So far their chat had been casual, but, as their conversation wore on, Dane became more convinced that there was a lot more to the Russian than met the eye. He had the posture and hairstyle of a career serviceman. His suit was pressed flawlessly, and his shoes were highly polished. Dane felt no immediate threat, however, and he decided to play along.

Ostrov felt Dane analyzing his every inch as they made small talk. He quickly decided he wouldn't be able to get any useful information without arousing serious suspicion. Dane was obviously no fool, and Ostrov suddenly felt naive to have ever entertained such an idea in the first place. He should have known that any friend of Koso's would be dangerously complex. If he wanted to succeed in extracting the information, he was going to have to be relatively honest.

"I'm going to be very honest with you," Ostrov started, his words escaping with the force of a noxious exhale.

Dane said nothing.

"As you know, the Russian economy is just beginning to recover from its tumultuous past," Ostrov went on. "Much of the lag in our economy's recovery is caused by a certain syndicate, and for the past five years, the Russian government has been working relentlessly to dissolve what some know as the IUS."

Dane said nothing.

"It's true, we've had some success in eradicating this syndicate, but each achievement has been temporary. For years now, we've known that the ultimate power of the IUS was in the hands of a single individual—a figure known as Krait. We have investigated Krait intensively, but have made little progress."

Dane's stamina changed instantly from groggy disillusion to upright concentration.

"You may wonder why I'm discussing this with you, in particular. To understand this, first I want you to know that I know from what our mutual friend Koso has told me that you are aware of Krait's existence. And I know you wish Krait dead."

An unsettling sensation of déjà vu gripped Dane's psyche. Only hours before it had been Koso sitting in front of him saying almost exactly the same words. He caught the Russian almost midsentence.

"So, you want to know what Koso told me before he was murdered?" Dane asked.

Ostrov smiled politely. "Koso told me of your sharp intellect. Yes, your presumption is correct. We believe Koso discovered Krait's identity, and I believe he was planning to tell me everything at our next meeting, which was scheduled just seven hours after his death."

"No," Dane said flatly.

"No, what?" Ostrov asked.

"No, Koso didn't tell me the identity of Krait."

Ostrov's expression changed from fiercely attentive to hopelessly washed out.

"He did, however, warn me to stay away. He warned me to give up my search. He was intent on stopping me. When he saw I wouldn't heed his warning, and I wouldn't back down, he told me he knew who Krait was," Dane said, his anger cooling. "Koso appeared torn by indecision of whether to tell me what he knew when his chest exploded in my face. So, no, he didn't divulge Krait's identity. The poor bastard died just for knowing." Dane staggered to his feet, glowering angrily at the Ostrov.

"I am sorry, Mr. Larusio. I didn't mean to upset you," Ostrov pleaded.

Dane ignored Ostrov. "One last thing, Mr. Munstrov, or whatever your name is. If the Russian government is so all-seeing and so mighty, then why is Koso no longer living?" Dane stormed from the café in a rage.

Long after Dane made his unruly exit, Ostrov sat, staring into his coffee cup. He felt lost. He had no idea where to go or what to do next. Finally he collected enough courage to make the dreaded phone call to his superiors. The line was not secured, but it didn't matter. The conversation would be short and insensitive.

"Sir, it's me."

"Yes."

"He knows nothing."

"Are you sure?"

"Yes."

"Where is he now?"

"I don't know, sir."

"I want him watched, and I want reports sent to me every twenty-four hours. He may know nothing, but he's still our only link."

"Yes, sir. I'll put one of our best men on him right away."

"Good, and make sure you get back here as soon as possible. Much has happened."

"Yes, sir."

The line went dead.

CHAPTER 12

THE RAT

One week later …

Using his CIA contact, Dane determined that the etchings on the back of Qui Trang's photo were phone numbers and dates. The phone numbers belonged to multiple locations in Europe, but the first set on the list led to a phone booth in Rome. Qui Trang was a known member of the IUS whose home was Southeast Asia, but certainly, he would travel to Europe to attend syndicate meetings. The phone numbers could well be links to these meetings—a long shot, Dane knew, but it was the only lead he had left and he was getting desperate. He had no choice but to investigate the possibility further.

Dane now patiently waited in the phone booth at the corresponding time. It was on a busy street corner, and a whirlwind of activity buzzed in every direction. Thus far, he'd fought off three people, all desperately wanting to use the phone. Now a fourth person approached—a massive hulk of a man.

"Are you going to be in there all day?" he bellowed through the glass with a strong French accent.

"Just a few more moments," Dane replied, somewhat timidly.

"That will be a few moments too long for me my friend," said the man.

Dane could do nothing but grimace as he was plucked from the booth and thrown onto the street. Grudgingly, he waited a few feet away and watched as the huge man crammed tightly inside. But before he could make his call, the phone rang, and he picked up. At that moment, there was a high-pitched whistling sound overhead. Instantly Dane recognized what it was, and without hesitation, he dove to the ground just as a rocket streaked from his left. The phone booth exploded into fragments.

Dane deduced two things in the same moment—one, he was alive, and two, judging from the trajectory of the rocket's trail, it had come from the opposite side of the street where there was only one building tall enough to get a clear shot with an RPG. He didn't hesitate; he sprang to his feet and ran. The shooter was now his only lead. Cars screeched to a halt as he flew across the street. The building was old and had only one elevator, in which an old woman was fussing. Dane instantly opted for the stairs. Crashing through the stairwell door, he quickly climbed, judging that he had at least eight floors to deal with before hitting the roof, where he hoped to find the shooter. His heart pounded as he rounded the fifth flight of stairs, but his ascent was brought to a sudden halt as he crashed headlong into a man descending in equal haste. Dane was as solid as a number-eight rugby player, and the other man—much lighter in physique—went flying headfirst over Dane's shoulder and crashed unconscious on the stairs below.

Still standing and feeling grateful for it, Dane checked the body for a pulse. He half-expected the man to be dead, but, to his surprise, the pulse was steady and strong. However, his surprise doubled when he recognized the fallen man.

The name burst from Dane's lips. "Sticks!"

Dane felt suddenly mortified. The last time he'd seen Sticks in the flesh was the day of the tragic bombing. Wide-eyed and almost afraid, he examined Sticks's face more carefully. Without a shred of doubt, the man was Sticks, his former employer. Dane breathed heavily, tying desperately to shake off a multitude of conflicting emotions. The oddness of the scene in its entirety was throwing his senses way out of perspective. Sticks's presence put an entirely new twist on everything. He opened the heavy bag that was thrown from Sticks during the fall, and instantly he discovered an RPG unit. He'd found his would-be-assassin, and, ultimately, a fresh link to Krait.

Noise suddenly erupted from the stairs below. Sirens resounded in the distance. Dane had to move quickly. He slung the bag over one shoulder and pulled Sticks roughly to his feet. With minimal effort, he half-walked him down the stairs and found his way to the back entrance. He propped Sticks against the wall, along with the bag, and strolled as casually as he could back through the front entrance, to where his rental car was parked. The police had not yet arrived at the scene, but they were coming. Sliding behind the wheel, he casually drove the car to the back entrance of the building and loaded Sticks and his bag into the boot. Moments later, they were speeding away to safety.

Dane didn't notice the curious eyes of Ostrov Putin's man, who was sitting on a bus-stop bench, watching the events unfold with mounting interest. Orange-tinted sunglasses hid his intelligent eyes, which followed Dane's every move with clinical precision.

When Sticks awoke, he was seated with his hands tied firmly behind his back, and his mouth was gagged. He tried tugging at the restraints, but the effort only made the bindings tighter. Cold fingers of fear crept up his spine. But it wasn't just the restraints that rattled him; it was something much deeper. Seconds turned into minutes before he realized exactly what it was—silence amplified by total darkness. Absolutely nothing broke the silence—not the distant hum of an air-conditioning unit, not the dull roar of traffic. The darkness was equally absolute. Not a single glow came from under a door or window. There wasn't even a hint of sunshine coming through a skylight. Surely he was blind. Time was frozen in an alien world of nothing.

It had been an hour since Dane had returned to his Rome apartment with Sticks. The apartment was in the older, northern end of Rome. Built on a terrace, it had large front windows overlooking the old city and a gated car park at the entrance. The apartment was a property he'd bought years before, but recently he had not used it at all, and he was getting ready to sell it.

Dane sat, quietly thinking on the uncomfortable Victorian couch, the only remaining piece of furniture. The other pieces had already been removed. The apartment did have one attractive attribute; it boasted a concrete bunker twenty feet below ground, a relic from World War II. The bunker was fully soundproofed, and was perfect for the task at hand.

Anxiously Dane glanced at his watch again. He was sure Sticks would be awake by now, and he felt slightly apprehensive about his next move. The situation was delicate. Sticks was a crystal ball—a window to an unknown knowledge. One wrong move could smash this fragile window. He'd never actually interrogated anyone, and he had to take a moment to wonder if he had what it took. Common sense dictated it would be a difficult, torturous job in which he would have to repress his conscience wholly. But he had no choice; Sticks would *have* to talk. His decision made, Dane's busy brain plunged into the sordid plans.

Sticks was slowly succumbing to the burdens of sensory deprivation, and panic began crawling up his bony spine. He knew this was precisely what was expected, but there was nothing he could do about it. Time lost itself in the silence; the darkness clawed at the shores of his soul. A single moment turned into eternity, and he slowly spiraled into a stupor.

By now he was convinced he was deaf. The fall had surely damaged his ears. Worse still, he began wondering if his eyes had been cut out, and he'd been numbed with powerful drugs. The thought mortified him, and he couldn't possibly imagine living with blindness. Again, he strained his ears for what seemed an eternity. He heard nothing. He was certainly deaf. He looked in every direction for a glimmer of light. Nothing again. He was certainly blind.

His throat was dry from thirst and fear. He'd relieved himself in his trousers some hours before, and the pungent odor of urine was adding to his discomfort. A burning pain shot through his wrists from the tightly tied rope. His legs were cramped and effectively useless from lack of movement. He would have been surprised to learn that a mere twenty hours had passed since his capture. He felt certain he'd been waiting days.

Carrying a large cardboard box that he'd had delivered that morning, Dane made his way to the basement. He smelled Sticks before he opened the door, and he couldn't help but hold his breath as he stepped down into the bunker. Déjà vu hit him relentlessly as the vivid image of the journey in the shipping container to Mongolia overwhelmed him. He stiffly shrugged off the bone-chilling memory and turned his attention to the crumpled, pathetic body of Sticks. He stood directly in front of him and looked with cool fascination into the eyes of a man who was obviously on the border of complete despair. Suddenly, in one quick motion, he tore the masking tape from his mouth.

For a few moments Sticks simply gasped at the foul air, his expression devoid of recognition. And then it hit him. "Dane," he croaked. He then lowered his gaze to floor again. "I don't get it," he said, obviously exasperated.

"Sticks, my old friend," Dane began, "what have you been doing with yourself all these years?"

Sticks just looked up at Dane, bleary-eyed. "What do you want?" he sniffed.

"Krait?" Dane demanded.

Sticks said nothing.

"Where I can find the infamous Krait?" Dane asked again. "You're all I've got right now, so you're the one who'll have to talk. Of course, I don't expect you to tell me right away, but I have little doubt that you will tell all eventually. You should also know that I hold you partially responsible for the loss of my father's legs and the death of my uncle. Consequently, I have no pity, mercy, or conscience in regard to your fate."

"I did nothing wrong. I only did what I was asked to do," Sticks mumbled.

"You did whatever the IUS asked you to do," Dane said.

Sticks said nothing.

Dane chose his words carefully. "I have no plans to kill you. In such a state, you'd be of no use to me. But I assure you that, the longer you take to talk, the more you'll beg for death."

Sticks's expression remained impassive, his eyes dark and goggled as if a giant hand had squeezed him. "I have nothing to say," he spat dryly with an undeniable note of conviction.

With direct, authoritative style, Dane retrieved a wooden chair from the corner of the bunker and banged it down in front of Sticks, beside the cardboard box. Producing some heavy pliers from inside, he sidled around to the back of Sticks's chair to his tied hands. Ignoring the odor as best as he could, he grasped Sticks's left hand, forced the thumbnail between the teeth of the pliers, and yanked hard. There was a brief moment of silence in which Dane imagined Sticks hadn't felt anything. But then it came—a scream, loud and completely free of shame. Dane produced a pair of earmuffs from his cardboard box, put them on, and sat down in his chair. Holding the pliers up for Sticks to see, Dane took his time, considering, watching, and waiting for the wailing to stop. Calm settled sooner than he expected, and the room was silent again.

"Will you talk?" Dane asked.

Sticks fixed Dane with a stubborn gaze of disobedience. He kept his thin, cracked lips pressed tightly together in determination and pain. Small bubbles of foam collected at the corners of his lips. He said nothing.

"You have no reason to be afraid of Krait. I have means to protect you," Dane said.

Sticks said nothing.

Dane decided it was time to step up the pain level. Silently, he reached into the box again and pulled out two more items. The first was a house-sized rat in a tiny wire cage. The second was a curious object that looked a lot like an ordinary two-liter soda bottle. On closer inspection, however, one could see the bottle had been specifically fashioned so that it could be separated into halves, and its surface was pierced with at least a dozen small holes. With great care, Dane reached into the rat's cage and removed it by its thick black tail. After separating the plastic bottle, he then placed the rat inside and sealed it tightly.

Sticks silently watched Dane's movements with growing agitation.

Finally, Dane took a tight hold of his mutilated thumb and forced it into the opening at the top of the bottle. He then strapped the bottle onto the arm of the chair, along with Sticks's arm. Satisfied with his work, Dane returned to his seat. The translucent container offered a perfect view of the rat as it scampered around its new environment, desperately trying to find a way out. But, as the minutes passed, the rat settled. Having realized that it was no longer in any immediate danger, it began to consider its second priority—food. Its tiny eyes began feverishly darting about, until they settled on Sticks's thumb. Understanding what was going to happen, Sticks began to sweat. He struggled hard with his bindings, but they would not budge.

The tiny black nostrils of the rat twitched as it sniffed at the delightful odor of fresh blood, and it scampered eagerly toward Sticks's mutilated thumb. It licked hesitantly at the oozing blood, and again, more enthusiastically once it realized there was no threat.

"I can protect you," Dane spoke again. "All of this can be stopped at any moment. Just tell me where to find Krait. It's up to you. How much of your thumb do you want to lose?"

"You cannot protect me," Sticks rasped.

Dane didn't like the edge of utter hopelessness in Sticks's voice. It indicated that he might actually be willing to lose his entire hand to avoid betraying Krait.

"I assure you, I have resources enough to acquire any protection you'll ever need," Dane insisted.

The rat's teeth slid into tender, pink flesh, and Sticks wailed. The rat backed off slightly, distracted and disturbed by the noise, but it edged back to the tattered flesh once it realized there was no danger. Sticks struggled, but the bindings would not budge.

"Please, please stop this. I can tell you nothing. It's true." Desperation was clearly evident in Sticks's voice.

Dane said nothing. He had Sticks exactly where he wanted him. Showing mercy now could bring the whole process to a halt.

Sticks's face was a mask of disgust, pain, and watery-eyed grief. The rat nibbled, oblivious to the pain it was inflicting; all it could detect was sustenance.

Dane had no idea how Sticks actually felt, and he hoped he never would. But he quickly decided that it would do Sticks good to have some alone time with his new friend. His conscience had worn thin—from voluntary repression, from lack of rest, and from anxiety. He'd worked himself into such a state over Sticks and Krait that he was literally numb to the result of his actions. He desperately needed a break from the basement. As he climbed the stairs, he couldn't help but hear Sticks calling, begging him not to leave. There were only a handful of men on the face of the planet who could stand up to such treatment, and Sticks wasn't one of them. Dane knew that when he came back he would have all the information he wanted.

For an hour, Dane sat on the Victorian couch, staring into the Rome streets, mulling over the implications of what he was doing. He knew he had crossed a threshold from which he could never return. Torturing another human being was something he did not believe he ever had the capability of doing, and yet, here he was. His mind was a whirl of emotion. He wanted to stop the torture, but some inner darkness stopped him rushing down the stairs and doing so. When the hour was up, a cool film of sweat covered his entire body. It was as if he had just awoken from a nightmare. As he stood, his body felt heavy and weary to the bone. All he wanted to do was to leave—to run from the horrors he'd created. But instead, he found his legs carrying him back to the basement.

This time when he stepped into the bunker, he was met by the sound of heavy, labored breathing and an even more repugnant smell of human excrement. He prayed the job would soon be over, and he forced his thoughts to order.

Sticks didn't register Dane's presence until long after he sat down. It was only then, between each labored breath, that he gargled a single word, "Siros ..." Another long, low, gargling breathing sound followed, and then the word again, "Siros."

Dane leaned closer, trying to get Sticks to focus, but he was way beyond that point.

"Siros ... Siros ..."

Dane noticed the bulging belly of the rat that was now trying to poke its head through the neck of the bottle to chew on the remains of Sticks's ragged thumb. His stomach almost turned, but he somehow managed to maintain his composure.

"Get this ... this fucking rat off me ... I'll talk," Sticks gargled, his words spat out like a wad of infected mucous.

Dane's frustration was overwhelming. It had been hours since Sticks had agreed to talk, but he wasn't making an ounce of sense. He kept repeating the word *Siros* over and over again, like an annoying parrot. Realizing Sticks needed to be made more comfortable, Dane made a phone call.

"Franco Valentino speaking."

People who didn't know Franco well called him Dr. Valentino, but he hated the title. He preferred to be called Franco—just plain Franco.

"Franco, old friend. How's life been treating you?" Dane answered.

"Oh, Dane, it's you. Until now, things were just fine." There was a pause. "I just got back from Greece and a very happy month in the sun. I was hoping to ease back into the working life, but I can see that's not going to be possible now."

"No, why is that?" Dane innocently asked.

"You know damn well why. I could tell the moment I heard your voice that you were going to have me patching up one of you or your friends' messes."

"It isn't always like that," Dane argued. But it was partially true. Twice in the past year, he'd had the doctor work on somewhat suspicious wounds. Once was when Koso had turned up to see him at his Rome hotel with a bullet wound in his leg. The other time was only a couple of months later, when Koso brought a complete stranger by with a crushed right arm. The doctor had not been able to do anything about that one and had insisted that the man be taken to a proper hospital.

"I know damn well what it's like. Now tell me how can I help you before I change my mind," Franco growled.

"I'm at my terrace apartment. How fast can you get here?"

"Shit," Franco swore, "I knew it. How fast do you need me there?"

"Now would be good. I'll make it up to you, Franco, I promise."

"Oh ... you'd better, son, you'd better." He paused a moment, deciding. "The drive to the apartment takes about thirty minutes. I'll be there in fifteen."

"Thank you," Dane said with apologetic sincerity, but the line was already dead.

Fourteen minutes later, Dane heard the sound of Franco's Dodge Viper pulling up outside. "Howard Hughes could have made a smoother landing in my driveway," he said, striding down the driveway to greet Franco.

Franco stepped from the car, wearing an Oriental robe, woolen boots, and an expression of sustained irritation. He was heavily tanned—a result of his latest trip to Greece, and his medical bag was clasped to his chest like his life depended on it.

"You look as fit as can be. What's the problem?" Franco said in the high-pitched, effeminate voice of an obvious sissy.

"It's not me who has the problem," Dane said, shaking Franco's hand. "Follow me."

Franco registered little or no shock at seeing the state of Sticks. He simply began his examination. The bottle and the rat were gone, but the scene was no less gruesome. Sticks was still babbling like a madman, but Franco seemed satisfied with the overall condition. He withdrew a hypodermic needle from his bag.

"Is he going to be coherent after the shot?" Dane asked.

"Dane, he will be considerably more coherent than he is at present. And you must know there are less barbaric ways of questioning someone," Franco said as he drove the needle into Sticks' wrist.

"One uses whatever resources one can lay their hands on," Dane mumbled.

"Tell me, what happened to the hungry little beast after he'd eaten his lunch?" Franco asked.

"I fed it to the neighbor's cat," Dane said nonchalantly.

"You always did have such a brutally concise way of dealing with things," Franco grunted.

"I like to think of myself as a man that wastes very little, and that includes time," Dane said, immediately regretting his words.

"I promise you I'll be out of your way before you know it."

Sticks visibly calmed as the painkiller took effect, and Franco went about patching him up. When he finished, he stood grimly. Taking his bag, he headed for the door. Dane followed.

"He's going to be fine," Franco said once they were back in the driveway. "But I should warn you, he's not as strong as he appears. Any further trauma could cause serious problems—even heart failure."

"I'll keep that in mind. Until next time then," Dane said.

"Don't you think you're forgetting something?" Franco said, giving Dane an exasperated look.

"It's already been deposited into your US account," Dane said.

"How do you know my fee?"

"I always know the fee," Dane said. "I'm sure you'll be more than happy with your next bank statement."

"Good!" Franco grumbled. Normally he'd stand around and argue a while after a job, but today, he was itching to get away from Dane and his sordid affairs.

Sticks was now in a lot better shape. The mumbling had stopped, and so had the trembling. This time, when Dane took his seat, he found himself looking at a man ready and able to talk.

"Siros. You were repeating this word over and over. What does it mean?" Dane asked.

"It's an island," Sticks spat. "It is the only contact I can give you for Krait, because it's the only contact I have."

"How do I know you're not lying?" Dane asked.

"Because, either way, I'm screwed, aren't I? If I don't talk to you, I'll be eaten alive by that fucking rat. And if I do talk, I'll wake up one night with a pair of hands around my throat. Because, Dane, I'd rather be strangled to death later than eaten alive now."

"So talk," Dane agreed. "I'm listening."

"I do not even know for sure if this is true. Most information surrounding Krait is merely rumor, and this is no different. Each year, for the month of October, Krait is rumored to holiday on the island of Siros ... The name of the hotel is the Hotel Vienna. This information came from a close associate of mine who is somewhat higher up the food chain. We were drinking heavily one night, and he told me this then." Sticks's shoulders sagged further, and he lowered his head, slumping into absolute defeat. His expression was hopeless; he was a doomed man, and he knew it.

Dane removed Sticks's bindings. "Okay," he said.

"That's it?" Sticks asked.

"That's it. From here you can feel free to clean yourself up, and either accept my services to protect you, or go your own way."

Angelica stepped into the evening Rome air. She'd slept fitfully the night before. In fact she'd not had a decent nights sleep in a week. During that time she'd made a few trips to police station to ask if they had heard from Dane. She had also turned over every stone she could think of to find him—but to no avail, he'd apparently disappeared. She was consumed with a dire need to be with him, but, being unable to satisfy this need, she decided to head for London and immerse herself in her work again. She hailed a passing taxi, and a driver wearing a broad-rimmed hat stepped out to open the door for her. She gave the driver her destination, and the taxi quickly pulled away.

"Your first time in Rome, madam?" the driver said in English, with a thick Italian accent.

"Much closer to my one-hundred-and-first time, I'm afraid," replied Angelica in Italian.

"Oh, but you shouldn't be afraid, madam. Rome is a city of romance and a million other wonderful things," the driver said, this time also speaking Italian.

There was a familiar edge to the driver's voice, but Angelica couldn't quite place it.

"People say love is most easily found in Paris, but to me, Rome is the best place to find love. For me, Rome is the home of love, no?" said the driver.

The driver kept on rambling, and Angelica stained her ears to peg the familiarity—and then the revelation hit her. Her heart raced at the impossibility of the driver's identity. It just couldn't be. She had to be sure. "What makes you so sure I'm looking for love?" she asked.

"Because of the look in your eye," said the driver.

"And what look would that be?"

"The lost and delirious look belonging to all people in love," he replied, expertly steering the car through the busy traffic with the skill of a veteran Rome driver.

Angelica's ears strained on his every word.

"To where do you fly today?" the driver probed.

"To London," she said.

"To your lover?"

"No," she said, exasperated.

"Ah, so it is just as I said; you have been in Rome for love, and now you are leaving," chirped the driver, his voice filled with mischief.

Angelica suddenly had no doubt. "It can't be," she said, astonished. "It's impossible," she exploded. She literally sprang into the front passenger seat to get a better look—and there, ragged and scratchy-looking as ever, was Koso. Angelica burst into tears. She couldn't help but throw her arms around him while he fought to keep the car under control. "I can't believe it. Koso, you bastard, you're supposed to be dead," she said, wanting to hug him and hit him all at once.

"I will be dead soon, and so will you, if you don't sit back and calm down," Koso growled, his Rome accent suddenly gone.

Angelica obediently sat back, but she couldn't suppress her smile. She stared at Koso as though he was a ghost, daring not take her eyes off him. He may not be dead, but it was clear to her that he'd been through a lot since she'd last seen him. His face was tired and gaunt. "Why, Koso?" she asked. "Why did you have to die?"

"I had no choice," Koso replied somberly.

She gave him a chilly, sarcastic look. "Why?" she asked again. "I feel as if I have the right to know."

Koso glanced sideways at Angelica, thinking for a moment before answering. "Only weeks ago, I discovered the identity of Krait."

CHAPTER 13

PURSUIT

One hundred nautical miles off Italy's west coast, a man with a missing thumb and a heavy iron wheel attached to one of his ankles fell though the air toward the deep waters of the Tyrrhenian Sea. He felt no fear as he fell, for he'd known his time was up the moment he'd crashed into the stranger on the stairs.

Dane answered his cell phone the moment it rang. "Yes?"

"As we speak, the sharks are enjoying their evening meal," said the person at the other end.

Dane smiled at the familiar voice of the pilot, who doubled as a specialist in waste disposal. "Thank you," he said.

"Will that be all, sir?" the pilot asked.

"One last job for the day. I need transport to the airport in an hour."

"Already on my way, sir."

Dane hung up and stretched out in his deckchair. He had three weeks to kill before his date with Krait. He needed somewhere to lay low and strategize his next move. He quickly decided that Siros would be the perfect place to plan his course of action; but first, he would need to pay a visit to his old friend and favorite arms dealer, Pipi Tellu. He needed weapons. He needed to go to Paris.

They were in a café, where Koso had spent the past hour explaining everything in detail while Angelica listened without interruption. The more she listened, the more concerned for Dane she became.

" ... As you can see," Koso finished, "we must find and stop Dane before he gets any closer to Krait. He has enough on his conscience without this."

"But why didn't you at least tell Dane what you knew before you did your disappearing act?" Angelica asked.

"I was about to, but there was a miscalculation with the shooter's timing," Koso said.

"Miscalculation is the understatement of the century. You must have damn near given Dane a heart attack."

"That's why I need your help. If I suddenly show up in Dane's face after having my chest blown out all over his lunch, do you really think he'll take me seriously?"

"And you really think he'll take *me* seriously?" Angelica retorted.

"He *will* listen to you," Koso insisted.

"I doubt that."

"He will listen to you, because he loves you. And if there's one thing that can change a man, then it's love. You're his only hope, Angelica. You have to confront him."

"Yes, yes," she replied, not quite knowing how to respond to Koso's revelation. "Do you know where he is?"

"I can tell you where he was right up to this very morning. With any luck, he'll still be there."

"Where?"

"He has an apartment here in Rome. If we're quick, we'll catch him there."

"What are we waiting for?" Angelica said, standing.

Leaving Koso in the car, Angelica walked to the security gate of Dane's apartment. She pressed the buzzer. There was no answer. She wondered if he might still be sleeping. She pressed it again, held it for a few seconds, and waited patiently. Two full minutes passed with no answer. She tried one more time just to make absolutely sure. "Damn you, Dane. Where the hell are you?" she cursed.

Koso replied to the misfortune with a colorful array of bad language that would have put a soldier to shame. They sat silently in the car, racking their brains as to what was to be done next.

"Do you have a phone number for Dane? I tried his old one and it's not working."

"I have the same number you have," Koso said.

"He must have changed numbers—but why?"

"If anyone knows where he is right now, it would be Bryant," Koso said.

"Who?" Angelica questioned.

Koso gave her baffled look, surprised she didn't know of Bryant. "Bryant Wilson is the CEO of Dane's company. If he doesn't know where the man is, then no one will."

"Is this lead as hot as the last one you had?"

"Do you give everyone such a hard time?" Koso asked.

Saying nothing, Angelica started digging in her handbag, smiling all the while.

Koso started the taxi. "What in God's name are you looking for?" he asked.

"My phone," she said, baffled. "I must have left it back at the hotel."

"What do you need the phone for?"

"Well, I would presume that the telephone is still the most effective way of contacting someone in this day and age. You do have a contact number for this Bryant, don't you?"

Koso pulled onto the main road. "As a matter of fact, yes, but, unfortunately, it's useless."

"What? Why?"

"Think about it. Dane leads a very private life; we both know that. Lets just say that Bryant is *not* the sort of man you just phone out of the blue, and you don't think he's going to just dish out information to a perfect stranger, do you? And I certainly can't talk to him. He thinks I'm dead."

"Crap!" Angelica's smooth features reddened with frustration. "Excuse my language, but can't things ever be easy?" she asked.

Koso sat silent and gave her a few minutes to calm down.

"So," she began several traffic lights later, "back to the hotel and then to the airport, is it?"

"Forget the hotel. It's straight to the airport and onto the next flight to New York," Koso replied. "Bryant will have to see me to believe I'm alive, and then I'm sure he'll be more than happy to tell me Dane's whereabouts."

Their flight touched down at JFK International a little after five thirty p.m., and they headed straight for Dane's office in the hope of finding Bryant before he left for the day.

Behind the reception desk sat a stiff, thin-lipped woman who gave the impression that the Gestapo had trained her. She must have weighed at least two hundred and fifty pounds—none of it fat—and had a temperament to match her muscle. Angelica stood to the left of Koso in a rather defensive fashion.

"I've already told you twice—Mr. Wilson is not here, and he sees no one without an appointment," said the receptionist with a thick Russian accent.

"Can you at least raise him on the intercom and let him know that Koso Dilerenso is here to speak with him?" Koso asked, desperately trying to restrain the anger.

"For the last time, he's not here," insisted the receptionist.

"I know Bryant Wilson very well, and he hasn't left his job early a single day in his life," Koso growled.

The feeling in the room was electric. Angelica found herself shrinking back and holding her breath.

In final defense, the woman raised her bulk and stared down at Koso. "Sir, *you need* an appointment," she said.

Koso was outclassed in every way, and he realized he wasn't going to get anywhere with the beast by talking, so he instead bee-lined it for Bryant's office door, vainly hoping he would make it through before he was stopped. As if anticipating the move, the receptionist from hell was on him before he'd taken four steps. Showing startling speed and agility, she grabbed Koso by his collar, lifted him from the floor, and headed for the exit. Koso looked like a kitten being moved by its mother.

Angelica seized the opportunity and headed for what was supposedly Bryant's office. She swept inside before the beast could recover, and she found herself face to face with a man who was obviously on his way out. The door closed behind her only to be thrown open again by the beast.

"Sir, I'm so sorry, but there was nothing I could do to stop her," the beast said.

Bryant was a very calm, cool-looking character in his early forties. He had short blond hair and the kind of overall appearance of an individual you would expect to find on a California beach rather than in an office running a global corporation. "It's all right Mrs. Coalthorp," he said. "I don't think we have any great threat on our hands, do we?"

"Yes, but you told me ..."

He raised his hand. "Mrs. Coalthorp, it *is* seven p.m., is it not?"

"Yes, Mr. Wilson." With that, she turned on her heel and headed for the door. She had the appearance of a wounded bull, and she didn't even so much as glance at Koso when he scurried into the office.

Angelica was in a perfect position to see the look of open astonishment on Bryant's face as Koso entered; she was completely forgotten as they embraced.

"I don't believe it. Koso, you old villain, aren't you supposed to be dead?" Bryant asked.

"At my age, I feel like I am supposed to be dead, but this old world will have to put up with me for a little longer yet. As for you not believing it unless you saw me with your own eyes ... well, that's exactly what I suspected, and precisely why I have had to come in person," Koso said, still recovering from the brush with the monster receptionist.

"I'm Bryant Wilson," Bryant said, introducing himself to Angelica.

"Angelica Skiathos. Pleased to meet you." Angelica shook his hand.

"Skiathos … Skiathos … Now where do I know that name from?" Bryant's eyes briefly reflected a cold look, as if he was registering an intensely disturbing thought. "Forgive me, please. There is obviously much to discuss. Please follow me."

They were led into a small elevator in the corner of the office, where Bryant entered a short code on a control panel. Immediately, the elevator rose. Moments passed in silence before they finally came to a halt. The door opened, and Angelica found it difficult to contain her astonishment. What they stepped into was not a richly decorated lounge or regular entertainment area, but a lush and breathtakingly beautiful garden of surprising proportion, considering it was all landscaped atop an eighty-story building. A waterfall cascaded at least thirty feet into a deep pool of crystal-clear water. All around the pool was thick foliage between large, exotic trees. Bryant explained that the trees were specially shipped from South American jungles. They had been too small for use as timber and were about to be burnt as trash when Dane had stepped in and saved them. Flowers and countless other plant species were everywhere, and the entire garden was enclosed in a massive, state-of-the-art bio-dome.

"I hope you don't mind this spot. When a dead man walks into my office, I can only presume he has something important to say. And this is one area where I know important things will not be overheard," Bryant began, taking a seat on an ancient-looking stone bench.

Koso and Angelica sat on a bench opposite to Bryant. A colorful monkey swung through the trees overhead.

"Unless of course, the creatures in your private jungle are eavesdroppers," Koso jested.

Bryant smiled. "Oh, there are over a thousand different creatures within our surroundings, but I can assure you, Mr. Larusio has screened each and every one of them."

Koso chuckled softly. Angelica just sat quietly, marveling at it all.

"We need to know where we can find Dane. There is something of great importance he needs to know, and as soon as humanly possible," Koso asked.

Being fully aware of Koso and Dane's relationship, Bryant knew better than to question his motives. "I'm afraid I don't have much to offer in the way of information. All I know is that he said he had some intensive research to do, and he needed somewhere private complete it. I don't even have a phone number to offer you. He insisted on complete privacy, even from me," Bryant said.

"He gave you no clue at all as to where he would be?" Angelica asked.

Bryant shook his head. "No, I wish I had more to offer you, but I don't. He did say that when he was done with his research, he would come straight to New York to see me. Why don't you just wait here until he's finished?"

"This cannot wait," Koso said.

They stayed and talked with Bryant for a short while longer, and then they decided on a good night's rest before considering their next move. They found a good hotel with the help of Bryant, but neither of them could sleep.

Koso rose from bed at around two in the morning and poured a glass of scotch. He looked into the cool, dark liquid as the wheels in his tired old brain began to loosen and turn. Suddenly there was a soft knock at the door. The noise startled him from his thoughts. "Yes," he inquired, his mouth half full of scotch, the words somehow finding their way through the tepid liquid.

"It's me," came Angelica's voice.

Koso grumbled softly and made his way to the door. Following an age-old habit, he checked through the spy hole before opening up.

"Hi," Angelica meekly murmured, inviting herself in and taking a seat.

"Hello," Koso replied, scratching his nose nervously, and taking a seat opposite her.

Angelica snatched Koso's glass and quickly downed the contents. "Okay," she began, "I've been doing a lot of thinking. He's going after Krait, correct?" she said.

"We have to presume that he is," Koso agreed, watching Angelica pour some more scotch. Realizing he wasn't going to get his glass back, he stood and retrieved another from the bar.

"He must need to pick up some tools for his job, correct?" Angelica continued.

"Correct," Koso agreed.

"And I think you'd agree that not just anyone has the tools he requires, yes?" Angelica asked.

Filling his glass, Koso began to see what Angelica was getting at.

"How many people in Europe could supply him with what he needs?" Angelica asked, her eyes fixed on the contents of the glass, as if the answer was lying within its depths.

Koso thought for a moment. "A thousand people could supply him with what you call tools, but if he'd learnt anything from me at all, then I know of only one dealer he'd actually use."

"Who?"

"Pipi Tellu!"

"Where?"

"Paris!" said Koso, reaching for the phone.

What most people saw when visiting the Paris was a fairytale-fantasyland where everyone, no matter who they were, would fall in love. *Paris, the City Of Love.* But when you looked a fraction below the shiny surface of the old city, with its restaurants, cafés, nightclubs, and theaters, one saw another world—a world filled with suffering and discontent; a world where you could buy a woman for half the price of a decent meal; a world where fear walked shoulder to shoulder with bliss.

Dane hated Paris. All the city was to him was a place where he'd meet Pipi Tellu, his European hardware dealer. Pipi was not the type of man who usually entertained clients at his home, but Dane was a known friend of Koso Dilerenso's, and Pipi had done business with Koso for decades. If Koso could trust Dane, then so could Pipi. The townhouse in which Pipi lived was situated in one of the darker corners of the city's east end. It was the fourth time that Dane had visited the residence, and as he rounded the corner of Rue Le Clemonce and into the gloomy alleyway, he promised it would be the last. The alley was long and narrow with six-story, sixteenth-century buildings that effectively cast the alley into perpetual gloom. Pipi's home, a building three stories in height and a good hundred years older than its neighbors, was at the end of the alleyway.

Walking down a small flight of stone stairs, Dane now faced Pipi's steel basement door. The door was red with rust and would have been more suited to an old tugboat. There was no visible doorbell, and Dane kicked the door instead. The steel on it was of a thickness that enabled his shoe to only make a dull, thumping noise. However, after a minute or two, the steel slid effortlessly down into the concrete, and he walked into a small, caged elevator, which began to smoothly ascend to the second floor. Here he was faced with a second steel door. He kicked again, and this time it slid to the side, revealing a room furnished in classic eighteenth-century style. He stepped inside to find Pipi seated at a beautifully handcrafted desk with a gold-trimmed leather top.

Pipi was a wiry man in his early fifties, dressed in an expensive but rumpled Italian suit and wearing a pair of tinted, round frames that effectively hid any indication of mood. His slicked-back gray hair was long, framing the chiseled face of a marathon runner. However, Pipi was not the type to run marathons. The amount of cocaine he used was no doubt responsible for his prominent jawline.

Dane helped himself to a chair and waited patiently for Pipi's full attention.

Pipi snorted another long line of cocaine from the leather desktop. "Dane," he finally pronounced in a high-pitched voice. "I think you'll find what you want in the corner." He lazily motioned to behind him with his left ear. "Everything else you asked for has been sent to the desired location."

Dane retrieved the suitcase and took his time examining the contents. Finally satisfied that everything was in order, he closed the case and set it aside. "Good," he said. He then removed a pouch from his pocket and dropped it on the desk next to two waiting lines of cocaine.

Pipi tipped the contents out, and a small pile of diamonds spilled onto the leather and shone brightly in the glow of a desk lamp. He spoke as he inspected the stones, "So, what takes you to the island of Siros?"

Pipi's only condition in business was to know in what part of the world his goods were being used and when. He did not want his business to conflict with others in the trade. And although Dane knew the risk, he'd honored Pipi's condition and told him of the island. However, he was not about to give the *exact* location. Instead he decided to brush around the subject as carefully as possible. "I've heard of an old church there with an interesting history. In the mid-seventeenth century the priest there used to hang local criminals from an olive tree." Close enough to the truth, he thought, and not exactly lying. The church was just across the bay from the Hotel Vienna.

"You're going to Siros to attend church?" Pipi asked, still looking at the diamonds.

"I'm very religious," Dane jested.

Pipi didn't pursue the subject further, and he studied the stones in silence. Most people would have put each one under a microscope and examined and tested them with the best of the diamond testers, but not Pipi. He just looked at them with his naked eye, occasionally picking one up and placing it closer to the lamplight. A smile teased the corners of his mouth. The phone then rang, and he looked momentarily destroyed by the interruption. He didn't answer it until the fifth ring. "Salome Cemetery, Julio speaking," he said in a none-too-strained voice. He listened for a moment and held his hand over the mouthpiece. "I have to take this call; please excuse me for a few moments."

Dane watched as Pipi slipped into the adjacent room through a side door, and he waited patiently. He chuckled at Pipi's greeting; the last time he'd heard him introduce himself, he'd been a parish priest.

Soon enough, Pipi finished his call and returned to his seat, his cocaine calm ever present; his life force crashing like furious waves on a beach. Only after continuing his study of the diamonds for several more minutes did he nod his content.

"So, we have a trade?" Dane asked.

Pipi sniffled softly and rubbed his nose. "Dane my friend, yes, we have a trade."

Dane didn't waste any time. He left Pipi to his sordid affairs and headed straight for the airport. Siros was waiting, and he desperately wanted to get out of Paris. He hated Paris.

"Pick up the phone, damn you!" Koso mumbled against the receiver.

"Salome Cemetery, Julio speaking," came the voice at the other end.

Koso instantly recognized Pipi Tellu's voice. "Last time I rang, you were a doctor. What will you be next time—a mortician?" he asked.

There was some shuffling and a long pause before Pipi replied. "Koso, you old dog, aren't you supposed to be dead?" Pipi finally said.

"If anyone asks, I *am* dead," Koso said.

"So what does a dead man want from the City Of Love?" Pipi asked.

"It's more a matter of who I want. Dane Larusio—have you seen him? Or has he been in contact with you?" Koso asked.

Pipi paused before answering. "Yes, I've seen him. He came here yesterday. I'm afraid you've missed him."

"Damn!" Koso cursed, all the while wondering how Dane could have seen Pipi yesterday, when he was still in Italy. Pipi was obviously lying, but why?

"He told me where he was going, if that's any help to you," Pipi offered.

Koso's ears pricked up. "Where?" he asked.

"If it were anyone but you, I wouldn't say a word."

"Where?" Koso pushed again.

"Siros."

"Did he say anything else?" Koso asked.

"He said something about visiting a church where the priest used to hang criminals—some kind of historical landmark. That's all."

"Thank you." Koso hung up.

"And?" Angelica asked.

"I'm not entirely sure how many people are playing this game, but I can tell you that Pipi Tellu just officially stepped into the arena."

"He knows where Dane is?" Angelica prompted.

"He says Dane is heading for the island of Siros." Koso had a look of deep worry on his face.

"Why do you look as though you have just seen a ghost?" she asked.

"Because Pipi said he met with Dane yesterday, but I know Dane was still in Rome yesterday," Koso said, his voice hollow with hopelessness.

"So, what does that mean? Why would he be hiding the truth?" Angelica asked.

"We go to Paris. We pay our friend Pipi Tellu a visit, and see what we can shake out of him," Koso said.

Five minutes after Dane left Pipi Tellu, another man showed up—an older man, wearing a straw hat and some orange tinted sunglasses.

"Hello," Pipi said, not bothering to address him by his name. The man in the straw hat was the type of man who needed no name.

"Hello," the man said, his voice neutral in emotion and accent.

"Siros," Pipi submitted. "He's going to Siros." Pipi hated giving the information away, but he had no choice, the visitor was Russian intelligence, and he was destroyed if he didn't give them what they wanted.

There was a certain tension in the air that Pipi couldn't quite identify. The man sat in total silence for what seemed an eternity, and Pipi felt as if he could physically feel his gaze and hear the wheels turning in his head. As if coming to some silent decision, the man purposefully stood and casually removed a pistol from his overcoat pocket. Pipi stared helplessly; the silenced pistol was pointed at his chest. He was paralyzed by shock. The entire moment was so unusually calm and peaceful, like a slow-motion scene from a movie. The first bullet took him in the throat and knocked him back in his seat. Finally, the shooter walked around the side of the desk and put one more bullet in Pipi's head. Evidently pleased with the job, the shooter pocketed the gun and moved toward the door. Once he was back in the alley, he made the call.

"Yes," came the steel voice of Ostrov Putin.

"It's me," said the shooter.

"You took care of him?"

"Yes. I'm on my way to Siros."

Ostrov thought for a moment. "Okay, when you find Mr. Larusio on Siros, and when he's completed what he set out to do, make sure that he never takes another breath. If he is the type of man who can hunt down and eliminate Krait, then I'd rather he'd be working for us or not working at all."

"Yes, sir!" said the shooter.

Who knew what it was that saved Pipi Tellu? It could have been the copious quantities of cocaine in his body that activated enough life-sustaining adrenaline. It could have been the sheer luck that the first bullet passed a fraction of a millimeter from his jugular, or the luck of the second bullet passing through his lower right cheek and exiting just below his left ear, brushing what the doctors later told him was a fairly inactive part of his brain.

Pipi would have certainly have bled to death had his cocaine dealer not paid his weekly visit only fifteen minutes after the shooting. More than anything, the drug dealer was more concerned about losing one of his best clients.

Upon discovering Pipi in a crumpled and unconscious heap, the dealer proceeded to calmly clear away the remaining cocaine. Not wanting paramedics or the concerned authorities to go snooping around Pipi's apartment, he stopped the flow of blood as much as he could and loaded him into his waiting car. Cursing loudly, he saw that Pipi was bleeding freely over the leather upholstery of his three-week-old BMW. He quickly removed the plates from the car, and ten minutes later, a still-unconscious Pipi was dumped at the local hospital's emergency entrance.

Pipi's apartment was sealed off with police tape when Koso and Angelica arrived. The scene baffled Koso, but a nosey neighbor soon explained that Pipi was in hospital and lucky to be alive. Without skipping a beat, Angelica and Koso made their way to the hospital room where Pipi lay.

Angelica looked on as the two supposedly dead men stared at each other for a full minute before either spoke.

"Hello, Koso," Pipi said.

"How do you feel?" Koso asked.

"Okay," lied Pipi. His voice hissed through his oxygen mask. The bullet had not damaged his vocal cords, but the swelling from the neck injury was severely restricting his speech.

"You should be dead by the look of things." Koso said. He wasn't lying about Pipi's appearance; he'd seen healthier looking corpses.

"Like yourself, I'm also not so easy to kill." Pipi took a long, raspy breath before continuing. "My guess is that you're looking for our mutual acquaintance, Mr. Larusio."

"Pipi, old friend, I was wrong about you. All that cocaine hasn't robbed you of your wits," said Koso.

"Well, being in here has given me wake up call. The doctors say that if I don't give up the nose-candy, I'll be dead within a year. Looks as if I'll have to walk the straight line for a while," Pipi said.

"Sounds like a wise move to me," said Koso.

Pipi suddenly went into a fit of wheezy coughing that lasted a full minute. Eventually he settled. His eyes were closed, and he looked as if he'd stopped breathing altogether.

"Pipi," Koso said.

As if on cue, Pipi's eyes flew open, and he inhaled a long, slow breath from the oxygen mask as a fresh spark of life flew through his veins. "He'll be on the island of Siros in October," he rasped. "That's all that I can tell you."

A doctor pushed his head through the door. "I think that will be about as much attention as our patient can handle for now," he said.

Angelica intervened. "Just another couple of minutes is all we'll need, thank you Doctor," she said, flashing her best smile.

The doctor didn't argue.

Angelica bent to Pipi's ear, "What exactly was it that you sold him?" she asked.

Pipi looked up at Angelica with his pale blue eyes. "Mostly an updated version of C-4 used only by Russian Special Forces. The rest of the stuff was nothing special," he softly whispered.

"What type of nothing special?" Angelica asked.

"Just a gun and ammunition ..."

"What type of gun?" Angelica asked.

"An automatic gun."

"Pipi!" Angelica urged, an edge of warning in her tone.

"Okay, okay," Pipi said. "Who the hell is this lady?" he asked, looking to Koso for support.

"She's the daughter of Limnos Skiathos," Koso replied.

Pipi looked back at Angelica, a look of sudden awareness and newfound respect evident in his eyes.

Angelica stared back, expectantly.

"An MT5 mini-gun, with 7.62-millimeter rounds, capable of firing sixteen thousand rounds per minute. The gun is the latest thing built by the Italian military, and although this kind of firepower has been around for many years, the Italians have halved the weight of its lightest competition," Pipi said.

Angelica stood wide-eyed in shock.

"Holy shit!" Koso exploded. "What in God's name would he want that for?"

"That's not my business," Pipi said.

"Did he say anything else, anything at all that may give us a better idea as to his whereabouts on Siros?" Koso asked, an edge of desperation in his voice.

Pipi thought for a moment. "He said something about taking a look at an old church, whatever the hell that means. He said the church had some historic value."

The doctor poked his head back in the door. Time was up.

"One more thing," said Koso. "Who shot you?"

"FSB." Pipi rasped. "I'm sorry, Koso. They pressured me. They knew Dane was coming to see me. They must be shadowing him. Look out for the Russians."

Koso's expression iced over. The look chilled Angelica to the bone.

It was too late in the day to do anything else but find a place to sleep, drink, and figure out what to do next, so Koso and Angelica came straight from the hospital and settled into the Hotel de Crillon, on Place de la Concord. They were seated at the bar, both somewhat at a loss. Koso unenthusiastically sipped on a scotch while Angelica downed her second glass of Pinot noir.

"I'll have to go to Russia," Koso finally said.

"What for?" Angelica asked.

"I know some people there who have back doors into the FSB. I have to see what their interest in Dane is."

"And what should I do in the meantime?" said Angelica. "I'll go mad if I just sit around thinking about Dane and how long it will be before he's killed by this Russian assassin."

"He won't be an assassin," said Koso. "Sure, assassination will be part of his job description, but the Russians are much too careful to simply put some rogue assassin on Dane. And don't worry; we have until October to find Dane. And I promise we'll get to him before the Russian does."

"I'll come with you to Russia," Angelica said.

"No I have to go alone. Trust me, you don't want to go anywhere near the places I'll visit," Koso insisted. "The best idea for you would be to go to Siros. Start looking for churches of historic value, but don't make yourself too conspicuous. I want you to try avoiding contact with Dane until I know more about the agent shadowing him."

"Okay, sounds like a fair enough plan. But what do I do if I do bump into Dane?"

"Tell him the truth. Tell him he has a Russian agent watching him, and as yet, his intent is unknown," Koso said.

Their course of action decided, they went their separate ways and retired for the evening.

CHAPTER 14

ALL THE PIECES

The Hotel Vienna was one of the older hotels on the Island of Siros. It was constructed of limestone tufa, much the same as any other traditional building in the area. Krait preferring such humble accommodations was something that Dane found difficult to understand. The rooms lacked any glass windows—they instead had wooden shutters that failed to keep out any significant amount of cold. But October was one of the warmer months in Siros, both night and day.

The floors were bare, but for a few simple rugs. The walls were bleached white and decorated with local paintings. The furniture was handcrafted and looked as if it belonged in a museum. The bed was a massive, four-posted structure, curtained with fine silk. The only plumbing was a commode, a shower, and a small basin. The shower was not closed off, but simply elevated and angled at the base, so the water would run into an ornate, iron drainage hole. Guests had the option of drawing a light curtain for privacy or simply enjoying the Mediterranean view through the nearby window while bathing. Dane decided the hotel had charm, even if it was somewhat rustic.

It was surprisingly cool for a September morning. Stretching back in his chair, he took another sip of coffee and watched as dew dripped from the rose bush growing on the balcony. He couldn't help but think that, within the next couple of weeks, he would have completed what he'd set out to do, or he'd be dead. Either way, he knew he'd be at peace. In the meantime, there was much work to do. He had to identify, beyond doubt, what room Krait would be staying in, and under what name. This was no small task, taking into consideration that he had no idea what Krait looked like.

Siros itself was about a hundred and thirty square kilometers in area, a fairly large island by Greek standards. It had twenty thousand inhabitants, and at the height of the tourist season, the numbers peaked at around twenty-eight thousand. The visitors came to enjoy the many quaint beaches and the classical Greek architecture. Dane was thankful that Krait did not holiday in peak season.

What Dane needed was information, and there was always plenty of that to be found through the Internet. First, he downloaded all the information he could find on Siros. He then compiled a file on the Hotel Vienna. It was amazing what he discovered, from floor plans, right down to what was served at the bar. Night and day he worked and worked, compiling data until he believed he knew enough to begin formulating a plan of attack. But how was he to locate someone neither he nor anyone else had ever seen? Which room would Krait be staying in, and under what name? And what was Krait's security capability?

Dane had very little to go on but a few simple facts—indeed, the fact that he didn't know for sure was whether Sticks had been telling the truth about the island or the hotel. However, it was also a fact that what Sticks had told him was all there was. He tried to imagine what a great detective would do in such a situation. Sherlock Holmes or one of the Agatha Christie greats would know what to do. Such characters could apparently pull answers out of thin air and then make it look as if the answer had been staring everyone in the face the whole time. However, Dane was certain the solution did exist, and all he had to do was find it.

But no matter how late he worked or how tired he was, he always found his thoughts returning to Angelica before he slept. What was she doing? Where was she? Had she forgotten him? This thought made him fiercely jealous—a feeling he wasn't used to.

Sticks had said Krait holidayed in October, but he did not say for how long. This meant Dane would have to take into consideration all those arriving and leaving the hotel that month. He needed help. He called John Williams, and with his assistance, he hacked into the hotel's computer and had a twenty-four-hour mirror of the registry on his laptop. He then meticulously compiled dossiers on each and every one of the October guests. He finally began to feel as if he was making progress. The hotel was small, like many others on Siros, and it hosted around seventy tourists when at peak capacity. With this knowledge, Dane then proceeded with one of the oldest and simplest techniques in the book—the process of elimination. There were eighty-seven October guests in total, and with meticulous care, he began to analyze the broad range of information on each of them—some with his own efforts, others by using John's invaluable ability.

The next morning, he sat again at the small wooden desk in his room and began the tedious work of whittling down the eighty-seven to just one. Although the IUS was a global syndicate, most of Krait's known activity centered in Europe and Russia. But Dane couldn't take a chance in assuming Krait's nationality; he had to consider everyone on the list.

There were Farsi-speaking Iranians.

There was a group of Chinese from Beijing.

There were three Australian tourists.

There was party of seven South Africans.

The list went on an on—fourteen separate nationalities in total.

What he had to do now was eliminate the people on the list who actually existed—and not just existence in the sense of having all the right papers and written records, but existence in the sense of possessing a real, personalized history. Evidence of this type was predictably very difficult to come by on the Internet. The things Dane needed to know were whether the subject had had difficulty with teachers at school, or if the subject had attended the local church since childhood. Those who had involuntarily formed their own unique backgrounds in which substantial evidence existed could then be discounted as potential Kraits. This was the most difficult, but crucial part of the process in which he could cross off the normal people, and also the most time-consuming. If he did his work right, though, he would be left with one not-so-normal person, a person who had a well-documented life, but with few or no other people to give firsthand confirmation of validity.

It took Koso four days to find the man he was looking for in Moscow. Under normal circumstances, he would have walked straight into Ostrov's office and demanded to know what the ultimate intentions of FSB agent following Dane were, and why he had shot Pipi Tellu. But Koso was supposed to be dead, and he wanted to remain that way for as long as possible—at least until he had a clearer picture of what the FSB was up to in regard to Dane, and at least until Krait had been dealt with. Therefore, he had to use the backchannels for information.

His contact was Feodor Demidov. Feodor was a retired KGB officer from the old days. He'd been retired unwillingly by a scandal involving him abusing his powers and importing American clothing into Russia when communism was still at its height. Feodor was seventy now. He made an official living by keeping an eye on a military aviation scrap yard on the outskirts of Moscow. This paid him enough money to live, but the sale of information was his real income. He knew hundreds of people in Russian intelligence's inner circle, and they all loved him. Feodor liked to think of himself as the oracle of Russian intelligence, both past and present. The FSB brass thought he was a pain in the ass, but, sometimes, even they grudgingly came to him for information; he was an evil they were afraid to do without, and Feodor knew it.

Koso climbed the stairs to Feodor's home, a gargantuan Antonov-124 cargo plane that had been converted into a house of sorts. It overlooked the vast graveyard of planes in various shapes, sizes, and states of decay. The wings of the Antonov-124 were gone—scrapped for use elsewhere—but the rest of the seventy-meter-long monstrosity was still intact and looking no less fearsome than it did when it took its maiden flight in 1982. An old artillery-shell casing with a chain and weight down the center hung near the door; it was what Feodor had decided would make a good doorbell. Koso rattled the chain, and the old casing gonged ominously. He waited patiently, and before too long, the door folded inward, and there stood Feodor. He wore army overalls, and casually held a bottle of vodka in his left hand. The buzz-cut of his graying head of hair was the same length on his face, and his piercing blue eyes and thin lips smiled when he saw it was Koso.

"I knew you were alive," Feodor said.

"If anyone asks, I'm not," Koso said.

"Come in and drink with me, old friend," he said. "I just plucked a fresh bottle."

Koso nodded his consent and followed the tall and lankily built Feodor into his home. The door opened into the plane's cavernous cargo area, which could easily hold a hundred and twenty tons. There was a crate of Stolichnaya Vodka just inside the door, together with a half-dozen other crates of various produce. The cargo deck had hardly been touched since the plane was decommissioned, but, as they climbed the stairs, it became obvious that the upper deck had been well adapted into a comfortable living space. On the port side of the plane's upper deck, the original windows had been removed, and in their place was a massive bank of plate glass windows that stretched twelve feet high and thirty feet in length. These windows overlooked the vast expanse of the scrap yard. Hardwood floors and rugs had replaced the original aluminum, and comfortable chairs and couches fronted the massive windows. The unique living arrangement intrigued Koso, but, at the same time, it made sense. The height of the plane gave the perfect view over much of the scrap yard. There was no obvious electronic security equipment, so the elevation of this view was imperative to the success of Feodor's job.

The last time Koso had seen Feodor, he'd been living in a southeast-Moscow slum, and his job then was working for a branch of the army, cataloging the dead. Considering they were in the middle of a war with Chechnya at that time, there was plenty of business. Now, as Koso looked around Feodor's new home, he clearly saw that life was much better—at least much more comfortable. Although he was living in the middle of a scrap yard, his accommodation was very much akin to one of Moscow's southwest, high-end apartments—plush and comfortable, with all of the modern amenities.

Feodor retrieved a glass from the bar at the starboard side of the cabin and poured Koso a drink. "I heard that someone was asking around about me, but I never dreamt it was you," he said. "Why all the smoke and mirrors? Why didn't you just ask Ostrov where I was?"

"The reason I didn't ask Ostrov is the reason why I'm here in the first place. I want to make my existence as little known as humanly possible, and I absolutely do not want Ostrov to know I'm still alive," Koso said, stretching back on a well-used-but-luxurious chesterfield sofa and sipping his vodka.

"You and Ostrov have always been close. What's happened?" Feodor asked.

"I died, that's what happened. Furthermore, I think he's shadowing one of my closest friends, Dane Larusio."

"The hotel magnate? The man who was with you when you were shot?"

"The same," said Koso.

"So what is it you want from me?"

"I need you to find out why Ostrov has an agent on Dane's tail. I need to know what that agent's objectives are. I need to know where Dane is right now. And I need to know all of this as soon as possible."

"You need to know a lot."

"I'd find out all of this myself in a heartbeat if I could risk being out in the open."

"Sounds like you've gotten yourself into a tricky situation. Should I be worried about being associated with you? Sounds risky," Feodor said.

"As long as you keep my name out of the picture, you'll be exposed to no risk."

Feodor picked up the bottle of vodka from the cocktail table between them and filled his glass, thinking. He downed the contents and looked out the window for a full minute before answering. "This is going to take time," he finally said.

"How much time?" asked Koso.

"I can't say exactly. Maybe a week, maybe more."

"Okay," said Koso, knowing he had no choice.

"I'll also need money."

"How much?" Koso asked.

Again Feodor thought for a long moment before answering. "Two million rubles to begin with. I may need more later, and I'll need cash."

"Naturally," said Koso.

"How can I contact you?"

"I was hoping I might stay here," Koso said, looking around. "And you obviously have no lack of space."

"I know a good hotel close by," Fodor said.

"Like I said, I'd rather stay under the radar as long humanly possible."

"I only have one bedroom."

"The cargo bay will be fine for me. I've slept in much worse places, and the cargo bay of a decommissioned An-124 is the last place anyone would expect to find a dead man such as myself."

They talked and drank into the evening before Koso made up a bed in the cargo bay. It was a large, airy space to sleep in, and it creaked and groaned in the wind, but he somehow found this soothing and he soon slept.

Angelica flew directly from Paris to Athens and took a small plane out to Siros. It was close to midnight before she booked into the Hotel Syrou Melathron, a small but luxurious hotel on the beach in central Ermoupolis. However, she hardly noticed the beauty of the hotel's neoclassical architecture. She was exhausted beyond reason, and the moment her head hit the pillow, she fell into a deep, dreamless sleep.

When she awoke the next morning, she felt well refreshed, but, at the same time, frustrated. She ate a breakfast of croissants, eggs, and coffee on the hotel's rooftop terrace and mulled over her predicament. Her role was mostly one of waiting for Koso to show up with the information needed to move forward. But she was a woman of action, and waiting for Koso was going to be difficult at best. Nevertheless, she knew Koso was right. Making any bold move on the island was like dancing on a minefield. If she did do anything, she would have to do it carefully, and she had to remain as inconspicuous as possible.

She had very little luggage with her. She had been on the move so much that most of what she had fit into a carry-on. If she was going to be on Siros for any length of time, she decided she would need a few supplies.

She spent the rest of the day shopping. She bought several sets of clothes and a new laptop, deciding that she would spend much of her time researching the island's hotels and churches—these being the only two crumbs Dane left on trail. By the end of the day, she was frustrated all the more by the many advances from young Greek men trying to take advantage of the fact she was alone, and she was immensely glad to make it back to the hotel and settle into her room for the night.

She had dinner on her private balcony, which overlooked Ermoupolis Bay, and when her appetite was satisfied, she went to work on her computer. She soon found that there were more than fifty hotels on the island, and although October was not peak season, there would still be around three thousand tourists at any one time. She was grateful it was not peak season, as, at its height, there were around eight thousand tourists during the daytime. She imagined the streets must be teeming with activity during such a time. As the sun wandered toward the horizon, she collapsed back into her chair, fully realizing that she was searching for a needle in a haystack. She needed more information, and she would have to wait for Koso to deliver it.

Dane decided he'd first focus on the German guests. At first, the task looked daunting, but he knew deep down he would succeed if he applied himself wholeheartedly. He tried to maintain the philosophy that nothing was impossible with the aide of time and patience. He picked up the first profile and began:

Andrew Renwant.
Born December 25, 1963.
Parents. Ethnic German.
Siblings. Two brothers. One sister.
Education. Six years at Berlin University, majoring in psychology. Graduated with honors.

Additional information:
Married with two children. Lives and owns own practice in Zurich, Switzerland. Checked into Liechtenstein dry-out clinic for treatment of long-term alcohol abuse. Treatment successful.

Dane smiled; this was exactly what he was looking for. He picked up the phone and dialed his first lead, a Zurich number. By his rough calculations, it would be about five p.m. in Switzerland.

A woman answered in thick German. "*Guten Abend!*"

"Er … *Guten Abend. Sprechen sie Englisch?*" Dane hoped she would understand him.

"Yes. 'Vot can I do for you?" she answered easily.

Dane gave thanks for the universality of the English language. His German was terrible. "Would I be able to speak to Mrs. Gretta Renwant, please?" he asked.

"This is Gretta speaking. How can I help you?" she asked again with a slight inflection of irritation.

Dane got straight to the point. "My name is Doctor Asti Ridoro, I'm from the Liechtenstein clinic. I wonder if you could spare me a few moments." He didn't wait for her answer. "This won't take long; I simply wish to check how your husband has been progressing since he was discharged. Nothing elab—"

"But I was rung only a week ago, I told Dr. Schrader everything then," she cut in, openly exasperated.

Dane had prepared for this response and answered without hesitating. "Yes, I understand a call was made last week. However, there has been an unforeseen accident, and your husband's former doctor will be indisposed for some time as a result. I am his replacement. We do, of course, have extensive records, but it's our policy to contact all new patients personally to familiarize ourselves with their circumstances and current status with respect to treatment."

"I see," she said.

"First, has your husband, to your knowledge, been in contact with any form of alcohol since his release?" he asked.

There was a shuffling sound and then an ear-piercing shriek.

"Das reicht! Hört endlich auf zu schreien!"

There was a clatter, and a child's voice babbled miserably in the background.

Dane rubbed his temple and switched the receiver to the other ear while he waited.

"I am sorry, Doctor ... What did you say?"

"Dr. Ridoro, madam," Dane reminded her, feigning impatience.

"Naturally, Dr. Ridoro. Please forgive me. My two boys are driving me crazy tonight."

"That's perfectly all right," he said, softening his tone.

Their conversation lasted a further five minutes, during which Dane didn't hear another peep from the children. By the time he hung up he was suitably convinced that Andrew Renwant wasn't the head of a global criminal network. In fact, the most he could be accused of was spawning two awkward babies that their mother did nothing but complain about. He crossed the psychologist off his list and immediately moved on. It was three hours and ten phone calls later before he'd eliminated the remaining two Germans.

This was how Dane spent much of his time. He made the calls at all hours of the day because of the time difference of many of the countries on the list. Some names took no more than five minutes to clear, and others took up to five hours. By the end of the first week, he still had many names to investigate. He was thoroughly frustrated with his lack of success. October 1 was looming, and his anxiety dramatically increased daily. At the end of the second week he finally made a breakthrough.

The name was Adrian Marino, a fifty-seven-year-old art dealer from northern Italy. Adrian had attended a very prestigious art school and married a rather famous professor. Other than that, her profile was very normal. Marrying the professor at twenty-three had fast-tracked her career as a dealer, and good things had happened to her ever since. But Adrian's past was *too* flawless, and this was exactly what Dane was looking for. Uncovering the contact information of her parents, he wearily picked up the phone and dialed their number. A charming gentleman was more than happy to answer any of Dane's questions. Indeed, he sounded a little too willing to give out information. His suspicions aroused, Dane decided to probe a little further—he called the art school. He barely managed to lie his way through to the director.

"Good evening, can I help you?"

Using the best Russian accent he could muster, Dane plunged into the conversation, "Yes, yes, hello. I'm Professor Yuri Marcolovitch, director of the Salsborough art school here in New York, and I wonder if you might be able to give me some information in regard to one of your former students?" he asked, hoping the mention of Salsborough, a very famous school in its own right, might loosen some tongues. It did.

The director's voice became very formal. "Hello, Professor. You've found the right person; I've worked here for twenty years, and I can tell you anything you need to know about any student who has studied under me. I also have a very extensive knowledge of the school's history, which, by the way, dates back to the seventeenth century. This school taught—"

"Yes, yes, of course my friend," Dane cut in as politely as he could. "I need information about an ex-student named Adrian Marino. Adrian has applied for a position on our staff, and we are in the process of doing an extensive background check on her."

It was the Frenchman's turn to interrupt. "Adrian Marino, you say?"

"That's right. Do you remember her?" Dane asked.

"This is a joke, yes? I'm tired, I haven't time for this."

"I don't understand," Dane replied curiously. "Believe me, sir, this is not a joke."

"Well, the only Adrian Marino I know is my son, and he is eight years old. Goodbye."

The line went dead. Dane was beautifully stunned. By the time he detached the telephone receiver from his ear and returned it to the cradle, a full minute had passed. "Adrian Marino," he said triumphantly. "Got you!"

Dane still had questions. First and foremost, who was Adrian Marino? The name didn't give a clear indication of Krait's sex. He had always assumed Krait was a man, but it was archaic and ignorant-minded to think Krait couldn't be a woman. Anything was possible, and as Koso often said to him: "When one doesn't know what to expect, then one should prepare for anything." Indeed, Dane agreed he should expect nothing to be exactly as it appeared. He was at a point where instinct had to take over.

It had been three weeks since he'd arrived in Moscow, and Koso still didn't have the information he needed. He'd been on the phone to Angelica for the past hour, trying to cool her anxiety. It was the fourth phone call in as many days. It was now October 6, and her stress was well warranted. She had him so on edge that he was about ready to pack his bags and leave right there and then, but Feodor then arrived home. It was late, and Koso had been wondering where he was. Feodor was never out late; it interfered too much with his drinking routine—a pastime he took rather seriously.

"I'll call you back soon," Koso said to Angelica. He didn't wait for her to argue, and he hung up.

"I have what you need," Feodor said, collecting a drink from the bar and taking a seat.

Koso's heart jumped. "Tell me," he said.

"You were right. He is being shadowed."

"By who?" Koso said.

"His code name is James Jones. He used to work for MI6, but he flipped back in the old days when the Brits screwed up and left him out in the cold too long. Now he's one of Ostrov's top agents, and he's rumored to be a no-nonsense guy when it comes to his work. He gets things done. And his specialty, amongst other things, is wet work."

"He's an assassin?"

"He's an assassin, and he's so much more. He's the human version of a heat-seeking missile. One of his greater exploits was his involvement with the capture of Ilrich Ramirez Sanchez ..."

"Carlos the Jackal?" said Koso.

"Indeed," Feodor said. "They say Carlos's takedown was purely a French effort, but James Jones had been on Carlos for months before the French made their move, and they only did so with James's consent."

Koso was feeling more anxious by the moment. "What else?" he asked.

"Dane's staying at the Hotel Vienna on Siros. But here's the real rub—James's orders are to observe Dane until he has killed the IUS chief, Krait, and then Dane is to be eliminated."

"Hell, how can Ostrov do that? Dane is no threat to him," said Koso.

"Hell is right. If I'd known this caper of yours involved the IUS, I'd never had answered my door when you'd showed up. Anyone I ever knew who tangoed with IUS affairs from outside their circle wound up dead. I'm not ready to be dead yet, Koso. Why weren't you straight with me from the beginning?"

"I'm sorry," said Koso. "I would have told you about Dane's involvement with Krait, but I had no choice. I needed the information."

"You owe me big-time. And I don't just mean money. When I come knocking on your door for a favor, I'll expect you come through," said Feodor, his face masked with worry.

"As long as you keep your head down for the next few weeks, I promise no harm will come to you beyond that."

"How can you promise that?"

"Because Krait will be dead, exposed, or imprisoned. Whatever the outcome, Krait will be powerless."

James Jones had a dozen other names and identities he used, but when all was said and done, he liked to think of himself as James Jones— British-born, British-raised. There had been a time when he'd worked for British intelligence, during the height of the Cold War. He'd been a high-ranking agent working in St. Petersburg, where he made a super-sensitive discovery of the Russian-military kind. He managed to get all the information back to London and stay alive in the process. But that was where his luck ran dry. He received word he was being investigated by the KGB, and he quickly decided it was time to get out. He sought refuge in a British safe house outside Moscow and quietly waited for word from his superiors. But word didn't come. The weeks slid into months, and hope slid into oblivion. It was as if his country had simply left him to rot in that cold, dirty, godforsaken city.

After four months, James snapped. He was convinced his country had abandoned him. He was finished. The borders were in a security lockdown, and he certainly wouldn't have made it to friendly ground on his own. He'd run out of food and money. He was starving and desperate, and he did what any warm-blooded man would have done—he defected. The Russians welcomed him with open arms, and after a lengthy debriefing, they even gave him a job and an apartment. Thus was the history of James Jones.

"Adrian Marino?" Ostrov Putin grumbled down the secure line.

"That's correct, sir. I have been tracking all the communications that Mr. Larusio has been making, and Adrian Marino is the name he's concentrated on the most. I've done a full background check on Adrian, and so far, I've come up with nothing but a skeleton cover," James replied.

"What is it that stands out most?" Ostrov pushed.

"Adrian Marino is eight years old. Adrian is booked into the hotel suite with an adjoining room—the occupant of that room is noted in the registry as 'partner,'" James said.

"Sounds too sloppy for Krait." Ostrov said. He still wasn't convinced, but he was never one to ignore any possibility, however remote.

"They all slip up in the end, sir." James offered.

"I hope you're right," Ostrov said, thinking for a moment. "Stay with Dane until he's finished with Krait. Make sure nothing interferes with what he's doing, and protect him at any cost."

"Yes, sir!"

"I'll look into this Adrian Marino's background more thoroughly and contact you when I have the results. In the meantime, don't let Dane Larusio out of your sight."

"Yes, sir!" James agreed. He took Ostrov's closing words very seriously.

Ostrov called the St. Petersburg Intelligence Office the moment he'd finished with James. The phone was answered on the first ring.

"Yes, sir!" The young female voice on the other end of the line was crisp and efficient, with an edge of steel.

Ostrov was not in the least bit surprised by the fact that she knew who he was before he even spoke; it was the FSB's business to know. "I need everything there is on an individual going by the name of Adrian Marino," he said.

"What country, sir?"

"Italy. Presumed to be an art dealer."

"Thank you, sir. I'll call you back on this number within the hour."

Ostrov hung up and slowly sank onto a beautiful eighteenth century, hand crafted evening chair. His thoughts were awry. After Koso had been killed, he'd thought any chance of finding Krait was over. Koso had been on the trail for years before he'd been shot, and the fact that he was now gone was a tragic loss. But when they'd looked more closely at Dane, the trail had grown warmer. The more they studied him, the more obvious it became that he was closer to pinning down Krait than anyone had ever been. If this were true, and if Dane's history was anything to go by, Krait's days were numbered. All Ostrov had to do was sit back and watch the fireworks. But was it all really that simple? What was the real reason Dane was on this private vigilante spree? Had Koso been correct in his theory that Dane was simply suspended in some kind of borderline, psychotic rage inherited from a tragic youth? Ostrov tried to imagine what he would do or how he would feel if he himself had unwittingly killed and maimed members of his own family. But how could one really imagine what was going through Dane's mind? How could one really know if he wasn't working for another government agency? He could even be some elaborate security decoy, set up by the IUS. Whatever Dane's motives were, they were extremely complex. Ostrov had uncovered dark layers in Dane's history that even Koso wasn't aware of. He had Sicilian roots, and his father had been a very powerful man. This meant only one thing—Dane was very capable, probably more so than he himself understood. The one thing that remained clear in Ostrov's head was the fact that every effort must be made to bring Krait down, and if Dane was the means to Krait's fall, so be it.

Ostrov was still deep in thought when the phone rang exactly forty-two minutes after his previous conversation. He picked it up right away. "Yes?"

"Sir, I have completed the search on Adrian Marino, and all I've found is a mere skeleton of records. The records I found would have been difficult to plant, requiring some people in very high places to bend the rules. But as you know, bending the rules is becoming cheaper and cheaper these days."

"What's your conclusion?" Ostrov said, growing impatient.

"If you were to ask my opinion, I would have to say that Adrian Marino is nothing more than a ghost," said the officer.

"Okay, thank you," Ostrov answered. "Please e-mail me any relevant data."

"It's already done, sir."

"Thank you again."

Ostrov hung up and wrote down the young lady's name in his notebook. Despite her brief ranting, he was impressed with her overall efficiency. He checked the files she'd given him and could clearly see what she meant.

Ostrov stretched wearily. He would call James Jones back in the morning and pass the information along. But, for now, he'd rest. He crawled into bed and fell into his usual restless sleep, filled with the familiar bone-chilling nightmare of a long-ago battle in Afghanistan.

It was five p.m., New York time, and Bryant Wilson answered the phone on the second ring. "Bryant Wilson speaking."

"Bryant old friend, it's Dane."

"Dane, good to hear from you. How's your research going?" Bryant asked.

"Never better, Bryant. In fact that's why I'm calling. I promised I'd let you know when I'd be finished."

"Soon, I hope," said Bryant.

"I'll be done here in the next few weeks. I don't have an exact date yet, but I think I'll be finished by the end of October at the latest."

"Good, because the Shanghai hotel is almost complete, and I know you never like to miss an opening ceremony."

"Don't worry, I'll fly directly to China the moment I'm free," Dane insisted. "I'll call you again when I have an exact date. I just wanted you to get the ball rolling on the preparations in the meantime."

"Good. Now, before you disappear again."

"What is it?" Dane asked.

"It's Angelica and Koso," Bryant said.

Dane was silent.

"They came by the office yesterday. They were looking for you," Bryant said.

"Koso's dead!" Dane demanded, naked annoyance in his tone.

"Yes, well, that's what I thought until Angelica Skiathos walked through my door with Koso in tow. If you were to ask me, I would say that the old villain is as healthy as the day he was born. We tried to call you, but we couldn't get through."

A whirlwind of thoughts charged through Dane's head. Koso was alive? But he'd seen the man shot right before his eyes. No mortal man could have walked away from that. He fired his questions and doubts at Bryant. "What was it exactly that Koso and Angelica wanted to see me about?" he pressed.

"Well, they didn't exactly say. Only that what they had to see you about was a matter of urgency," said Bryant.

Long after the phone call was over, Dane's mind was awash with confusion, and he wished he'd not called Bryant to begin with. His entire thought process was now in a tailspin. He thought about the blood flowing freely from Koso's body when he was shot at the restaurant in Rome. He thought of the grief that followed. He thought about the last conversation he'd had with Angelica and how badly she'd wanted him to stop what he was doing. He thought about how he'd left her and how much he missed the warmth and comfort of her arms. But mostly, he thought of how close he was to completing his epic objective. Like a professional sprinter on the track, nothing had a chance of breaking his tunnel vision. All he could see was the ribbon at finish line.

CHAPTER 15

KILL THE RUSSIAN

Dane imagined many ways to assassinate Krait. The more he thought about the task, the more confused he became. First he had thought of poisoning the food or water. He also thought of filling the room with gas. Finally, he pondered the possibility of creeping into Krait's room in the early hours of the morning and using the faithful blade. But all these ideas were far too risky. The gas might not be effective enough in such a well-ventilated room, a food tester would render poison useless, and it was also impossible to determine just how extensive a bodyguard there was, and exactly what surveillance measures had been taken. In the end, Dane decided a bomb was the only sure way.

But the bomb method came with its own set of problems. First and foremost was finding a way to isolate the target in order to limit collateral damage. A delicate calculation was required in order to know exactly how much explosive was needed. Finally, he had to know that it was Krait he'd actually killed. This meant he would have to go in and check after the bomb detonated. But how was he to get in and see the bodies without attracting the attention of authorities? The hotel was at the eastern end of the island, though, which was not very populated. The nearest police station was at least a thirty-minute drive, so authorities were not a massive problem. He'd have plenty of time to make himself scarce once he'd completed what was necessary.

He still had serious problems that had to be solved in only a few days. By then, Adrian Marino would have arrived, he would have finally put a face to the name, and he would have to make his move.

Dane was on the veranda of his hotel room, wearing nothing but a pair of white boxers. He'd been moved into the new room, which had an extra-large balcony to accommodate his daily workout. Most importantly, the room was directly under Adrian Marino's. His body glistened in the noonday sun as he pounded the bright red boxing bag hanging from a stand.

"Everything is ready," Dane said, talking under his breath. He threw in another heavy right and followed through with a left uppercut. He backed off for a moment, keeping his forearms close and his fists at the ready. He looked more like he was in the ring with a deadly opponent rather than having a regular sweat session on the bag.

"The explosives are in place." He danced a little more, measured the distance with his left, and came right in close with lightning speed to deliver a sharp, hard-right elbow, which sent the bag flying almost clean off its chain.

"The research is flawless." He came at the now aggressively swinging bag and dodged it like it was a blow of a sparing partner.

"The back-up plan is in place." He pounced, leading with his left foot, as he always did, and delivered a long series of crippling blows to the now-buckling imaginary opponent. The last blow came in low and hard from his right and sent the bag flying off the hook and off the balcony. "Where the fuck is Adrian Marino?" He continued to shadow box.

Dane wasn't used to having such sudden and seemingly uncontrollable outbursts of rage. Suddenly realizing his state, he stopped and forced himself to relax. Several deep breaths of the cool breeze helped greatly, and he found his usual calm returning. But indeed there was a problem—Adrian Marino should have already arrived. It was October 7 already and, with each passing day, the reality of an arrival was becoming duller and duller. As his heart rate returned to normal, so did his regular thought pattern. Logic, as it always did, prevailed. There was nothing to be done except wait. How long would he wait? Well, that was simple—he would wait until the end of the month.

Leaning over the banister, Dane breathed in the cool, evening air.

"This yours?" The voice came with a thick Italian accent.

Dane looked down from the second-floor balcony, and found a bull of a man staring up at him, boxing bag in hand. He was about six-foot-four in height and must have weighed at least a hundred and fifty kilos. He looked none too pleased about Dane's bag falling from the sky.

Dane quickly gathered his senses. "Yes," he said, apologetically. "I'm sorry, it's the chain. It broke halfway through training. I hope I didn't cause you injury."

The gorilla's stony look suddenly changed to one a little less aggressive, and the trace of a smile spread across his face. "I'm not sure which, but you either need a stronger chain or a heavier bag," he said. With one hand, he swung the bag through the air, like an Olympic discus thrower. It sailed up and landed back on the balcony next to Dane.

Dane was completely dumbstruck by the action. Before he could utter a word of thanks, the gorilla disappeared into the hotel. "Shit!" he said, exasperated. There must be only a handful of men on the face of the planet who could have thrown a thirty-six-kilo boxing bag fifteen feet into the air, and he'd just met one of them. A thought suddenly struck him, and he rushed back into his room to his ever-present laptop. He quickly logged into the hotel registry. He smiled broadly at what he saw—Adrian Marino had checked in two minutes ago. Undoubtedly, the gorilla was Krait's bodyguard.

The young hotel manager was sitting in the garden below, going over the details of the month's up-and-coming events in her notebook. She watched the exchange between Dane and the gorilla with detached interest. But she didn't care about the gorilla. Her real reason for being in the garden was the view of Dane's glistening physique as he worked on the bag he'd ordered from her. Her face was a mask of lust, which, from her point of view was well warranted. She discretely snapped a picture with her phone and wondered if he was single.

The horny young hotel manager wasn't the only one spying on Dane as he boxed. A few hundred yards away, curious eyes peered from a dusty loft, atop an ancient, abandoned villa. James Jones was the unblinking observer. He'd settled there with an ample supply of food and water, anticipating a wait he hoped wouldn't be long. He couldn't help but grin as he watched the short confrontation between Dane and the near-stricken gorilla. His work would soon be finished, and soon, he could go home again. Home was Astrakhan, a small city in southern Russia. There he had a young wife and daughter. Ostrov had had him continuously working in deep cover on Krait for two years, and he'd not seen his family the entire time. Oh, how he longed to play again with his daughter and make love to his wife in their little house by the Caspian Sea.

His orders were firm and without question—follow Dane until he'd killed Krait, and then kill Dane. However, for the first time in memory, a most unusual feeling began to evolve within James. He was beginning to imagine how easy it would be to go against his orders and steal the glory. He'd been tailing Dane for weeks and hunting Krait for much, much longer. He felt tired beyond comprehension. Killing Dane would be easier than knocking a toddler from a rocker. But that plan just wouldn't do at all. Why shouldn't he carry out the assassination of the infamous Krait himself? He knew every detail of Dane's attack strategy, and it would be so simple to take over the job. Besides, it was ridiculous entrusting such a task to a rank amateur such as Dane Larusio. The man was no more than an overrated resort tycoon with an unusual hobby. If Dane were to bungle the assassination, Krait would simply vanish. James would never forgive himself if such a thing happened.

No, the entire plan was far too risky. The solution was simple; James would take over, and when Krait was dead, he would kill Dane.

He stretched back in the rickety, wooden chair and took another long pull on his bottle of vodka. Peering through his binoculars toward the hotel, he watched and waited.

He hated waiting.

Waiting always reminded him of the months he'd spent in that British safe house, and that was a time he never wanted to remember. Something had changed inside of him while he was there. He'd lost something, and it was only now that he realized what it was—he'd lost his pride. Sure, Russia had given him a new home, a family, and a fresh chance at life, but they'd never given him his pride back, and they never could. Before he'd flipped, his pride was the glue that held him together.

The more he thought about the matter, the more he was convinced he was doing the right thing by taking down Krait himself. He could make up any story for the brass. He could tell them Dane had fouled up the assassination, and he'd had to take over and finish the job. For succeeding, he'd receive a major promotion. He'd finally get out of the field and into a nice command position where he'd give orders and watch others put their lives on the line.

He could almost smell the leather on his new office desktop. He could imagine the smile on his wife's face when he told her he would now have a job where he'd come home at the end of the day and not at the end of the year or longer. He could finally be proud of the man he was and of the future he'd created. He could taste that freedom. It was only days away. All he had to do was watch and wait for the right opportunity.

He hated waiting.

For the hundredth time, Dane reviewed the calculations for the explosives he'd set. There was a series of five different charges, and it hadn't been an easy task setting them. First, he had to silently hand-drill holes into his ceiling so there was only one inch of floor remaining between the explosives and Krait's room. They were engineered so they would explode upward and outward; first through the remaining inch of limestone, and then through the flesh of Krait. Dane was sure that the bomb would only damage the allocated room, but he wanted to avoid unnecessary risk. He needed to limit the number of people in the hotel as much as possible before he blew the charges. He'd imagined a dozen different scenarios in which the other guests could be provoked to evacuate their rooms, but all seemed too risky. However, he was not going to let his chance slip away. If he was forced to detonate while there were still people in the hotel, so be it.

One more thing worried Dane—it was already October eighth, and thus far Krait hadn't so much as stepped outside the suite. Dane hoped he'd have a chance to actually lay eyes the elusive villain, but he'd so far had no such luck. There was time. He didn't know exactly how long Krait's holiday was going to be, but he was certain Krait would have to get out and round at some stage.

Dane was tired. He had been intensely focused since Krait's arrival, and he realized he had to risk a walk and a breath of fresh air before he went insane with cabin fever. But, as he exited the lobby, the manager hailed him.

"Mr. Larreno, excuse me?" the manager, at the front desk called.

"Yes," Dane replied, halfway out the door. He'd always found it hard to remember his alias when he used one. Jeff Larreno was the name he'd chosen to use while he stayed on Siros; it belonged to a Rome banker.

"For you," the manager said, leaning across the desk and exposing a generous portion of what were undoubtedly her greatest assets.

Dane took the envelope and thanked her before stepping into the refreshing evening air. He tore the envelope open and read:

Tonight. 7:00 p.m.

All guests are invited to our annual masquerade ball. This ball is to be held at the citadel ruins on the beachfront. Entertainment and refreshments will be provided, with a jazz band specially flown in from New York. The mystery singer complimenting this band is a surprise that you will have to discover yourself. Each guest in attendance will be required to wear the traditional mask, along with formal evening dress. Please bring this invitation with you for admittance.

We look forward to entertaining you,

Management

Dane spun on his heel and returned to the reception. His walk was going to have to wait. The manager gave him a broad grin as he approached. "This masquerade," he said. "Is this an event that will be popular?"

"Oh, yes, Mr. Larreno. The masquerade is something not to be missed. I myself will be off duty this evening, and you can be sure that I'll be there, enjoying the celebrations along with all the other guests."

"Really," Dane said, an idea beginning to form. "So then, *everyone* in the hotel will be attending?"

She looked at her computer screen a few moments, punching a few keys. "It looks as if you're the last on the guest list to confirm."

Dane had to be sure of what she was saying. "You say everyone on the guest list. Does that mean everyone in the hotel is going to be there?"

"Yes, sir." There was a hint of curiosity in her tone. "Why do you ask?"

"Do you really want to know?" Dane said with as much guilt as he could muster.

"Yes," she pursued.

"Well, the fact is, I've been cooped up here in the hotel for the last three weeks working on a business proposal, and I haven't had a chance to enjoy any of the island's beauty or attractions."

The manager's expression changed to one of aghast sympathy.

"Anyway," Dane continued, "the fact of the matter is that I don't think I could stand one more night at the keyboard. I believe this masquerade may be just the thing to take the edge off." His mind was running at ten times the speed of his voice. If he were to attend the masquerade, he would attract less attention if he arrived with a date on his arm.

"So then, it's settled. You'll be there, correct?" asked the manager.

"Well, the thing is, I really have nothing to wear," Dane said.

"Well, there's an excellent tailor in Ermoupolis who'll handcraft you anything you require surprisingly quickly," offered the manager.

It was time for Dane to make his move. "What would you say if I asked you to show me where this tailor is?" he asked. "I'll buy you lunch."

The manager visibly rocked on her heels.

"Bu ... buu ... but," she stuttered, nervously tugging at a worn gold bracelet. "I have to work."

"I'll buy you a gown for the ball," he said.

She picked up the phone, and for a moment Dane, wondered if he'd pushed his luck too far. He watched expectantly as she dialed a number.

"Yes, hello. Is Sarah home? Hello, Sarah, I was wondering if you could come in early and cover me at the hotel?" There was a long pause. "I promise I'll make it up to you."

Dane looked on, patient as always.

"We can leave in ten minutes," said the manager, hanging up.

"Ten minutes will be perfect," Dane said, relieved.

"Oh, by the way, I'm Andrea Zinnetti," said the manager.

"Andrea," Dane repeated, "please call me Jeff. And it's a pleasure meeting you."

Two hours later, they were seated in a small, dockside restaurant, eating lobster and chatting, while the tuxedo was being cut. It was mostly small talk, but, all in all, Dane was sure that the young woman would be more than pleased to go along with him to the masquerade. When he did get around to asking her, she instantly accepted with a helpful smile.

Koso touched down at Siros's Demetrius Vikelas National airport at a little after one in the afternoon and met Angelica at the gate. He noticed how tired she looked the moment he saw her. The wait had obviously taken its toll. When he'd called her from Moscow, she'd insisted he give her Dane's location right there and then, but Koso had told her it was best if they approached him together.

Angelica had rented a small Volkswagen. "Okay, now tell me—where are we going? What hotel's he staying at?" she asked when they were seated in the car.

"Hold your horses," Koso said. "I know you're feeling a little anxious right now, but let's not rush into this."

"A *little* anxious? I've been sitting around for the last three weeks, waiting on you. I'm not anxious; I'm half out of my mind. Now, tell me where he is," she demanded.

"Okay, before you get carried away, you should know that Dane has a Russian agent watching him at this very moment, and we have to be very careful how we proceed. Yes, we have to proceed quickly, but Dane's life is on the line. We have to neutralize the agent before we confront Dane."

"Neutralize?" Angelica asked.

"We need to kill him, okay?" said Koso.

"How in hell's name are we going to do that?" Angelica asked.

"Just let me worry about that bit."

"And what am I supposed to do, more waiting?" asked Angelica, looking more agitated than ever.

"You need to find a way of making sure that Dane is at the hotel. Otherwise, we're just wasting our time. What we need to do is have a look at the layout of the hotel area."

"I can do that from here," Angelica said, reaching over to the backseat and producing her laptop.

"Just what sort of details can you get?" Koso asked.

"I can get you *any* details you need on the area."

"I need to know where an agent would be potentially surveilling Dane from. I need an aerial view of the area."

"I can do that," Angelica said. She booted up the laptop and had a Google Earth image of the address Koso had given her within minutes.

Together they studied the image. The hotel was fairly small, the grounds covering about three acres. Built in a classical Greek style, with oversized red-clay tiles on the roof and large open balconies, the hotel was obviously ancient. It was rectangular and long and had been built into the belly of a small, horseshoe-shaped bay. It had gardens fronting the main building with two fountains at each side and a wide driveway approaching western front end of the building. A small beach sat before the gardens.

"Can you zoom out to give us a better look of the surrounding area?" Koso said.

Angelica did so, bringing an area of about three square kilometers into view. There they saw two outstanding features, both built on the beachheads at the tips of the bay. One was an old church with a massive tree in front of it. The second structure looked like the remains of a medieval castle.

Koso saw nothing of significance. "Zoom back in to about a kilometer surrounding the hotel," he said.

Angelica tapped away at her laptop again, and they studied the image once more. They then saw what Koso was looking for—at the eastern edge of the bay, gloved within a thick grove of wind-beaten pine trees, sat a villa. Its location gave the perfect view of the front of the Hotel Vienna, facing its front from about a hundred meters away and at a 45-degree angle.

"What do you see?" Angelica asked.

"What I see is a place where I'd be if I were keeping an eye on someone in the hotel without them knowing. But I need to get a closer look to be sure," said Koso.

"What do you propose?"

"Okay," said Koso, "like I said, we have to be careful how we approach this. We're going to have to split up. I suggest that you go and make sure that Dane is actually staying in the hotel. While you're doing that, I'll check the villa. I need to know if our Russian friend is there. When you've confirmed Dane's presence, go straight back to your hotel. I'll meet you there. And, Angelica, I beg you, if there is any way you can avoid it, don't approach Dane yet."

"Don't worry, I won't."

Their course of action agreed upon, Angelica started the car and they drove eastward around the coast toward the hotel. There was a warm breeze blowing in from the Mediterranean, and the sun was shining, making the tips of the gently rolling waves sparkle dazzlingly. On any other day, the drive along the dramatic coastline could have been a spectacular pleasure, but the beauty of their surroundings was far from either of their thoughts.

Angelica dropped Koso off at the church, as he insisted on walking the remainder of the way and approaching the villa on his own. Now, as Angelica drove along the hotel's driveway, her heart thundered with a mixture of anxiety, adrenaline, and anticipation. She had no idea how she was going to find out if Dane was at the hotel. Simply going room to room, knocking on doors wasn't going to work. She realized she had to get a look at the computer. But how—how could she get behind the desk and have a look at the guest list without being thrown out? All this was at the forefront of her thoughts as she drove into the hotel parking area.

The hotel was small. She judged that it had forty rooms at most. There would probably be no more than two staff members in the reception area. All she had to do was get them outside for a couple of minutes.

She quickly realized what she had to do. The Volkswagen she was driving had an alarm, and the key had an emergency alert option.

She parked the car in a space next to three other cars and got out. Next she walked into the garden area in front of the hotel. From here she activated the emergency alert from her key ring. The car alarm was deafening, shattering the relative silence of the area, and she didn't have to wait long before a young lady dashed from the lobby to investigate. Angelica wasted no time; she skipped into the lobby behind the young lady's back and scanned her surroundings. She was alone. She wasted no time congratulating herself on the success of the diversion; she had a job to do and all she saw was opportunity. She leapt over the low door, which was the only security the reception desk offered, and immediately attacked the computer. She had the guest list on the screen in seconds. Quickly she scanned it.

"Larusio … Larusio … where the hell are you?" she mumbled, not seeing him anywhere. She quickly realized Dane would never use his real name. She was going to have to resort to plan B and go knocking on all the doors after all. Koso had warned her against the idea of her confronting him alone, but she had no choice. The computer indicated a total of thirty-six rooms. The search wouldn't be easy.

A door closed somewhere nearby, and Angelica's heart almost jumped from her chest. She then saw it, pinned to the back of the desk. It was a photo taken from a fair distance, but there was no doubting the subject. The man in the photo was wearing only shorts and boxing gloves, obviously in the middle of a workout while unsuspectingly being photographed. The man was Dane.

Footsteps sounded on the stairs, and Angelica leapt back over the low door. No longer needing the diversion, she punched the key ring button to turn the car alarm off. She took a seat on a nearby couch, trying desperately to look relaxed. Down the stairs came a man the likes of which she'd never seen before. He was a massive, hard-looking character with eyes as cold as stone—eyes that drilled deeply into everything in their path. Atop of this, Angelica could not help noticing the armful of ornate masquerade masks he carried.

Aldo was returning some unwanted masquerade masks to reception. He didn't like to leave the view of his employer, but he wanted as few people as possible coming to the room. He was surprised to see just how quiet the hotel was. The foyer was all but empty, except for a single woman who sat alone. She was stunningly beautiful, but it wasn't her beauty that caught his attention. Her face looked startlingly familiar, but he couldn't quite pick where he'd seen her before. He nodded a hello to her as he placed the masks on the reception desk.

"Do you mind if I ask what the masks are for?" Angelica said, unable to stifle her curiosity.

"A masquerade," Aldo answered. For some reason he'd always been overly anxious around women, and he was suddenly eager to escape back upstairs.

Angelica wasn't going to let him go that easily.

"A masquerade. Really." She beamed one of her best smiles. "I'm just checking in, so I didn't know. May I ask where and when this masquerade will be?"

Damn the woman, Aldo thought. He turned back to face her, making a mammoth effort to be polite. "At the citadel on the beach tonight," he said.

"Well, thank you," she said, maintaining her smile.

Aldo nodded and made good his escape.

It was time for Angelica to leave. She had what she'd come for. She walked from the lobby and gave the young lady she'd seen earlier a casual wave and a hello. The lady smiled in return, but when she saw Angelica climb into the Volkswagen and drive off, her expression turned to one of annoyance.

Angelica drove back to the church, and there she waited for Koso, mulling over the complication of the photo of Dane behind the hotel reception. A spark of jealousy fired through her veins. Had Dane taken up with another woman so soon? Half of her wanted to speed back to the hotel and confront him there and then, but the other half clung to Koso's rational warning. This emotional tug of war continued until Koso arrived.

Koso made his way cross-country toward the hotel area. He felt, for reasons of stealth, that this was much wiser than simply taking a stroll though the entrance. He tried to think from the agent's point of view. If *he* were going kill someone in the hotel, how would he approach such a task? As he walked, he checked his pistol. It was a .22-caliber Baretta 70S, a favorite lifelong companion. Reaching the top of a knoll and coming in full view of the hotel, he decided to take a short rest and think things over. His old bones were suddenly feeling their age. He sat on the soft grass so he could just to see over the top of the tiny hill and toward the hotel area. The hotel itself was only about a half-kilometer away, and his position gave him an excellent view of its every feature.

Koso had to assume for the moment that the agent wasn't staying in the hotel. He had to assume he would be following and watching

Dane from a distance, and the villa was the perfect vantage point to do so from. Koso had to assume many things, and assumption was something he hated. He pulled a pair of small, but powerful binoculars from one of his pockets and began to scan the entire area. The hotel itself was set in a shallow cul-de-sac. Soon his focus shifted to the villa, which was nestled in amongst a pine grove. A few of the roof tiles were missing, and the windows had rickety shutters, some also missing, and some hanging loosely from single hinges. Two-stories high, and made entirely of stone, the building had obviously once been grand affair, but now it was nothing more than a crumbling relic. It was the perfect observation post.

Koso got brusquely to his feet and began walking toward the deserted villa. The sinister glare of the hollow windows watched his approach. If he were lucky, he'd have a bullet in James Jones's brain within the hour.

He entered the building from a side window. Like many of the others, the shutters and glass of the window had long since vanished. The inside was large and eerie. There was old furniture scattered around the floor—none of it any good. The wind whistled loudly through the house, making ghostly sounds, but Koso felt glad he had some noise to cover his approach. He was sure that, if the agent were in the house, he would have taken up a position on the upper floor; but he was never one to take chances. Systematically, he checked all of the rooms on the ground floor first. He came across nothing of any great significance—old chairs, tables, a piano, but mostly dust.

Now sure that his back was covered, Koso approached a spiral stairway that ascended from the main hall. There were a total of six rooms on the upper floor, but, as he peeked around the doorframe and through the first doorway, he made the discovery he was looking for: an empty chair sat near the window, but it was the empty bottle of vodka sitting next to the chair that caused him to investigate further.

He flipped off the safety catch on his pistol and stepped inside, sweeping the barrel around the room, ready to fire if need be. There was no one there. Crumpled under the chair was an empty packet of Aohchou Tabak cigarettes. Koso recognized the Russian brand. There were also a few discarded butts on the floor. He picked one up and took a sniff. It smelt freshly burnt. He now felt certain he was on the right track.

But where was the Russian agent?

Koso spent a few more minutes looking around the villa. He found nothing else of any significance, and he soon decided he'd better leave. He felt it was best he reconvene with Angelica before making any further moves on the agent. He needed to know what Dane's position was, and with any luck, Angelica would have that information by now.

While Angelica waited for Koso, she called the Hotel Vienna and inquired further about the masquerade. An idea was forming in her head, and the more she thought about it, the more it made sense. If she wanted to approach Dane without attracting the attention of the Russian agent, a good place to do it would be in a social environment. But she needed to know if Dane would be attending the ball, and if the ball was open to the public.

It didn't take more than a couple of minutes to gather the information she needed from the hotel manager. Indeed, the masquerade was an annual event, organized by the hotel, but it was also open to outsiders who were willing to purchase an invitation. Furthermore, all of the hotel guests *were* attending—Dane *was* going to be there. No sooner had Angelica finished her phone call than an exhausted Koso showed up.

"You look like you've just run a marathon," Angelica said as Koso climbed into the car.

"I'm not the man I once was," Koso said, getting his breath back.

"And the agent, is he the man he once was?" Angelica asked.

"I located his post of observation, but sadly, I didn't locate him," said Koso. "How did you go? Is Dane staying at the hotel?"

"Oh he's there, all right," Angelica said. She explained the discovery of the photo behind the hotel reception.

"How would you like to go to a masquerade?" Angelica asked Koso as they drove back to their hotel.

"I'm not in the dancing mood," said Koso.

Angelica explained about the ball and how Dane would almost certainly be attending, and Koso quickly cottoned onto the rational she was driving at.

"I'll need a new tuxedo," said Koso.

"And I'll need a new gown," said Angelica.

Chapter 16

Masquerade

A gentle breeze blew off the Mediterranean and lightly stirred the Siros shoreline. On a rocky outcrop not far from the shore stood the remains of an ancient citadel that had seen its last day of service more than five centuries earlier. The walls were all but crumbled, with the exception of two sturdy watchtowers standing at the northern corners. The two towers stood a good sixty feet high and twelve feet in diameter. Between the towers were drawn two massive, deep-green, satin curtains, behind which was the stage where the musicians would perform. The cobbled courtyard floor within the citadel remained intact, and it looked as though it had at least another millennium of service to offer. It was within this courtyard that the guests of the masquerade were beginning to assemble. Masks sipped champagne and listened to a mesmerizing clarinet player, who set the atmosphere alight with a mysterious tune. Overhead, a million stars were performing, and a full moon hung from the heavens. No cars pulled up to the entrance. Guests who were not staying at the hotel parked in the hotel car park before walking a leisurely distance along a lantern-lit path to the citadel. In the midst of these festivities were Krait and Aldo. If ever there was a time when Aldo was more on edge, then he couldn't remember it.

Krait's mask was in the form of a giant serpent with blood-dripping fangs. Aldo's mask was a little less elaborate, but equally as sinister; it was simple black silk with two eyeholes and an iron crown to hold it in place. Despite its simplicity, he managed to look as fearsome as ever. He constantly scanned the crowd, desperately trying to assess any threat. The clarinet player was only a few feet from where they stood, and the noise only added to Aldo's confusion and to the ever-increasing difficulty of his work. He hated the clarinet. He would rather listen to a cat being strangled.

Aldo's attention was suddenly captured by a figure making an entrance. He instantly recognized the dazzling young lady he'd seen in the hotel foyer earlier. She wore a shoulder-to-ankle, white silk dress that fit her body like a glove. Her white porcelain mask was fashioned Chinese-style and had fine, intricate art around its edges that formed a flowered vine. The tiny flowers were painted red, and matched perfectly with a massive ruby pendant that hung from her neck. She'd been attractive earlier, but now Aldo couldn't take his eyes off her. Suddenly she turned and their gazes locked. Aldo felt instantly uneasy, and he forced his attention back to his job.

It was only eight p.m., and already the venue was nearly full.

James Jones walked briskly along the path toward the masquerade. For reassurance, he brushed his hand over the lump in his jacket, feeling the .22-caliber pistol firmly holstered under his left arm. He glanced at his watch; he was well ahead of schedule. He'd done his homework—he knew exactly how Dane planned to kill Krait, and he knew of both sets of explosives and exactly where they'd been set. The only thing he didn't know was exactly when Dane was going to execute his plan; but that didn't matter anymore.

James marveled at the plan's effective simplicity. At ten p.m. sharp, there was going to be a massive fireworks display. However, the fireworks, with a little help, were going to be set off sooner than planned. Dane had planted a small explosive charge, just powerful enough to detonate the very large shipment of fireworks. This would be all that was needed to send Krait's bodyguard into panic. If Dane's plan was successful, Krait would be hustled back to the assumed safety of the hotel, only to be blown to hell by a second set of explosives.

James's plan was simple too—acquire the detonation transmitters from Dane and execute the plan himself. Gaining control of the transmitters wouldn't be an easy task, but if all went to plan, he'd have them by the time he reached the festivities.

As he approached the entrance, he realized his nerves were more than a little on edge. So they should be. By the end of the night, one of the world's most wanted criminals would be dead, and James Jones would be responsible. He would be a hero.

Dane was beginning to wonder if he'd made the wrong decision in pairing up with Andrea. It was already eight p.m., and she still wasn't ready. He checked his watch for the tenth time in as many minutes and made a decision. If she wasn't prepared to leave in five minutes, he'd go on his own.

When the knock came, it startled him. "Finally!" he grumbled. He opened the door to reveal a smiling, expectant Andrea.

"Well," she asked, doing a full turn to show off her gown. "What do you think?"

I think you're very fucking late, Dane thought. "I think you look breathtaking," he said.

"Do you have your mask?" Andrea asked excitedly.

Dane collected his jacket and mask and headed for the door. It was in Phantom-of-the-Opera style, made of fine porcelain.

Andrea's was fashioned in the shape of an Egyptian cat. Although it was of exquisite design, it somehow failed to compliment the clinging red gown she wore. To top this off, Dane only now noticed how tall she was. With the heels, she towered over him in a way that was almost intimidating.

Angelica sipped her third glass of champagne and declined yet another invitation to the dance floor. The drinking was beginning to go to her head, but it did little to take the edge off her ever-increasing anxiety. She had arrived at the event on her own. Koso had one last piece of business to take care of; he was going to have one final shot at the Russian agent, after which he'd promised to meet her at the masquerade. But it had been half an hour since she'd arrived, and as yet, she'd not seen Dane or Koso. The only person she did recognize was the gorilla she'd seen earlier in the hotel. However, her impatience finally lessened as she watched a man wearing a massive red dragon mask weave his way thorough the crowd. The familiar stoop in his posture, and the fact that he declined the offer of champagne, instead opting for scotch, left no doubt in Angelica's mind that Koso had finally arrived. As relaxed as her frayed nerves allowed, she made her way toward him. Koso almost jumped clean out of his skin when Angelica tapped him on the shoulder.

"A little jumpy, aren't we?" she said.

Koso kept his mask in place, hiding his grim expression. "Over there," he said, regaining his previous calm.

Angelica slowly looked around. "What? Where?"

"By the bar opposite us—the man with the black mask in his hand." Koso twisted his head in the general direction.

Angelica spotted a man in his early fifties, making no effort to hold his simple mask in place. "The agent?" she whispered.

"Yes!"

"You didn't get him?" she whispered.

"No," Koso said, "but I promise you I will."

"Is he tailing Dane right this moment?" Angelica asked.

"I don't know."

"Have you seen Dane?" Angelica asked.

"That's exactly what I was about to ask you. I've been busy focusing on the agent. I followed him directly from the villa after almost bumping into him when he was on his way out." Koso said, lifting his mask and taking a long swallow of scotch. "I've no idea where Dane is."

"You don't know much of anything, do you?" Angelica ruefully growled.

"What do you know?" Koso asked, begrudgingly.

"Not much," Angelica admitted. Her eyes then lit up and were suddenly glued to the entrance.

Koso followed Angelica's gaze to a tall young woman collecting a glass of champagne before seizing the arm of what would appear to be her date. The man was substantially shorter than the woman—

not because he was short, but because the woman was *very* tall. By anyone's standards they made a superbly odd couple.

"That's him!" Koso said, finally understanding Angelica's silence.

"Yes," she replied, her voice hardly audible.

Angelica recognized the woman on Dane's arm as the lady from the hotel she'd seen earlier. And this explained the photograph behind the reception desk. Had Dane so easily forgotten her? A million questions and accusations flew through her head until she thought it would burst from the pressure. She suddenly found she could barely think. The glass in her hand began to tremble out of control. She had to leave.

"I hate the bitch," Dane mumbled for the hundredth time. He had made a huge mistake by taking her as a date, and he racked his brains as to what madness had possessed him to do so in the first place. Andrea had nagged him continuously from the moment they'd left the hotel, and she showed no signs of letting up. Dane was sure he wasn't going to get a moment's peace from her the entire evening. He decided an extra shot of scotch would do him good, so he headed for the bar.

Andrea clung to Dane's arm. "Where are we going?" she demanded.

"To get a real drink," Dane replied, making no effort to hide the distaste in his voice.

As they shuffled toward the bar, they were almost knocked down by a woman running toward the exit. The woman wore a white mask, and although the mask effectively concealed her expression, Dane could sense her distress. He immediately dismissed the collision, however, and proceeded in claiming his drink.

Between making numerous attempts at dislodging himself from Andrea, Dane scanned the crowed in search of Krait's bodyguard. If he could locate the bodyguard, he might get a chance to see Krait— or, taking the mask into consideration, he'd at least see most of Krait. At little after nine thirty p.m., at Andrea's bidding, he moved a little closer to the clarinet player, and there he saw the giant man he'd seen at the hotel. Dane tried to scan the people surrounding the bodyguard, but he could not focus around Andrea's infernal chatter. It was always: "Oh, have you tried the hors d'oeuvres? We had a chef especially flown in from France to do the catering. And I'm not sure about the champagne. I like the Henriot, but the Dom Ruinart is terrible, don't you think? I must remember to choose something else next year. What do you think? Do you like the clarinet? Why won't you dance with me?" She just wouldn't stop. Dane *had* to get away from her. He had to get a better look at those surrounding Krait's bodyguard.

His luck finally changed when Andrea excused herself to go to the bathroom. Dane felt deeply thankful for the break and thought little of it when she failed to return. He hoped she'd finally picked up on his obvious distaste, and he congratulated himself on getting rid of her. Finally he'd have the opportunity to examine all those in close proximity to the bodyguard. But the more he looked, the less confidence he felt that anyone near the bodyguard was a globally powerful villain. There was a drunken man holding a mask in his left hand and a wine glass in his other, who had the nerdy appearance of an aged computer geek. There was a large woman in a shapeless dress wearing a massive mask, which gave no clue to the features beneath it. There were two boys of about twelve, with their mother all wearing masks of jesters. The list went on. No one really stood out, aside from the gigantic bodyguard.

Soon Dane gave up looking and decided to focus on the matter at hand. It was time to detonate the first charges. Calmly he headed toward the exit, where he waited for the precise moment. He plucked a glass of champagne from a passing waiter, and while he sipped, he slipped his hand inside his jacket pocket, feeling for the first transmitter. His fingers felt only pocket. He checked the other—still nothing. His heart skipped a beat as he checked all his pockets. The transmitters were gone. Panic washed over him. What in hell's name had happened to them? He thought carefully for a moment, forcing his mind to calm. He knew he had the transmitters when he'd left the hotel, so they had gone missing since then. Suddenly, a grim realization swept through him like a fowl wind—Andrea.

There was suddenly a massive explosion.

As he'd promised, James handed Andrea a bag of money in exchange for the transmitters at the masquerade entrance. James had told her they were two-way radios, but she didn't really care what they were. She was too focused on the healthy sum of money he'd offered, and she'd earned every penny. Now all she had to do was make good on her departure. From the money she'd made from James, she'd be able to take an entire year off work and do whatever she pleased. But, as she walked along the path back to the hotel, a massive explosion erupted behind her, immediately followed by a crescendo of smaller explosions.

Andrea's heart leapt in panic, and as she always did when nerves got the better of her, she impulsively ran her hand over her right wrist, where she wore her mother's gold bracelet. A second wave of nerves shook her. The bracelet her mother had given her as a child wasn't there. The possession she treasured most was gone. Time stopped, and her head spun. All thought of the explosion was gone. She then understood; it must have fallen off her wrist when she was at the ball. In a half-run, half-stumble, she headed back to the masquerade. She *had* to find her bracelet.

Koso stood about thirty feet from the fireworks, and he was almost knocked off his feet by the explosion. A thousand different colors danced into the sky, and sparks flew in all directions. People screamed and scrambled for the exit. But then, as suddenly as it had begun, it was over. The remains of the fireworks fizzled and died, and the thick smoke drifted out to sea. The panicked crowd stopped their flight and chatted like a gaggle of excited geese.

"Ladies and gentlemen! Please, there's no need for panic," came a voice over the loudspeaker. "The explosion that just occurred is the result of a technical problem with the fireworks. We assure you there's no danger, and the remainder of the evening will continue as scheduled. I repeat—there is *no* danger. Please accept our sincere apologies for the interruption. In absence of the fireworks, we're delighted to offer you something just a little more special. Ladies and gentlemen, thank you for your attention, and please welcome to the stage, all the way from the United States, Celine Dion."

Koso watched, still stunned from the explosion. As the artist took the stage and began to sing one of her most popular hits in Italian, Koso realized the announcement was nothing but a cover-up. The explosion he'd heard wasn't only from the fireworks; they had been helped along with a charge of plastic explosives, and he knew it. The difference in sound could be detected by anyone with a military background. He had to find Dane. He only hoped that he wasn't already too late. Making his way quickly through the crowd, he looked for the mask that he and Angelica had seen only moments before. The more he looked, the more confused his eyes became. Soon all the masks looked exactly the same, blending into a stew of madness.

For the second time in five minutes, someone bumped into Dane as he tried to exit the masquerade. This time the klutz was a man wearing a finely crafted mask in the shape of a dragon.

"I see you're still as clumsy as ever," Koso said, revealing himself.

Dane's eyes almost popped out of his head. "Koso?"

"You look like you've seen a ghost," Koso jested.

"Why?" Dane mumbled, exasperated.

"Why aren't I dead? I'll explain later. Right now, we have bigger fish to fry. By the way, I remember you having far better taste in woman."

Dane looked confused for a moment and then realized what Koso was referring to. "Oh, the girl you saw me with; she was nothing," he insisted.

"Try telling that to Angelica," Koso growled.

"Angelica's here?" Dane asked.

"She *was* here until she saw that hideous creature on your arm."

"Where is she now?" Dane asked, still in shock from seeing Koso alive.

"Who? The creature or Angelica?"

"Angelica, of course!"

"She ran off a few minutes ago. But you can stop thinking about her for the moment. There are other things to deal with that cannot wait. Let me explain," said Koso.

"Explain why you're alive?"

"No, you idiot. Explain about Krait," said Koso.

Dane was exasperated. "You're not going to stop me from killing Krait. I already told you this."

"If you can live with killing your own mother on your conscience, then go ahead, I *won't* stop you," said Koso.

"What ... what do you mean?"

"I mean the person you know as Krait—the head of the IUS, the infamous villain you're hell-bent on killing—is none other than your mother."

James waited at the masquerade entrance for few minutes after the first explosion. He didn't see anyone make an exit during that time, but he was sure that Krait must have returned to the room, most probably by way of an unknown route. He knew it was time to return to the villa and blow the second set of charges at the hotel. He trotted off up the path, anticipating his next move, when suddenly a figure materialized from the gloom. He wanted to step into hiding, but there was no time.

"Mr. Bradburn? James, is that you?" came a voice.

James breathed easy. It was Andrea. James Bradburn was the name that he'd given her. "Andrea, what are you doing out here? I thought you'd be long gone by now," he said.

Andrea didn't like the icy edge in James's tone. Warning bells sounded in the back of her head. "I left something at the party. I must go back and get it," she said.

James was also hearing warning bells. What was she going back to the party for? What reason could possibly be important enough to risk being seen by a man she'd just robbed? Had she sold him out? An old rule sprung into his mind—a rule taught to him by British Intelligence during his initial training. He could still hear his instructor's words as if they'd been spoken only moments before.

He uttered the words aloud, "If there's ever any doubt at all, then there is no doubt."

"What?" Andrea asked. There were then hands around her neck, and she could speak no more. She kicked hard, but her moves were feeble, and James easily pinned her to the ground. Her head swam, her eyes fogged, and she blacked out.

Angelica sought solitude on a bench atop a low hill not so far from the path leading from the masquerade. She was so immersed in her grief that she hardly heard the explosion when it thundered through the night. She sat, sobbing in the gloom, tears streaming down her cheeks. Why had she so foolishly trusted another man? But soon her anguish was interrupted by the sound of approaching footsteps. She still desperately wanted to be alone, so she decided to move a little farther into the shadows. Her heart skipped a beat as she watched a young woman come into view under the glow of a lantern. It was the same girl she'd seen earlier with Dane. At that same moment, an older man came into view from the opposite direction. Angelica was riveted to the spot in silence as she watched the two exchange a few words. The man's hands were suddenly around the woman's throat, and he was pinning her to the ground. All anger Angelica felt toward the girl vanished. Now all she saw was her father, alive again, his hands around the throat of her mother, during one of their fights. Rage seized her. She leapt to her feet, kicked her heels aside, and rushed silently toward the scene.

Spread randomly alongside the path, tin lanterns sat atop wooden poles. Angelica swiftly plucked one of these lanterns from its perch and headed straight for the predator. Preoccupied with his sordid act, the man didn't notice her approach. Coming right behind him, she swung the lantern in a sweeping arc toward his head. The blow connected, but not well. However, it was enough for the man to release the lady, and badly dazed by the onslaught, he stumbled off along the path.

After two years of pursuing and trying to kill Krait, Dane was now on a mission to accomplish the opposite. The implications of what

Koso had told him were massive. How had this happened? Was it really true? A million questions flew through his head as he and Koso jogged toward the hotel. They had to get there in time. They had to get Krait out in time.

"So who is this agent on my tail?" Dane demanded.

Koso was finding the jog a little more laborious than Dane. His words came in short gasps. "His name is James Jones. He's working for Russian intelligence."

"I wish you'd contacted me sooner," Dane said.

Koso didn't have a chance to answer. Rounding a corner, they were suddenly face-to-face with Angelica. She was on her knees, leaning over the prone figure of another woman.

Dane recognized Andrea, and for a moment, panic pounded in his chest. Had Angelica killed her?

"Dane," Angelica looked up. The look on her face wasn't a happy one.

"Angelica, what in God's name did you do?" Dane asked.

There was then a massive choking cough. Andrea's body convulsed, and she began gasping for breath. The three of them looked at the woman, whom they'd believed to be dead.

"What happened?" Koso asked.

Angelica looked up at Koso, only now realizing how things looked. "You think it was me who did this?" she asked, exasperated.

"What happened?" Koso asked again.

"I was sitting out here, minding my own business, when I saw this woman meet another man on the path, and then the man's hands were around her throat. So I grabbed a lantern and hit him over the head. That's what happened," said Angelica.

"Where is he?" Koso asked, looking around.

"He ran away."

"After you hit him over the head with a lantern," Dane said.

"It wasn't a very good shot. It's a little dark around here, if you hadn't noticed."

"What did this man look like?"

"I can tell you," Andrea croaked, and she then described James.

All the while, Dane looked on, momentarily dumbstruck by the entire situation. "Did you give the transmitters to him?" he demanded.

"The transmitters?" Andrea asked.

"The devices you took from me. Did you give them to the man who tried strangling you?"

"Yes," Andrea croaked quietly, glad to be alive—but not at all glad to be alive in her present situation. "He told me they were radios."

Suddenly, there was another explosion. But colorful fireworks didn't follow this blast, and this time, it came from the hotel. Dane's worst fears were realized in a flash, and he began desperately running toward the hotel.

"Stay here with the girl," Koso said to Angelica. "If you can, get her back to the masquerade, but don't leave her on her own just yet. I have to go after Dane, and I don't think it'll be safe for you at the hotel yet."

Angelica reluctantly nodded her consent, and Koso sped off.

Had the impact to his head been an inch further forward, James would surely be dead, but the blow wasn't serious. He was bleeding and feeling none the worse for it, but he forced himself to focus his attention on Krait's room from his position in the villa. It was situated at about ninety degrees to the left and front of the hotel, and the position gave James a 45-degree view directly into Krait's room from a distance of about a hundred meters. Soon, the lights came on in the room, and using this as his cue, he detonated the second set of explosives and watched as the room caved in from the blast. He'd done it. His head pounded in agony, and blood continued to trickle freely from the wound, but he was alive. And, if his instincts were correct, Dane Larusio would arrive at the hotel any second now. With luck he'd walk right into the line of fire.

James's head swam. It was becoming harder and harder to focus on the hotel. Putting a live cartridge in the chamber of his rifle, he perched the weapon on the window frame, wiped blood from his right eye, and peered through the scope. He wondered if he could really make such a shot in the condition he was in. But this was the only chance he'd get; he *had* to make the shot. He waited patiently. The cool, concrete floor pressed into his hip uncomfortably. He was glad that the wait would soon be over. When the dust settled, he'd have a clear view of Dane, and then he'd get his chance to fire.

He hated waiting.

When Dane reached the hotel, he was surprised to find that there was very little fire. He walked to the front of the building, where he found Krait's suite collapsed into his own. The explosives had done just the amount of damage he'd anticipated, minimally affecting the rest of the hotel. A massive dust cloud shrouded everything, and using the wreckage of a banister dangling from his balcony, Dane climbed up through this dust and into his room. His eyes watered and his lungs clogged, but, through the haze, he soon spotted a gray lump near the crumbling eastern wall. He reached the object, and summoning his courage, he knelt down and looked. His heart missed a beat when he found that it was only a mattress corner. Immediately he began searching elsewhere—but there was nothing. Everywhere he looked, there was nothing but rubble. The more he searched, the more convinced he became that his mother was buried. Panic welled inside him. Broken furniture, tattered pieces of material, and other items—that was all there was. There must be a body. He had to know for sure. Using his hands, he franticly dug in all directions, not caring when the broken glass and tiles tore into his flesh—still nothing. The more Dane searched, the more hope faded. He finally sat, defeated, in the middle of the destruction. All his remaining energy drifted off on the breeze along with the dust. His hopes were dashed; his mother was certainly dead.

"If it hadn't been for Aldo here, you'd find me buried under that rubble," came a voice.

The words startled Dane. They came from the crumbling doorway that led into the hallway. It was his mother's voice. He squinted into the dust and the gloom, but couldn't see a thing. Two people then stepped into the dull light that glowed from a nearby blaze; one was the gorilla Dane had almost crushed with his boxing bag; the other was none other than Dane's mother. In one blinding flash, Koso's revelation materialized into reality. The very oxygen Dane breathed stuck in his chest. Words failed him, and he was frozen to the spot in shock.

Celia Larusio looked at her son, raw malice stabbing from her eyes. "You never did forgive yourself for what happened to your father and uncle, did you? Let me tell you something—what happened to them was *never* any fault of yours," she said.

"Mother," Dane mumbled vaguely.

Her features hardened further. "You know, what happened to your father and uncle ended up being the best thing that ever happened to the family business."

Dane's tongue finally began to loosen. "What? What do you mean?" he pleaded.

"Please, you don't still actually believe that your father made his money from his shoe business, do you? Let me tell you something about your father—something he never had the nerve to tell you." She took a few careful steps toward him as she spoke. With the strength of a woman half her age, she pulled a battered chair from the rubble and elegantly sat. The gorilla followed her every move, a massive pistol held loosely at his side. "Your father was born into one of the oldest Mafia families in Sicily. Sicily was where we fell in love and got married. Your father had a rare and powerful opportunity, but to the disgust of many, he ignored his heritage and left Sicily without looking back. Oh, sure, he did some business here and there; he had to feed his family. But he did nothing that would ever give him the respect his family had so painstakingly built over eight generations. He was a soft man, a weak man—not the man I thought I married at all. When there were times he needed to be a little more forceful, he always backed off. Each time he backed off, he lost business and respect."

Dane was becoming increasingly mesmerized. He desperately tried to absorb what his mother was saying without completely breaking down.

"Finally, not long after you were born," Krait continued, "the family cut him off almost completely. I could no longer stand by and just watch things decay. I began to take more of an interest in the business, at first offering only advice. After a time, however, your father began seeing the results of my advice, and he let me take more of a direct hand in things. I returned to Sicily, and the family greeted me with open arms. They were overjoyed about what I was doing on the mainland, and they offered me their full support. By the time you were in your early teens, I was mostly running things."

"I was working for you back then, and I did not even know it?" Dane asked.

"Your father wanted you to have no part of the business, but I knew you'd be the family's greatest asset if you were handled correctly. Yes, you were working for me. You don't really believe that meeting Gioberto and Osvaldo—or Sticks and Stones as you may have known them—was a coincidence, do you?"

"But what about uncle Dino? Why did he have to die? What about father?" Dane asked.

"Your uncle was the same as your father—weak. He too wanted you to remain legitimate. As for your father, well, the moment he was out of the way, I was guaranteed complete control," she said heartlessly.

"You had me bomb uncle Dino and father?" The bewilderment Dane felt was transforming into rage unlike any he'd known before.

"Not exactly. That was a mistake our mutual acquaintance Sticks made. He was simply told which building to blow and when to blow it. You weren't the one I chose to help him carry out his task. The man who was supposed to help Sticks was passed out drunk, and therefore useless. Sticks made the simple mistake of coming to you instead of finding someone else." Krait uncomfortably moved her bulk in the rickety chair.

Dane now saw everything in crystal-clear detail. From the very beginning, he'd been set up by his mother. He kicked himself for not seeing the truth earlier. How could he have been so blind? The woman who'd left the meeting room just before he and Angelica had been kidnapped and shipped to the Gobi desert—that woman had been his mother. She'd been right there in the same room, and he'd failed to realize it. "And what of the money that I found?" he asked.

"Oh yes, the money. A considerable sum, if I remember correctly. The money was your father's. He'd had access to massive sums of money when he ran the business, and my guess is, the cash in that suitcase was profits he's skimmed over the years. The irony of the situation is, the money was destined for you in the first place. Your father was in that bank that day to set up an account that would give you the independence from the family business he so desperately wanted. Later, my sources informed me that you were involved in extensive business in Jamaica. I wondered where you'd acquired the resources to do what you were doing, but your father put two and two together, and one day, he told me. After the accident he'd put his feelers out, trying to find out what happened to his suitcase. There was actually CCTV footage of you rummaging through the remains of the bank. The authorities had never been able to ID you from the footage that had come from a camera on the opposite side of the street; the images weren't very clear. But when you father acquired the tape, he instantly recognized you by the way you moved and the style of your clothing. He'd succeeded doing what he'd set out to do, and was happy, despite becoming crippled in the process. And when he finally revealed the truth about you, I'd accepted your departure and wished you every success with your accomplishments."

"What do you mean? Are you saying that you had a hand in the success of my business?" Dane asked, exasperated.

"No, I did nothing to interfere with your business. Although, there was one thing—I had your CEO fired from his previous job, then placed him in a position where he had no choice but to be hired by you."

Dane was further shocked. "Bryant Wilson is working for you?"

"We shouldn't be here," the gorilla insisted. "We need to finish this and leave."

"What's wrong, Aldo?" Krait asked.

"I don't know for sure if there's anything wrong; I just have a very strong feeling that we shouldn't be—"

A shot then rang out.

James grinned, knowing Dane's fate would soon be sealed. He felt the warm steel of the trigger under his forefinger and waited for the right moment. He watched as the hazy outline of Dane came into view and disappeared again behind a piece of broken wall. Dane was obviously searching through the rubble for Krait's body, which was certainly buried. All James needed now was one clear shot, but there was thick dust, as well as broken furniture and wall obscuring any clear view. James tried to relax his breathing as much as possible and be patient; at the same time hoping he'd zeroed the rifle correctly. Sharpshooting had never been his strength in the field. Still, the distance wasn't great, and he felt confident he could hit the target once the dust settled a little more.

"Just give me something to shoot at," he said aloud. But this seemed too much to ask. Every time he caught sight of Dane, there was only a fraction of a moment before he disappeared again.

"Shit!' he said as Dane made another pass before vanishing behind a piece of crumbling wall. "Shit!" he swore again.

He had to have a clear shot. He couldn't afford to miss; to do so would be to sign his own death warrant. Dane was now moving franticly, unpredictably in every direction. James then saw two new figures step through the remains of the hotel room's doorway—a man and a woman. James could hardly believe his eyes. He stared through his scope carefully. The man he recognized was the bodyguard booked into Adrian Marino's suite. He knew that this man was a bodyguard—undoubtedly Krait's bodyguard—from information he'd received after sending his photo to Ostrov. But what was he doing alive? James had seen the light come on in Krait's suite; Krait and the bodyguard had surely been there when the charges had blown. But now it seemed as though he was wrong with this assumption. And now, there with the bodyguard was a woman. And, judging by the way the bodyguard was shielding the woman, she had to be Krait.

"Impossible," James breathed.

James cursed these unforeseen complications and racked his brains for answers. But there was no time to think. *Kill them all,* he decided. He had no choice; it was all or nothing.

The newcomers were apparently preoccupied in conversation with the obscured Dane. And due to the angle at which James faced the suite, much of the woman was obscured by the bulk of the bodyguard. James decided the bodyguard would have to go first, and then he'd have a clear shot at Krait. With any luck, the onslaught would draw Dane into open. James wondered what the group could be talking about in such a dire situation. By his calculations, the authorities would be no more than twenty minutes away. But that didn't really matter now. He had a job to finish. Carefully, he took aim at the ever-alert bodyguard. Carefully, he squeezed the trigger.

Dane watched, shocked as the gorilla took a bullet in the head and crumpled to the ground in a lifeless heap.

"Get down. Don't move!" The words came from the garden below.

Krait took cover behind the remains of a heavy wooden desk, but not before snatching the revolver from the dead gorilla's hand. "Who in hell is that?" she whispered hoarsely.

"The Russians," Dane replied, cursing himself for being so careless. He drew his own revolver and chanced a look over the wall. He was rewarded with a second shot from the sniper. A massive chunk of the desk, behind which his mother crouched, exploded into fragments. "Explosive rounds," he grunted.

"Who is that?" his mother called again.

Another shot exploded through the night air. This time the bullet tore into Dane's wall. "The Russians," Dane repeated. "This is what you get when you mess with a country that knows exactly how to play the game you play."

"No, not them—him," Krait said, candidly poking a finger in the desired direction.

Another shot rang out, obviously intended for Krait's finger, but it missed and smashed instead into the doorframe. Krait pointed her revolver over the top of the desk and vainly emptied it in the direction she guessed the fire was coming from.

"Get down and stay down!" came the voice again.

"Koso, is that you?" Dane asked.

Between shots, Koso had scrambled up and into the room the same way Dane had. But he'd settled in just behind the wall at the opposite side of the room from Dane. A heavy standalone wardrobe and much debris separated them.

"Stay where you are," Koso replied.

There was a loud crash, and Dane watched as another large piece of the doorframe behind his mother fell away.

"What the hell are we going to do?" Dane whispered. "We can't just sit here. If this guy has another dozen rounds, then he's sure to get one of us."

Another shot rang out. This time it hit the remains of his mother's cover. A short groan followed, and Dane could see that shrapnel had hit her in the right leg. An average woman would be screaming in agony, but, apparently, his mother wasn't average. Still, blood flowed freely from the wound, and despite the circumstances, Dane couldn't help but feel a degree of compassion.

Koso peeked his crazy wash of gray hair around the corner of his wardrobe. "The gun, where is it?" he whispered.

Dane held his revolver up sideways for Koso to see.

"No, you idiot. Where is the mini-gun?"

Dane's heart leapt in understanding. In the insanity of the past minutes, he'd completely forgotten about his insurance. Only now did he realize how close Koso was to the weapon. "Right in front of you," he whispered back.

"Right in front of me where?" Koso asked.

"In the wardrobe," Dane said. "But the door's on the opposite side of where you are. One of us will have to break cover to reach it."

Dane was at the western front-side of the room, and Koso was at the eastern front-side. They both had about a meter and a half of intact wall to take cover behind, but between the wardrobe and Dane there was little to no wall left to protect him. It had been destroyed during the blast, and this open area was where the wardrobe door was.

"Damn my luck," Koso cursed, considering the problem. "Okay, I'll do it, son, but you're going to have to cover me."

"Okay," Dane agreed. "Let's see if you're as lucky as you say you are," he jested, trying to take the edge off the tension.

Koso gave Dane a wry smile. "Okay, let's get this over with. Our Russian friend is holed up in that decrepit villa southeast of our position. That's where you'll have to fire. On my mark, old friend." Summoning all his courage, Koso began the count: "One ... Two ... Three ..."

To increase accuracy, Dane chanced a hair's glance over the top of his cover before firing his last rounds furiously at the Villa. Just as he finished shooting, the sniper fired back and Dane was thrown into the rubble. Stunned, he was dangerously out in the open, and precious seconds passed before he managed to scramble back behind his cover. He was just in time. The sniper fired again, but this time the shell only hit rubble.

"Are you okay?" Koso asked.

"Yes," Dane answered, and pain hit his right shoulder with fiery intensity. "No," he said. He looked and found blood flowing freely from a gaping wound. Though it was no scratch, it was instantly apparent that the shell had made a clean exit. In a vain attempt to slow the bleeding, he took out his handkerchief and applied as much pressure as he could without passing out.

"It's time to even up the score," Koso said. It took only seconds for him to pull one of the mini-guns from the wardrobe, and in less than a minute, he had it ready to fire. Despite the new, lighter design, the entirety of the weapon looked massively clumsy against Koso's wiry frame.

"Can you fire again to give me a moment's cover?" Koso asked, awkwardly strapping the gun's packed ammunition onto his back while keeping as low to the ground as possible.

"I'm out of ammunition," Dane grunted painfully.

Koso reached inside of his jacket and pulled out his own gun. He checked to make sure the safety was on before throwing it to Dane. "Use this," he said.

Dane struggled to pick up the weapon. The movement almost made him pass out.

"On three," said Koso. "Just put the barrel into view this time. Also, fire a little slower. I have to get a good look and make sure of where he's shooting from."

Dane counted, "One ... Two ... Three." He slid the barrel of the revolver over the top of the crumbled wall and began firing. He got three shots off before the sniper fired again. This time the bullet whistled over his head and exploded into the rear wall.

In the instant the sniper fired, Koso spotted the bright flash from the barrel and perfectly pinpointed the agent's position. He leapt to his feet and braced himself as hard as he could into the waist-high, crumbled wall. He pulled the trigger with all the finesse of a skydiver pulling the ripcord.

Dane had the perfect view of Koso. An insane stream of tracer flew from the revolving barrels as the mini-gun roared into action. He chanced a look at where the fire was being drawn, and in the moonlight, he watched the entire front of the villa disintegrating from the assault. Debris flew in every direction. The overall effect was horrifying. It was all over in seconds.

Koso's vision remained tunneled toward the target, as if he were hypnotized by his task. The gun's ammunition was spent, but adrenaline still pumped through his veins. Only the noise of the still-revolving barrel broke the silence of the night.

Dane stood and stumbled to Koso's side. "Koso? Koso?" he urged, shaking his arm, summoning him back to reality.

A loud crash erupted from the villa and the entire front of the building collapsed to the ground. Finally Koso became aware of Dane. He let his hands relax, and the barrels of the mini-gun ground to a halt.

For the first time in memory, Dane realized that Koso was truly shaken. "I think you got him," he said.

Koso's eyes suddenly regained some life. "Yes, I think we did," he said. He carefully put down the gun as if he were handling an armed bomb.

Fires began burning in the destroyed villa, and the distant sound of flames crackled, their sound the only noise disturbing the still night air. Dane suddenly remembered his mother. He turned from the dazed Koso and walked back to where the remains of the desk were. He prepared himself for the worst, but she and the corpse of the bodyguard were nowhere to be seen. He looked in all directions for any sign of her, but found only bloodstains. Some inner sense told him she was long gone. The feeling gave him little comfort. He then saw something strange sitting close to where she'd been crouched. Picking up the object, he saw it was a beautifully made mask in the shape of a serpent. He instantly realized its significance, and his comfort augmented. Krait's greatest armor had been shed. The name now had a face.

"Dane," came a woman's voice.

The voice snapped Dane from his melancholy. He turned to find Angelica standing in the broken doorway. Krait's mask fell from his fingers. Angelica walked slowly toward him, intense compassion in her eyes. All the pain from his shoulder and the horrors of the past vaporized as they embraced.

EPILOGUE

Dane, Koso, and Angelica sat quietly drinking coffee at a bayside Siros restaurant, in downtown Ermoupolis. Franco Valentino, Dane's doctor friend, had just departed. Dane had flown Franco in, amid the usual performance, to take care of the bullet wound in his shoulder. Ironically, the bullet had entered in the exact spot where he'd been stabbed only months before. His arm was now in a sling and would remain so until Franco told him otherwise.

"I can see you have room for one more," said a voice laced with a thick Russian accent.

They all looked up to see an elderly gentleman wearing an exquisitely tailored suit, his head topped with a white fedora hat. The man bore an uncanny similarity to a certain stylish detective from an Agatha Christie novel. The only thing missing was the bulbous belly—this man was wiry and athletic.

The newcomer sat down and looked squarely at Koso. "Hello, old friend."

Koso said nothing, his expression unreadable.

"Aren't you supposed to be dead?"

"Not right this minute," Koso said.

"Never mind, we'll get to that later." A waiter came, and the stranger ordered coffee in an all-too-relaxed manner.

Angelica looked at Dane and he at her. They both looked expectantly at Koso, who in return looked at the newcomer.

In a display of decision, Koso stretched his hand toward the stranger. "Hello, Ostrov," he said, firmly shaking his hand.

"It's good to see you alive," Ostrov said. "And you too, Mr. Larusio."

Dane didn't shake hands with him. "Last time we met, your name was Alex Munstrov," he said.

"Yes, well, please forgive the deception. I was only doing my job," Ostrov said.

"And what job is that?" Dane asked.

"I'm not here to give you a description of my professional position, Mr. Larusio," Ostrov said.

"He's here to decide if he should let you live. He's possibly here to recruit you," Koso said.

"Recruit me. Possibly kill me. What the hell for?" Dane growled. "Who in hell's name is this man?" Dane could no longer hide his annoyance.

"He's Russian intelligence," Koso bluntly replied.

Open astonishment swept across Dane's features. "You mean to tell me that this is the man behind that bloodsucking assassin trying to kill us last night?" Dane's annoyance was turning to raw, unbridled anger.

"You're quite right," Ostrov said. "It was I that put that agent on you."

"First you try to kill me, and now you want to hire me?" Dane growled.

"Okay, everyone, please just calm down," Koso said, realizing the scene was about to explode.

"I'm calm," said Ostrov. "It's your friend here that seems out of control. And this is very interesting, considering the magnitude of his achievements over the past couple of years. I put that agent on you, Dane, because you're obviously a very dangerous man, a man we would have liked to have working for us or not at all. However, from what we learned, you're not the type who works for anyone but yourself. Therefore, we decided to eliminate you."

"I haven't changed," Dane interrupted.

"You still have hunting to do?" Ostrov asked.

"No, I have other business to attend to. My hunting days, as you call them, are over."

"So you say. So you say," said Ostrov.

"Krait's dead," Koso lied, injecting some tension of his own into the already explosive atmosphere. He was taking a massive gamble that Krait's capability was now nullified by the exposure of her identity, and she'd melt into obscurity and never be seen or heard of again. In such a case, Ostrov would never know he'd lied about her death. But one thing was for sure—he couldn't give Dane's mother up to the FSB.

Ostrov was visibly rocked by Koso's words. "You've killed Krait?" he demanded.

"Dane killed Krait, and I saw the body. And I know it was Krait, because I'm the only one who knows what Krait looks like," Koso said.

"This is an astounding turn of events," Ostrov said. "You mean to say that, after all these years, you finally identified that scum?" Ostrov said, astonished.

"Yes," Koso said.

Silence settled over the table. Ostrov sipped his coffee in silent thought. Dane eyeballed Koso suspiciously. Koso remained impassive and directed his stare toward Ostrov, trying to anticipate the outcome of the moment. Angelica, silent since Ostrov's arrival, slid a small .38-caliber pistol from her purse. She had just gotten her man back, and she'd be damned if anyone was going to take him away again.

Ostrov suddenly rose with decisive intent. Downing the last dregs of his coffee, he threw some cash onto the table. "Koso," he said, "if you're telling me that Krait will no longer be doing business in Mother Russia, then your word is good enough for me."

"Thank you," Koso said, openly relieved.

"No, thank you. And thank you too, Mr. Larusio. You don't know how deeply the IUS had its claws in the flesh of our black market," Ostrov said, brushing an unseen wrinkle from his suit. "And, Koso, can I count on you for keeping our friend here out of trouble?" he asked.

Koso stood and offered his hand. They shook. "I don't think that'll be a problem," he agreed.

Ostrov then tipped his hat at Angelica and departed with the same grace with which he'd arrived.

As the tension waned in Ostrov's wake, Angelica plucked up an object lying amid the cash that Ostrov had left. "Somehow I don't think we've seen the last of our Russian friend," she said.

Dane looked at Angelica quizzically. In response she dropped the object she held into the middle of the table. Dane instantly froze. Staring back at them was a photograph of a ruined hotel, and amid the ruins was the clear and present image of his mother, wounded but obviously alive. It was a clear warning—only Dane didn't know exactly how to interpret it. One thing was for sure—the Russians knew that Krait was his mother and that she was alive.

Dane still hadn't had the time to process the fact that Krait *was* his mother. He couldn't kill her; he knew that much. But anything beyond that he simply couldn't make his mind up about. He had gained a degree of peace from what he'd achieved. His youth had been steered in the direction of disaster by his mother's ambition. It was now obvious that he'd had little protection against that. He could live with himself easier now, but there was still work to do, and he felt certain that Angelica was an integral part of that work. She calmed him. Even now, as the Russian made his departure, leaving uncertainty in his wake, Dane had to but look at Angelica, and an overwhelming feeling that everything would be all right rose within him. No one knew what the future held, but there was hope.